COVO FAMILY SAGA

FORGIVEN
A NOVEL

BRUCE J. BERGER

Black Rose Writing | Texas

ISBN: 978-1-68513-673-4
LIBRARY OF CONGRESS CONTROL NUMBER: 2025938136
PUBLISHED BY BLACK ROSE WRITING
www.blackrosewriting.com

Printed in the United States of America
Suggested Retail Price (SRP) $22.95

Forgiven: A Novel is printed in Book Antiqua

*As a planet-friendly publisher, Black Rose Writing does its best to eliminate unnecessary waste to reduce paper usage and energy costs, while never compromising the reading experience. As a result, the final word count vs. page count may not meet common expectations.

Praise for
FORGIVEN: A NOVEL

"Bruce J. Berger is a writer of epic stories about family and place, stories that extend beyond generations within the tradition of Faulkner and Milan Kundera. I know his craft, his language, but beyond all this, I admire the dignity he brings to his books, his compassion and understanding of the human spirit. I have read his novels and heard him read from them, and with each experience I have felt my heart expand with greater love for the world."
–David Keplinger, author of *Ice*

"*Forgiven*, Bruce J. Berger's new book in the Covo family saga, authentically captures the impact of the Holocaust on successive generations of a family. He explores how family members, faced with their own personal challenges, struggle to rely on each other – and sometimes outside forces – to accept forgiveness and find purpose. I was particularly struck by Kayla, a former concert pianist who must trust in herself and others to find a way back to her music. *Forgiven* is an important and powerful read."
–Bonnie Suchman, author of *Stumbling Stones*

"*Forgiven: A Novel* … insightfully navigates the intricacies of relationships and depth of various theologies."
–Rabbi Michael Werbow

Further Praise for
FORGIVEN: A NOVEL

"In a quiet early scene of Bruce Berger's *Forgiven,* Kayla, a Jewish musician and composer whose career has been arrested by schizophrenia, tries to create a sonata, a musical piece for one instrument, the piano. Just prior to the sonata attempts, Kayla successfully focuses on composing for string quartets. Quartets are easier because, after all, no one can ask her to perform a quartet alone. If she composes a sonata, however, she could be pressured to perform. Alone.

As I enter Berger's world of *Forgiven,* I am Kayla. It's challenging but natural to enter the multiple world views of the characters. The characters are quartets and ensembles with differing but understandable wrestlings with God – even the atheists wrestle with God. I believe Nicky, atheist, Jewish, Psychiatrist, saved from the Holocaust by what he believes is a miracle. I believe Helen, longing so much for her daughter to live. I believe Sarah, cancer, too young. I believe beautiful brown child, Jackie, playing his music. I believe Theodora, a nun in Greece, born Jewish, rescued from the Holocaust by Christians. I believe Max, lawyer musician, Kayla's brother. But what the text asks me to do is gaze at the world views of them all, and wrestle with God, even the non-God of the atheists. This novel then asks me to search for ONE. Alone. I have to create my own wrestling with God from these quartets and ensembles. I am persuaded to take up my questions again and again, every time I open the text of *Forgiven.* 'What shall I believe this time.' I ask myself again, yes, I am wrestling with God again. Bruce, I love your good stories, I love how you tuck in the different world views so that I accept them without realizing them. I love the task of figuring out where I am in the context of your story."

–Carolivia Herron, author of *Thereafter Johnnie*

Praise for
TO SEE GOD

Finalist -- National Indie Excellence – Religious Fiction

"To See God peers boldly through a dark glass at a mysterious human striving. A well-conceived, absorbing, and unpredictable sequel to *The Flight of the Veil."*
–Cheryl Anne Tuggle, author of *Lights on the Mountain*

"Bruce J. Berger writes about belief like no other writer: his characters have ecstatic visions and undertake divine missions. They struggle to act on their beliefs, even as such beliefs are challenged, not by adversaries, but by the people closest to them. *To See God*, asks profound questions about how to live in and accept the world as it is, not as we see it in our dreams."
–Stephanie Grant, author of *Map of Ireland* and *The Passion of Alice*

"Readers of Bruce J. Berger's two previous novels will be rewarded with this … volume [too]: . . . the story of Jewish siblings separated by time, continents, and religious traditions but joined by complex histories. … Berger moves deftly among matters of faith and spirituality, miracles, mental illness, and the scars of war. The crisp dialogues virtually spring off the page as his complex characters wrestle with demons both sacred and profane."
–Roberta Rubenstein, author of *Literary Half-Lives: Doris Lessing, Clancy Sigal, and Roman à Clef.*

Praise for
THE MUSIC STALKER

"What drives the characters of *THE MUSIC STALKER* to their highs and lows, their togetherness and their times apart, is also what artfully holds them locked in patterns of an intricate harmony. The heliotropic center of this novel is desire: desire for the Other; desire for talent; desire to be seen; desire to be held; desire for safety and peace of mind; even the desire to be left alone. Bruce Berger exhibits a sensational knack for imagining lives, real lives lived with triumph and weakness, mental illness and ordered reason, as well as daily flubs and foibles. His skills make for a page turner …"
-David Keplinger, author of *The World To Come*

"Although Berger's work [*THE MUSIC* STALKER] is replete with depictions of life with mental illness, it's never reductive or one-dimensional. Instead, it immerses readers in the lives and perceptions of those with psychological differences. It's also about the power of family members to pull loved ones back from isolation and distress, even when they're suffering themselves. … A tale that shines a light on the redemptive power of religion and relationships."
-Kirkus Reviews

"Bruce J. Berger's *THE MUSIC STALKER* is a thoughtful, enjoyable story and an interesting study of mental illness, spirituality, and artistic genius — and the possible relationship between them. … [He] writes with warmth and attention to detail, bringing the Covo family's experience to life. His exploration of mental illness makes Adel a fully-fledged character, a woman aware of her brain's misfirings and yet helpless against them in many ways. And if Kayla's own mental imbalance is obviously telegraphed, his exploration of its connection to her rapturous, effortless musical genius is fascinating."
-IndieReader Reviews

Praise for
THE FLIGHT OF THE VEIL

Winner—Illumination Bronze Award in General Fiction
"A well-crafted tale about trauma and miracles."
–Kirkus Reviews

"In the intelligent historical novel *THE FLIGHT OF THE VEIL*, a psychiatrist returns to places that were treacherous in his childhood, reconciling internal contradictions."
–Clarion Reviews

"Berger has created a compelling Everyman, who must wrest with grand theological questions: in times of great calamity, why does God save only some?"
–Stephanie Grant, author of *Map of Ireland* and *The Passion of Alice*

"The text skirts between fantastic realism, real realism, and a protagonist who has not taught himself how to go entirely insane …"
–Carolivia Herron, author of *Thereafter Johnnie*

"Provocative character discussions span a variety of topics, including religion, mental health, and family and love, achieving an enlightening balance between logic and emotion … Illustrative language is used to render the Greek landscape in gorgeous terms. An intelligent historical novel."
–Foreword Reviews

"With deft, vivid prose, Bruce J. Berger's *The Flight of the Veil* takes the reader on the searing and inspiring journey of Nicky Covo, a man who thinks he has buried his World War II memories, only to have them demand his attention again with news of a possible modern day miracle."
–IndieReader Reviews

Praise for
RETURN TO SENDER:
224 UNANSWERED LETTERS TO
THE WHITE HOUSE
(NON-FICTION)

"Well Worth It! Well written. Eloquent. Unanswered. A perfect chronicle of [Trump's] presidency. Bruce says what the majority of the country was thinking at the time."
–Amazon Review

"I love Bruce's wit and eloquence. A damn shame he writes to someone unable (or unwilling) to read."
–Amazon Review

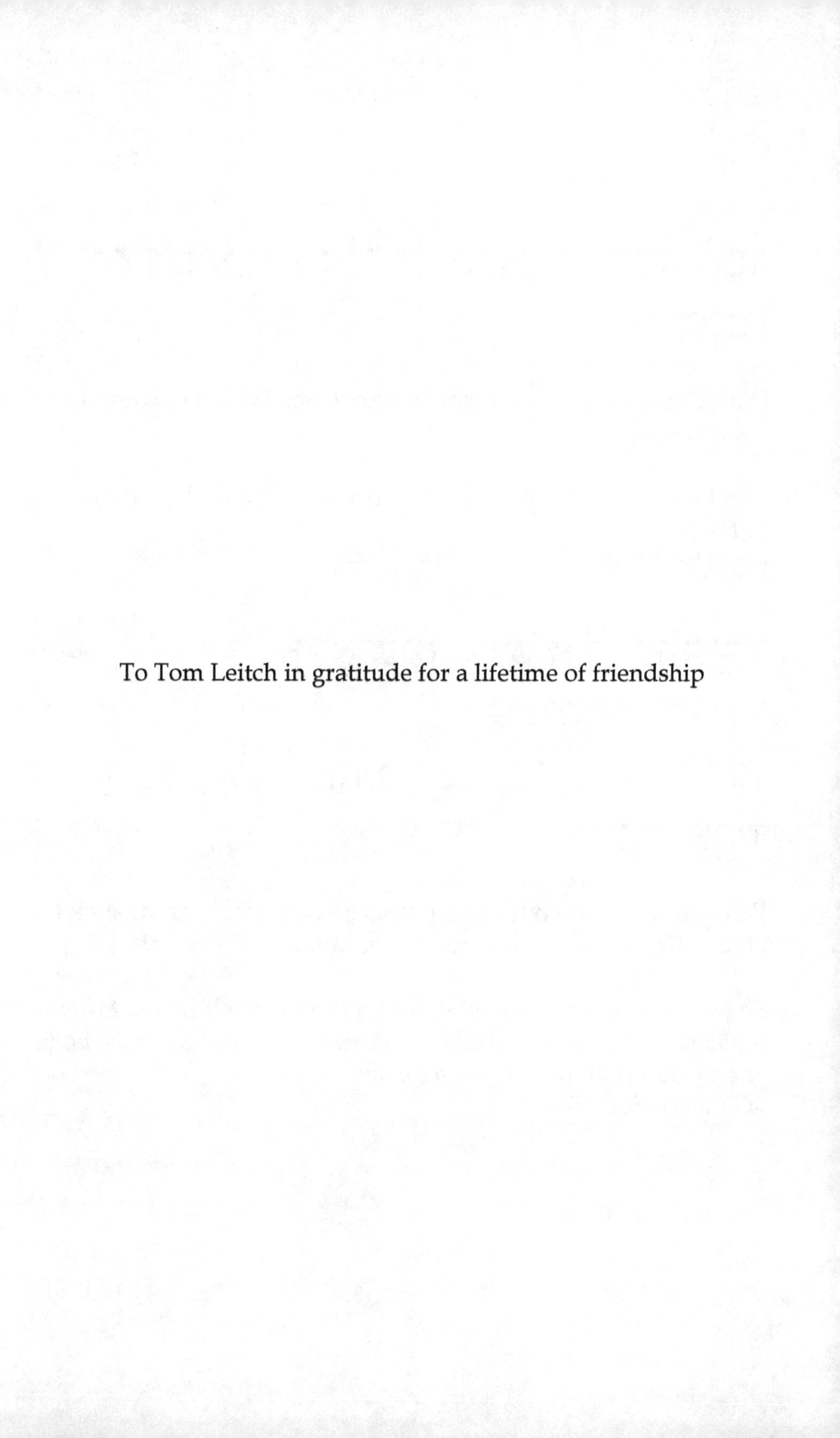

To Tom Leitch in gratitude for a lifetime of friendship

יַרְבִּים מַכְאוֹבִים לָרָשָׁע וְהַבּוֹטֵחַ בַּיהֹוָה חֶסֶד יְסוֹבְבֶנּוּ:

[Yarabim machovim larasha, v'haboteach badonay chesed y'sovivenu]

Great is the pain of the wicked, but love will surround those who trust in Hashem.
–Psalms 32:10

וְלֹא־עָמַד אִישׁ אִתּוֹ בְּהִתְוַדַּע יוֹסֵף אֶל־אֶחָיו
וַיְנַשֵּׁק לְכָל־אֶחָיו וַיֵּבְךְּ עֲלֵהֶם וְאַחֲרֵי כֵן דִּבְּרוּ אֶחָיו

[V'lo amad ish ito b'hitvadah yo-sef el-echav … vayanshek l-chol-echav vayevik alehem, v'acharay chen dibru echav …]

So no one stood with him when Joseph made himself known to his brothers…. And he kissed all his brothers and wept over them, and afterwards his brothers spoke with him.
–Genesis 45:1, 15

Dramatis Personae

Dr. Nicky Covo – Born in Salonica, Greece, he left his family at age 14, in 1943, to hide from the Nazis just before they began to deport Jews to the death camps. Later, he fought with the partisans against the Nazis and should have died in a grenade explosion, but miraculously lived to continue fighting. After the war, he made it to the United States, got a college education, went to medical school, and became a psychiatrist. He married a former patient (Adel) and had two children with her, Max and Kayla. Three years after Adel's death, he married an old friend, Helen Blanco.

Max Covo – Nicky's son, who at the time of this novel is 28 years old, a lawyer in a New York law firm. He is divorced, and his two children live on the other side of the country. His sister, Kayla, and her biracial son, Jackie, who is almost eight years old, live with him.

Kayla Covo – Nicky's daughter, 26, a former piano prodigy who lost the ability to perform due to paranoid schizophrenia. She has become a successful composer of classical music. She is an observant Jew, a member of a local *Chabad* community, and she is raising her son, Jackie, to be observant as well.

Jackie Covo – Kayla's son, going on eight. His father is August Sorel, a Haitian-American concert violinist.

Helen Covo – Nicky's second wife. Helen became Nicky's good friend when her family sponsored him into the United States in 1946. Helen and Nicky had lost touch with each other for many years, until they ran into each other in 1990 (both having lost spouses) and resumed their friendship. They married in late 1990.

Sister Theodora (formerly Kal Covo) – Nicky's younger sister. To escape the Nazis, her family sent Kal into hiding with a young Orthodox Christian friend of the family, Alex, but he died giving Kal her chance to escape. Kal was hidden and protected by a priest and later saved from certain death by the miraculous intervention of the Theotokos, the Mother of God. From the age of six, following her adoption of the Orthodox Christian faith, she has lived at a monastery in northern Greece.

Abbess Fevronia – The abbess who brought the Monastery of St. Vlassios, which lay in ruins, back into operation in the early 1950s, discovering there the young woman (Kal Covo) whom she named Sister Theodora.

Abbess Zoe – As of late 1990, the new abbess of the Monastery of St. Vlassios, replacing Fevronia after the latter's death during a trip to the United States with Sister Theodora.

Andros – A villager living near the monastery. He was a friend of Abbess Fevronia, helped her rebuild the monastery in the 1950s and later helped her find Nicky Covo, Sister Theodora's brother, in America.

———

Forgiven: A Novel takes place in 1991.

FORGIVEN

Complications

An Ongoing Concern

When the phone rang at nine in the morning, Helen Blanco Covo was momentarily unsure where she was. She lifted her head from the pillow – the pain of a rare hangover making her wish she'd not indulged in an extra glass of red wine the night before – still thinking she was in her house in Highland Park. Then, she blinked and realized she was in Nicky's apartment, in his bed, in their bed, and that she had stupidly overslept. What was it she'd been intending to do? She dimly remembered Nicky getting up early to drive to his office in Brooklyn. He'd said something to her she couldn't recall, something about the streets being treacherous? A glance out the window showed a dark sky and raindrops beaded on the pane. Right. A day of heavy rain had been forecast. She picked up the receiver, and it was Nicky.

"Helen …"

She rubbed her eyes, which only intensified her discomfort. "Oh, Nicky, my head is killing me. I …"

"We've got trouble. I'm being sued. Some yoyo process server just pushed a summons into my hands. *Gamóto!*"

"This couldn't wait until you got home?"

"A patient killed himself. I don't even remember him. Jesus, I don't believe this."

Helen swung her legs out of the bed, whispering her usual prayer upon awakening, "*Modah ani l'fanecha, Melech chai v'kayam, she'hechezarta bi nishmati b'chemla, rabah emunatecha."* (I thank you, Living and Forever King, for returning my breath to me in your great faithfulness.) Doctors get sued all the time, she thought, and Nicky hadn't escaped the occasional malpractice claim. He'd been luckier than most psychiatrists, and his insurance carrier had managed to settle the few lawsuits against him. He'd given a few depositions, but had never had a case go to trial.

"Well, we can talk about it … where are my slippers?... oh … let's talk when you get back this evening, can't we, and …"

"You don't understand, Helen. Listen. This complaint claims I *knew* this patient was going to kill himself and deliberately did nothing to prevent his death. His parents are suing."

Helen stuck her feet into her slippers, wondering if she would need to barf. "Your lawyers will take care of it though, won't they? Like before?"

"I can't concentrate on seeing patients today. What if these charges are true? What if these things happened and I've blocked it out of my mind because …"

"Nonsense." With difficulty, she stifled a major, sour burp. "Come home. Cancel your appointments. Come home."

"But the name is somehow familiar."

"What name?"

"Yahon. The patient – the alleged patient – who died. His last name was Yahon. I know it somewhere, but I can't for the life of me remember …"

"You checked your files?"

"Immediately. No one by that name."

"I think you've mentioned that name. It'll come to you."

"I'll see what I can cancel and call to let you know when I'll be back. Oh, God. Why me?"

"Get hold of yourself, Nicky. Lawyers file all kinds of nonsense cases. Against doctors and against social workers too. It's one of the worst diseases of our country, of our society. So we'll talk."

Helen took two Tylenol capsules with a smidgen of water, sat perfectly still for ten minutes, and finally decided she would not throw up. As she dressed in blue jeans and a Mets sweatshirt, thinking about Nicky's call, Helen debated whether she should call Kayla, his daughter, or Max, his son, who was a lawyer but not one who handled medical malpractice cases as far as she knew, let alone psychiatric. Perhaps Nicky wanted to tell them about this himself. He had been unusually upset. Maybe his angst was due in part to the fact he'd been slowly reducing the number of patients he saw in preparation for retirement later in the year. The lawsuit would obviously force him to keep his mind wrapped up in his practice, even if he did retire, unless it could be resolved quickly.

Suicide. It was an ongoing concern, not only for psychiatrists, but for social workers. Helen recalled at least two of her own clients who had killed themselves, one of whom had been in the middle of therapy. She hadn't been sued, *Baruch Hashem*. And even though Helen felt these suicides were not preventable – both clients had consistently denied having suicidal ideations – she had still felt guilty. She had wracked her brain for clues she might have missed, hints she might have ignored. She had even seen a therapist herself a few times after the first of these tragedies. But then she'd been able to move on and, in doing so, continue to help others as the committed social worker she'd been.

A lawsuit filed against him would make it much harder for Nicky to move on, at least until it was resolved. And what if, against all odds, this was a case that actually went to trial? And what if, *Hashem* forbid, the case went against her husband? Nicky's fragile ego could shatter.

Suicide. Nicky had twice tried to kill himself. Twice that she knew of.

Jewish Visitors

Sister Theodora sat on her cot, rereading the letter she'd received a few days earlier from her brother. It was late afternoon in early March 1991. The weather had been cold and cloudy, and the light in her cell was barely sufficient for her to make out the writing, but thoughts about Nicky's letter had interrupted her immersion in daily prayer. She finally decided to stop praying and figure out what in Nicky's letter bothered her so much. On its face, it was a typically chatty missive, just the thing she'd come to expect from Nicky in the few months she'd been back at the monastery following her visit to America, although it did bear bad news.

"My Dearest Kal,

So much has happened here I wanted to tell you about. You'll be most interested in Jackie. He keeps asking about you and insists we must visit you in Greece. A seven-year-old doesn't quite understand what a monumental trip that would be, but Kayla and I told him – we had to in order to placate him – we'd think about it for this summer. I hope, if we visit, we will be able to spend a good deal of time with you and that our visit won't inconvenience you or the monastery. Jackie keeps talking about Abbess Fevronia and how you took her back to Greece in a box. He knows the word coffin, but keeps saying box. One thing he hasn't mentioned recently is how you believed he was the reincarnation of Jesus. Just as well he forget that. He's making good progress in his clarinet playing, by the way, and wanted me to tell you.

The worst news is that Helen's daughter Sarah has had a recurrence of her ovarian cancer. Things don't look great. I've tried to be supportive of Helen and her family. It's downright scary to think this wonderful young woman, with three children, might be taken from us. She's only 42. If you can say a prayer for her, please do. Now, you'll think that's an odd request, coming from an atheist. Yes, I still think of myself as such, and yet, knowing of the miracles you undoubtedly wrought, the miracle that saved my life, I can't help but ask you to seek divine intervention for Sarah. Thank you in advance for doing so.

And the last news is about Max, and maybe about a nightmare for him. Max is scheduled this summer to assist in a major trial in Chicago. It's so important for him, a new partner in the firm, and he's only second chair, but, as he tells me, that means he does most of the work and gets most of the blame if the case goes poorly. So the anxiety and stress are eating him up. I don't know how much you're aware of our crazy legal system here in America, but, to listen to Max, juries don't care about facts and only want to make sure someone gets the money otherwise sitting in the bank accounts of large corporations. We could do well without lawyers. I'd like to say I hate them, but I hate only the plaintiffs' lawyers. Max is one of the good guys.

Kayla will probably need a lot of help watching after Jackie when Max is gone. She hasn't been feeling well herself lately. She seems irritable, but, yes, I think she's still taking her meds. At least I hope so.

With that, I wish you well.

All my love,

Nicky"

Theodora wondered what in Nicky's letter worried her most. Sarah's illness? Theodora had talked quite a bit with Sarah, a lovely person, at Helen and Nicky's wedding the previous fall. Sadly, she was dying unless a miracle occurred. Theodora should have offered up a prayer to the Lord Jesus Christ for Sarah's healing, and she regretted not having done so yet. She'd thought about it and had come close to trying, but something had prevented her, something she could not explain. Perhaps that bothered her.

Or maybe it was Nicky's reference to her strong conviction that Jackie was the incarnation of the Second Coming. Nicky wanted Jackie to forget, as if God's message to Theodora, the message she'd misinterpreted but that led her to visit America, was something to be embarrassed about. Then why ask her to pray? What sense did it make for Nicky to deny God, yet try to have her do the difficult work of beseeching God to save a life?

Or maybe what gnawed at Theodora was the possibility the Holy Monastery of St. Vlassios might receive Jewish visitors from America in the coming months. Who exactly? Certainly Nicky and Helen, Jackie and Kayla. Theodora loved them all, but how long would they want to stay and what effect would their visit have on her daily prayer? Since her visit to America, Theodora's prayer had deepened, and she often felt herself at one with her Lord. She prayed often at Fevronia's gravesite, next to the stream Microdermis, a place where Theodora experienced the greatest peace.

Would the visit of her American relatives disrupt that blessed state?

Curveballs

Helen had attended the morning *minyan* at the West Side Institutional Synagogue as had been her habit when she had the time, and then she'd marched to Zabars to pick up bagels, rolls, rye bread, and cookies. She and Nicky had developed a weakness for these delicious baked goods and had lately gained a few pounds. But, she thought, what is life but to enjoy oneself while one can? Who knows when the end will come? Nicky's first wife, Adel, had died of a heart attack. Abbess Fevronia, while visiting America with Sister Theodora, had died of a heart attack too. A character in *Hamlet* – was it Horatio? – had remarked that the readiness was all. Helen was ready, if *Hashem* so willed, but she much preferred to be granted many more years of healthy living, wanting the joy of spending time with her grown children and watching her grandchildren grow up. In the meantime, she could still enjoy a toasted bagel with cream cheese.

Gritting her teeth and holding the large paper bag against her raincoat to protect it from the elements, she headed out of the shop. Although the weatherman and WABC promised temperatures would rise into the sixties by the afternoon, it was still raining and very cold by the time Helen got back to the apartment. With the wind compounding the chill – her umbrella had been useless – she felt she'd never get warm. Helen's headache had faded, but shivering kept her miserable.

An hour later, during which she dusted and vacuumed, wondering why Nicky failed to see the need for more frequent cleaning of his apartment, her husband arrived. He seemed somehow smaller than the six foot two inches to which she was accustomed. She switched off the Hoover, chucked it into the utility closet, and hugged him. His return hug was weaker than she'd been hoping for.

"I'm glad you came home early. Take off your hat and jacket and loosen your tie and tell me if you want a drink, even though it's still morning."

"I'd prefer coffee, if we have a pot going. Otherwise, just a glass of water."

Nicky made himself more comfortable as she'd instructed, opening his briefcase to pull out a bunch of papers, and sat on the living room sofa. A minute later, she brought him coffee in a gray Bellington mug, the music school's name in bright blue letters.

"So look at this shit." He handed her the complaint, and she read carefully. The patient, Shimon Yahon, had hanged himself in his family's Brooklyn home three years before. He was twenty-two, a college dropout, and had been involuntarily committed twice. His principal psychiatrist was Jonathan Waller. The lawsuit alleged Waller contributed to Yahon's suicidal ideation by talking to him about the conflicts in his own life and by approaching Yahon sexually, details of which were, apparently, recorded in a diary kept by Yahon and found by his family after his death. Supposedly, Waller purposely induced Yahon to take his own life, because Waller was afraid Yahon would disclose Waller's improprieties. Nicky was named as codefendant because he'd been taking a shift at Maimonides Medical Center when Yahon was brought there in extreme distress two days before the suicide. Nicky had allowed him to be discharged from the hospital the morning after his admission. Amazingly, the lawsuit alleged – as Nicky had told her – he knew Yahon was about to commit suicide but intentionally did nothing to prevent that occurrence.

"Outrageous," she said after handing the complaint back. "I didn't even know you had worked at Maimonides."

"It was only for a short time, just after Adel died, a few extra shifts on the psych unit. I was trying to … I don't know. Keep my mind busy. When I wasn't working, I was in a state of shock, grief …" He seemed about to break down.

"Easy, there." She hugged him again as they sat and kissed him on the side of his head. "It's totally normal, when you lose a spouse, to find ways not to think about the loss. I was in denial for a long time about David."

"I suppose so." To Helen it seemed as if Nicky's frown deepened at the mention of his long-ago friend. "So, I was working at Maimonides at the time this fucking complaint says I was there. I checked my records."

"And how many patients did you admit and then discharge? Any memory?"

"I was there for about four months, on and off. It happened a few times, I guess, when the day shift attendings were tied up and I was still around. I did mostly admissions, and usually the day shift attendings would review my notes, obviously talk to the patients, talk to the patients' families, and either keep or release them. Sometimes, they'd get me on the phone later, right after I'd gotten back home, to ask my opinions."

"Obviously, these are medical judgments. And how can you prevent someone from committing suicide if they're intent on doing it? You can't."

"You can keep them in the hospital, where they can be watched."

"You called your insurance company and reported this complaint?"

"Of course."

Helen wanted to assure him the case would be thrown out quickly, but hesitated, feeling that doing so would lead to an argument, the last thing she wanted. They had recently argued about a lot of things, the most serious of which was whether Nicky was adequately attentive to Helen's needs. A lot was going on in Helen's family, with Sarah's cancer by far the scariest. And then Helen thought maybe she could avoid an argument by reminding him simply that *Hashem* was fair and would protect him. He didn't believe in *Hashem*, or at least he didn't admit to any such belief, but he respected her own devotion. Before she could speak, though, he rose and walked into the kitchen, opening the bag she'd brought back from the bakery.

"I'm starved," he said as he found the cutting board and bread knife.

"Then let's toast two bagels."

"Right. We can't think clearly on empty stomachs about the ridiculous screwballs life throws us."

"I think the idiom is curveballs. But screwballs, sure. Fitting for psych patients. Let's go with screwballs."

Helen popped open the toaster oven, while Nicky seemed to stare at the knife longingly for a second before slicing into the first bagel.

To Clear One's Head

Kayla Covo sat at her upright Steinway piano, where she did her composing. On the low table next to her she had placed the blank staff paper, and next to that the *yeled tov kiddush* cup holding three sharpened No. 2 pencils, their pointed ends spreading outward as did the top of the Hebrew letter *shin*. *Shin* for *Shaddai*, she thought, *El Shaddai*, a name for *Hashem* meaning the All-Powerful Life Giver.

She'd bought the cup for Jackie when he'd turned five, made a big deal of teaching him the Hebrew phrase emblazoned on it and assuring him he was a very good boy. For more than a year, Jackie used the cup every *Shabbat*; it had held only grape juice, not wine. Then, not long after Sister Theodora returned to Greece, Jackie announced he no longer wanted to use the cup. He very much loved the cup, he said, but now – so suddenly – he wanted to use a more adult *kiddush* cup, just like those Kayla herself and Uncle Max used.

She removed a pencil and jotted down a few measures, then turned to the piano and played for what might have been the fourth time that morning. Her idea had been to write a piano sonata, her first. But for months, every time she sat to compose, she struggled to conjure more than the first three or four measures before becoming discouraged and crumbling her work into the wastebasket. She often wondered why it had been so much easier over the past eight years to compose for string quartets and other small chamber ensembles in contrast to composing for the piano alone. The only reason she could fathom was that the performing career she'd been forced to abandon still menaced her like a dark storm cloud. No one could rationally ask her to perform a string quartet, so she had been prolific in composing for that genre. But a new piece for solo piano would remind her audiences she had once been a prodigy, had shot to the highest tier of virtuosity as a teenager. Wouldn't she be asked to perform her own composition? In fact, wouldn't venue managers demand this? She knew she could no longer perform to the standards of perfection that had characterized her short career. And yet she still wanted to create for the solo piano, the voice of her soul, the closest link she had found between music and *Hashem*.

Kayla had heard about writer's block, but not about composer's block. Nothing like that had happened to Mozart, as far as she knew. If composer's block accurately described her problem, she had no idea how to get around it. She'd read that various authors had their peculiar ways of getting started. Some advocated not pushing, but just giving up on an unproductive day and starting anew on the morrow. She'd given up plenty during the past months, though, and that had not enabled her creativity. Some recommended taking a walk to clear one's head. Kayla walked daily in her hilly neighborhood, for exercise and for listening to the birds sing. The walking had kept her reasonably fit, but it hadn't opened any doors to new music.

Or a change of scenery, she thought. Hadn't Antonin Dvořák toured the United States for months as inspiration for some of his finest composing? Kayla had been through much of Europe on her final solo tour – Moscow, Rome, Copenhagen among the other cities she'd visited. She had no interest in returning to these places, where she'd hallucinated she was being stalked by a murderous fan. But then the obvious answer occurred. Why hadn't she thought of it earlier? She needed to go to Greece, to Sister Theodora's monastery, maybe to listen to the nuns singing their chants of the Psalms. Maybe to walk with Theodora through the valleys and hills of which her aunt had talked so movingly during her visit. A change of scenery, indeed, was just what she needed. And it would make sense to take Jackie to Greece when Max was going to be away anyway on his trial.

She would mull it over a while, but if it still seemed reasonable, she'd mention it to her father and Max. And Jackie, for sure. She had no doubt he would love to see Theodora again. Whether that was good or not for Jackie, she wasn't sure. But it could be a good thing for her. If it took a miracle to rediscover what Kayla had felt she'd lost, perhaps it was a miracle only Theodora could bring about.

A One-Off

Max and Kayla delayed dinner – although Jackie was permitted a yogurt snack in light of his demanding hunger – until Nicky and Helen arrived from Manhattan. The purpose of the visit was to discuss the lawsuit in which Nicky had been named a defendant. Although Max did not handle professional negligence cases, he felt confident enough about his general knowledge of law to be able to provide useful counsel. At least, he could listen sympathetically.

Kayla, who had received Nicky's initial call about being sued, worried about her father's mental health. He had sounded weird in a way she felt unable to specify. Perhaps shocked or stunned? Depressed, certainly, as if he had already lost the lawsuit, paid millions in damages, heard expert witnesses belittle his professional judgment, and been forced to give up what was left of his career. She felt she could do nothing more important than cheer up her father.

Jackie was excited that Grandpa and Helen would visit, although he was mildly upset dinner had to wait. On the other hand, *Ima* had given him permission to watch television, something that rarely happened on a week night. He had just begun watching *The Wonder Years* – conscious now, as he had not been the year before, that all characters were white – when Grandpa and Helen arrived. So much for television.

Over dinner, Nicky briefly repeated the main allegations of the complaint, careful for Jackie's sake not to use the words "suicide" or "killed himself" but referring instead to the "event." When he concluded, he handed Max the well-folded copy of the complaint he'd been referring to, and Max flipped through it quickly. "Terribly distressing, Dad, although I dare say from my own experience that everyone who's sued feels crappy, even when they know they've done nothing wrong."

"Your experience? Personal?" asked Helen.

Max sniggered. "Sorry to say. Last year some asshole in Texas – sorry, Jackie – sued our firm and the lawyers including me who defended Britten Industries on a toxic tort claim. They alleged nonsensical violations of … get this … insurance law. For defending a client. At best, it was a bad joke, and we got the suit dismissed in a few months, but being sued bothered the hell out of me, even when I knew the allegations were absurd. And, damn, frivolous lawsuits drive our clients nuts as well, knowing they're the victims of a litigation game having nothing to do with justice. Any successful company paints a big target on its back for plaintiffs' lawyers."

"You know, Max," observed Kayla, "you effectively started your legal career when you stood up for me about the contract with the Bellington people. We were plaintiffs. We'd been wronged. We were the ones who needed justice. So I'm surprised you ended up at a defense firm, I must say, and a large one, too. You represent the kinds of companies you used to want to sue yourself."

"Not true, my darling sister. Well, of Bellington, but not true otherwise. Anyway, come on. We're not here to talk about my career, but about Dad's problem. What can I tell you, Dad, from my perspective?"

"How do I get out of this quickly? And cheaply? And without having to be deposed? And without embarrassment? That's all I want."

"I wish there were an easy answer." Max picked up the complaint again to reread a paragraph or two, then shook his head. "Sometimes, in mass tort litigation, cases go away more quickly if the first few trials go badly for the plaintiffs, end up in defense verdicts or minimal recoveries."

"I guess there's a 'but' coming."

Max shrugged. "Well, this isn't a mass tort case. It's a one-off. Very strange as well."

"Which means, practically?"

"There might be no easy way of getting rid of it. But let me keep thinking."

Signaling

Kayla didn't know how long he'd been looking at her. Was it only this morning, or had he been doing so across the *mechitza* for days? Or was it even weeks? All she knew was that this man's focus had been on her and that she felt creepy when she became conscious of his gaze. She was not there to be gazed at, and he was not there to be gazing. They were both at the West Orange *Chabad* to pray.

She had noticed him also a few days earlier, as she left the *minyan* and he glanced at her while he spoke with Rabbi Beck. She didn't know his name. As a rule, men and women did not chat with each other. The twelve or thirteen men who usually attended would gather in one corner of the sanctuary as they put on their *tallesim* and *tefillin*. The women – two besides Kayla occasionally attended – meanwhile moved to seats on the other side of the *mechitza*. Only one-third of the room was allotted to women, who could not be counted as part of the *minyan*; still, there was more space for them than needed. When the *minyan* concluded, when the rabbi finished the lesson of the morning and the *kaddish de rabbanan* and mourner's *kaddish* had been recited, the women would leave quickly, speaking only to each other. So it was unusual, Kayla thought, that any man there would notice her.

He wore a black suit, a white shirt, a dark blue tie, and *tzitzit*. He was tall, maybe a touch over six feet, had dark but thinning hair, and she considered him reasonably good-looking. He had a full beard and mustache, both neatly trimmed, and wore golden wire-rimmed glasses and a black *kippah*. He had once or twice responded to a question posed by Rabbi Beck, his voice intelligent and cultured. When he'd used the Hebrew terms, he didn't affect what Kayla understood was the exaggerated Eastern European accent many of the other men used. His comments also showed he was well informed. He'd spoken about *Parsha Parah*, to be read on the coming *Shabbat*, which dealt with ritual purity. Kayla had been studying it by herself, and everything this man said – what was his name? maybe she had in fact heard it? – accorded with her own understanding, that there was no rational basis for the law; it was *chukkah*, to be done solely because *Hashem* had commanded it: a rare red heifer without blemish was to be slaughtered to help make the impure pure once more.

Purity had often been on Kayla's mind lately. She'd spent a lot of time cleaning the house. *Pesach* was coming, and she couldn't bear the idea of being impure in any way as the holiday and the *seders* approached. But it was a big house, especially when it had to be cleaned, and she was but one woman, and, even after the cleaning service had been there on Monday, she still saw signs of dirt and disorder. They'd used the wrong cleaning agent on the kitchen floor, and its tiles had developed an unpleasant-looking scum, which Kayla, on hands and knees, had spent more than an hour wiping off. Then she'd gone through Jackie's drawers, looking for cookie crumbs and candy and anything else that might make the house *chametzdik* for *Pesach*.

That's when she'd stumbled upon the icon, hidden behind Jackie's underwear and under a winter sweatshirt he'd crammed in. The icon was wood, roughly three and one-half inches by one inch, it looked hand-painted, and it depicted Jesus, wearing red and blue robes, holding a book in his left hand and signaling with the fingers of his right hand, the third finger touching the thumb.

Kayla had thought she might faint and sat quickly on Jackie's bed. The icon must have been given to him by Abbess Fevronia or Sister Theodora during their visit. Jackie had certainly not acquired this on his own. Kayla was tempted to throw the icon in the trash along with the half-eaten, ossified Mars bar she had collected near it. The icon wasn't *chametz*. It was worse. It made the house morally unfit, a place where a true *Pesach* couldn't be observed.

But then she wondered how, if she threw it away, she'd be able to question Jackie about it. If she were to confront her son, wouldn't she need to show him the evidence of his crime?

Aharon. That was it. Rabbi Beck had called him by name when he'd raised his hand to comment on the *parsha*. And what was the last name? She now recalled seeing his picture somewhere. It hit her suddenly she'd seen a photo of him in one of the monthly *Chabad* bulletins, which she kept in a tidy pile on the small desk in her bedroom. She rifled through them, anxious to have a full name to associate with the man whose eyes had locked onto her. And there he was. Of course, he was a teacher at the *Chabad* school, but teaching grades higher than Jackie's. He was *Hamoreh* Aharon Pottinger. How could she not have known? And she knew he was single. He would not have glanced at her otherwise, not a pious, *Chabad* Jew.

Was he near her age? Did it matter? Was he looking for a wife? And, if he was, what would he say if he knew that a pious nun in an Orthodox Christian monastery, none other than her Aunt Kal, had believed Kayla's son was the Second Coming of Jesus Christ?

Punishment

He hadn't intended to hide it from *Ima*. When Sister Theodora had given him the picture of Jesus painted on wood, she'd just said "This is Our Lord, Jesus Christ, the Savior," and he'd understood immediately she was just telling him what she believed. He had made it clear to everyone that *Hashem* couldn't be seen, that for Jews *Hashem* was not also a man. Yet, he'd been warned to respect the contrary beliefs of the visitors from Greece. He'd been told more times than he could remember how important Sister Theodora was to Grandpa, that she was Grandpa's sister, that she had been in *HaShoa*, and that anyone who survived *HaShoa* was to be shown the greatest care and love, no matter what they believed. So, he'd taken the icon from her, glanced at her as if to get further instruction on why she was giving this to him, but she'd smiled warmly and turned away to continue her prayers. He thought the man could not have been *Hashem*, but put the icon into his drawer and resolved not to worry about it.

He knew he'd put it all the way to the right side of the drawer, in the back, and it had remained undisturbed for weeks. Every so often he felt for it, to make sure it was still there. It wouldn't do for him to have lost this gift, even long after Sister Theodora returned to Greece. And then he'd forgotten about it entirely.

On this morning, however, he remembered the icon again and once again felt for it. When he realized it wasn't in its corner, he pulled the drawer out farther and checked a wider area. Thus, he discovered it in the center of the drawer, still in the back, but now behind his t-shirts. He was certain the icon had been moved and that *Ima* had found it. Now, he dreaded what was undoubtedly to come: she would yell at him and punish him. Even though he didn't pray to the man painted on the wood, *Ima* would feel his keeping the gift in his drawer was an unforgivable sin. His consciousness of guilt was so severe that he instantly developed nausea and a headache. While still in his clothes, he got into his bed and pulled the covers over his head.

Inevitably, *Ima* called from downstairs to tell him supper was ready, and he couldn't respond. Within minutes, she was in his room, feeling his forehead with her hand. He had to be feverish, he thought. How could he not be inflicted with a disease as punishment from *Hashem* for what he had done? The only way to escape *Hashem*'s anger was to confess. The confession couldn't wait for the next *Yom Kippur*. By then, he would be dead.

"I'm sorry, *Ima*." He could hardly get the words out before breaking down. But he didn't have to say more. She knew what he'd done.

She leaned over him and kissed him on the head. "Shush, my son. There's no need to cry. I understand."

The File

Nicky stared glumly at the lawyer assigned by his insurance carrier to handle the claim against him. The card he'd been given after he was ushered into the lawyer's midtown office had been entirely superfluous. He already knew the lawyer's name – Martin Edelmann – and address. How else could he have shown up in the right place and the right time? He was annoyed as well that he'd had to give up an afternoon of seeing patients to meet with the lawyer. The interview could have been conducted with equal effect, if not better, by telephone. But Edelmann had been persistent. Meeting in person at the outset of a case "was the way he did business." He had "wanted to get off on the right foot."

Nicky had been obliged to comply. His malpractice policy made such requirements explicit, Edelmann had reminded him. Comply with the lawyer's requests or lose coverage.

"I do thank you for coming in."

"It's not terribly convenient, particularly having to park in a garage around here."

"No. I'm sure it's not. May I call you Nikolas?" he asked, glancing at his notes.

Nicky sighed. He much preferred strangers to call him Dr. Covo, but he understood it would not serve his interests to insist on such a formality. "I go by 'Nicky.'"

"I'm Marty to you."

"Great. So, if we can make this quick …"

"Oh, yes, certainly. Why don't you just start by telling me about your background?"

He had to be kidding, Nicky thought. The carrier had covered his malpractice claims for over three decades. They had every single document on his background. Was this Edelmann too lazy to read through the file? Did he even bother to find out what was in the file? Nicky sighed. Just get it over with, he told himself. Give Edelmann what he wants. Make it short and sweet.

"Naturalized American citizen in '55. September 30. I remember, because of the swearing-in ceremony. I had to miss the third game of the World Series. Tickets on the first-base line."

"The World Series?"

"Dodgers and Yankees?" Edelmann looked young enough not to have even been born by the time the Dodgers won their first World Series.

"Not a baseball fan, I'm afraid. So, continue please. Your psychiatry background is what I'm interested in."

"Robert Wood Johnson Medical School '52, completed my residency in psychiatry in '55. I've been practicing psychiatry in Brooklyn since then. At the beginning, part of a small group practice, but on my own since '59. Board-certified in neurology and psychiatry since '60."

"Published articles?"

"A few, back in the sixties, but I sent you my resume. I assume you've read it."

"All right, then, tell me about this allegation."

"You lawyers. You make up shit, if you don't mind my French."

Edelmann nodded knowingly, as if this was a conversation he'd had a thousand times. "Dr. Covo, I mean … Nicky … I didn't file this complaint, and I'm trying to defend you from a serious allegation. I agree with you that too many lawyers file weak claims, trying to shake down insurance companies. But we won't get very far here if all we do is disparage the legal system. It's the system we have, it sucks, and yet we have to deal with it."

"Fine. I don't remember this particular case, Yahon, although I know the name. There was a family by that name living near us in Salonika, before the war. That's Greece, by the way. A common enough name in our community." Nicky pointed to the complaint lying on the corner of the conference room table. "As to these ... outrageous charges, I've taken hospital shifts on and off over the years, and I was taking even more back then, to keep my mind busy. Did I sign the discharge papers for a Shimon Yahon? I probably did, but I haven't seen them. I don't think anyone would forge my signature."

"Well, I have the file here. Look for yourself."

Edelmann removed a folder from the leather briefcase he'd placed on the table and handed the folder to Nicky. Nicky flipped through the few pages and found what he was looking for. "Yes, that's my signature on the Discharge Summary. You'd probably find another few from that night in similar circumstances."

"The circumstances here don't ring any bells?"

"You're kidding, right? A patient who's in psychological distress brought in by family members? That's all we saw." He looked at the page on Admissions. "Threatening self-harm? Nothing particularly of note there. Like I said, routine. That was the business of the ER, to funnel the crazies to the psych staff, and it happened repeatedly."

"What do you know of Dr. Waller in this case, whom plaintiffs named as a co-defendant?"

"I've known Jon maybe years. Or more. A big player in Brooklyn psychiatry, but retired now, I think."

"He's deceased. Two years ago."

"Really? I hadn't heard that."

"Apparently neither had the Yahon family's lawyer, because they were still trying to serve him as of last week. They've now served the executor of Waller's estate, so the estate's now officially a co-defendant. But what kind of contact did you have with Waller?"

"Oh dear. At times we referred patients to each other. He was more willing to work with children and young adult patients than I was. Although I did plenty of those too. But if someone called me with a child psych problem, I would occasionally give them Jon's name. And he would send me an occasional geriatric patient." Nicky stopped to think for a moment. "Other than that, no special relationship."

"You co-wrote an article, didn't you?"

Nicky thought for a second, then grimaced. "Of course we did. I'd forgotten completely. That was a long time ago, and … wow … I don't even remember what we wrote about. A case study, most likely. Yes, if memory serves, I did most of the writing, but he was listed as senior author. He did have ten years on me."

"Any hard feelings?"

"Because he was senior author? Hardly. I couldn't even remember the damn article a second ago. Can't truly remember it now. And what does this have to do with the claim against me? If you would be so kind as to tell me."

"Probably nothing, although there are serious allegations here about Waller, as you know. I'm going to have to track down the article, unless you have a copy."

"I don't think I do. I most likely put it out of my mind as soon as it was accepted. I probably never even read it in its published form."

"It's unfortunate Dr. Waller isn't with us."

"If he was having a sexual relationship with Shimon Yahon – and you can be sure I'd have no knowledge – I'm glad he's not here."

"Hmm. Maybe. Although, if he were here, he could deny it. I assume, from what you've said, you didn't correspond with him or talk to him at all about the case?"

"Why would I have? Correspond? As in writing? Highly unlikely. There would be no reason to do so. I doubt very much I even knew Waller was this patient's psychiatrist."

"So, tell me please, as a matter of general practice, what you do with patients such as this Yahon when you're the attending? How do you decide whether to refer them for further treatment or release them?"

Nicky picked up the chart again and read it more carefully. Putting it down, he thought for a minute before answering. "All right, Marty. I talk to the patient, I talk to the family members who are at the hospital, as I must have done here, where there's a note about the patient's father. I talk to nurses who may have interacted with the patient. If the patient was admitted before my shift, I talk to the admitting physician when he's available. He or she. If there's someone with pertinent information available by phone, I call them. We do the obvious. We ask whether the patient formulated a specific plan. There's no evidence here that Shimon Yahon did. We assess the degree of agitation, if any. We try to see if there are hallucinations, if the patient is talking to someone not in the room, hearing things no one else can hear. That kind of thing. No evidence here of hallucinations." He stopped for a few seconds to catch his breath. "In fact, no evidence of psychosis, other than what's on the admission form. Here: 'Talking crazy. Wanting to kill himself.' Unfortunately, no additional detail re observations. 'History from father.' Pretty bare bones, but not unusual. The hospital's a busy place. Honestly, when we fill out our charts, we don't have time to enter all the details, although we should. We being the attendings."

"Can a suicidal patient hide his intent?"

"Obviously. If he's smart enough. Or any patient, like Yahon, might talk about ending it all and not mean it at the time of observation, but might decide afterward they do mean it. Then they form a plan and execute it only after you've released them. Human beings are complex, as I'm sure you appreciate. Just like … a witness, perhaps, the types you deal with in your profession. You may think he's going to say X and …"

"And he gets on the stand and says Y. Quite true. It does happen."

"So, this witness totally screws up your case, and you can get sued for legal malpractice, right? It's a bitchy world."

"I hear you, Nicky, and I agree."

Legalese

Kayla could not fall asleep, and the more she tried, the more agitated she became. She couldn't remember if she'd taken her meds. Would the bizarre thoughts still run rampant through her mind if she'd been more careful? She vowed to do better. She'd sworn to the judge in Jackie's custody case, just months before, that she'd do better, had sworn to Jackie, had sworn to everyone. Yet, maybe she had skipped a day or two. Aharon had been on her mind.

Now, as she lay in her bed, unsettled and uneasy, she was frustrated by her inability to relieve herself sexually. That had never happened before. When she'd given up the effort, she'd drifted into sleep with a vivid dream sequence. She saw the grotesque mask of a young German soldier in excruciating pain. It was a picture she'd formed from the story her father had told her, one that had plagued him as well following his harrowing experiences in the war, his miraculous escape from certain death. The dream soldier spoke to her, but made no sense. She'd never studied German nor performed in a German-speaking country. And then this soldier became Max, and Max was yelling at her, lecturing her about something. "Take your pills," the dream Max commanded, leering at her. That, at least, she could understand. But he was also angry. Why else would he tell her so forcefully to "go away"? Where did that come from? Where could she go? This was her home, and Max wanted her gone? What would happen to Jackie if she left Jackie with Max? Then she was in a tall building in an apartment that must have been hers after she had left Max's house. Jackie was near an open window. He climbed up on the edge and glanced back at Kayla. He said goodbye. He said now you will learn your lesson. She had struggled to stop him, but could not move. Jackie disappeared.

She jumped up, fully awake, her heart pounding as if it might explode. Her room was dark, save for the faint light creeping under her door from the hallway. She tried to remember the dream, what the dying soldier had yelled at her in German, and why in particular Max wanted her to leave. He didn't, she realized with a large measure of relief. He wanted her to stay. So why dream the opposite? And why was Jackie in danger? Why did Jackie feel so distant from her he'd push himself out of a window? She would take her pills. She would no longer threaten the life of the son she loved more than anything else in the world. She saw the purpose of the dream was to remind herself of her solemn obligations, the only way to fight the schizophrenia that had ended her performing career.

Kayla glanced at her clock; it was only 11:00 pm. She had slept for only five or ten minutes. Trying to sleep again would be futile. She donned her large blue robe, one of the few things of her mother she'd kept, and left her room, intending to drink a glass of warm milk, when she noticed the light in Max's office. Still up, still working hard. A twinge of guilt trickled through her, because she felt she'd not adequately been supportive. Max was surely in a lot of stress with the trial coming, the stress was growing, and she'd never even given him a chance to unload to her. Should she knock? Offer to bring him coffee if he intended an all-nighter? Would she disturb his train of thought, as he occasionally disturbed hers when she was trying to compose?

She knocked lightly and heard no answer. Then she knocked harder, and the door, which had not been fully closed, pushed open far enough for her to see that Max was asleep, his head back on his chair. He looked uncomfortable. She felt he'd be much better off sleeping in his bed. She walked in, put her hand on his shoulder, and gently nudged him awake.

"Kayla? What time is it?" Then he looked at his watch. "Damn."

"You should get in bed. Sleeping here won't help. If you have so much work, at least get an hour or two of shuteye before you get back to whatever you're doing."

He shook his head, despairingly. "I don't know. I'm supposed to put a draft on Phil's desk when I go in tomorrow morning. He said have it there by seven. He said make sure it's perfect. I've barely started, and it's a piece of shit."

"Don't say that."

"Here. You can read what I've done so far." He pulled a few sheets of paper from his printer and handed them to her. "A motion to exclude expert testimony." He shook his head again, this time with a look of resignation. "A mess."

She sat on the chair next to his desk, a captain's chair decorated with the Fordham Law School logo. "It's legalese." She read the three pages again, then handed them back. "You should write like you were talking to me. Simple. I haven't been to law school and don't know about your judge, but he'd probably appreciate something he could understand the first time through and not have to reread it."

"The judge is a she. Sharon Metcalf."

"Whatever. She'd appreciate."

He reread what he'd written, then grabbed a pencil and started marking up the draft. "You're right. Thanks. I think I'll keep at it now."

She watched him work for minutes. It appeared as if he'd forgotten her presence. Then he turned to her, puzzled. "You're still here. There's something you want to talk about?"

She pulled the robe closer around her, uneasy it had slipped open slightly while she'd watched him. "I dreamed … just now … you were angry with me. You wanted me to leave. To leave this house. I know it's silly, but …"

"You can't really think I want that. With you gone, this house would feel so incomplete, empty. I don't want to be alone; you know that as well. I want just the opposite, for you to stay as long as you want to, forever, if you want to."

They stood simultaneously, as if drawn from their chairs by a clever puppeteer, who then yanked them together. Kayla pulled him as tightly against herself as she dared, sorry for the dream and for having told him about it. Their hug lasted a full minute. Max pressed his chin against the top of Kayla's head, resting it on her fine brown hair. Then they separated, embarrassed. They hadn't hugged like that for months.

He smiled finally, and she thought: he loves me like a brother should. How can I leave him? "Max ... my dream ... Why would I think you wanted me to leave? What does it mean?"

"I'm just a lawyer, you know. If you want an interpretation of your dream ..."

"I know ... talk to Dad."

"Talk to Dad, right. He has a theory for everything. Now please let me get back to work."

On Her Sarcasm

To her great surprise, it appeared Aharon knew a lot about music and about her. But first things first.

They had agreed to meet in no less auspicious place than Rabbi Beck's house, or at least in what he and his wife called their "Florida room." It gave them both a modicum of privacy and the sense they were carefully chaperoned. Rabbi Beck had assured Kayla – and hence, she assumed, Aharon – that neither he nor his wife would dream of eavesdropping. He also told her with a chuckle that she should scream if she needed help, but this last directive had been unnecessary. Kayla was sure she would scream if she needed to.

"You look lovely," Aharon said, standing, as Rabbi Beck escorted her into the enclosed porch.

It took Kayla a second longer than was seemly to acknowledge this compliment with a polite, if uninspired, "Thank you." His comment immediately made her think of all the thousands of fans who had approached her when she signed programs or CDs for them after a concert and how they often started with similar inanities. "I've caught you looking at me more than once at the *Chabad*, you know."

"I wanted to meet you long ago, it's true. The famous Kayla Covo. When …"

"Wait. What did you say?"

"I wanted to meet you long ago?"

"No, after …"

"That I wanted to meet the famous Kayla Covo?"

"Famous, because …?"

He could not believe she wanted to play this game. "You are of course the pianist. I would've recognized you anywhere. I saved the two *Life* magazines with your picture on the cover. I'm one of your biggest fans, but honestly until I came back home I didn't know you lived here. So … why do you want to pretend you're not she?"

"I'm not pretending anything." She was put off by his lapse into fandom. She couldn't tolerate being of interest to him only because of her career as a pianist. And yet his reference to the *Life* covers brought back that longing she still felt, to be in front of audiences again. Aharon – intentionally or not – had reminded her of what had kept her going for so long, the adulation of her fans.

Aharon continued, "I mean, it's your business, but I would have never asked Rabbi Beck if I could meet you if I thought my talking about your music would be painful."

"No, it's not painful. Well, not very. You just caught me off guard. I didn't realize our meeting had anything to do with my having been a pianist. This comes out of the blue."

"I didn't say to Rabbi Beck that was my reason. I didn't give him any reason for trying to set this up, other than that I wanted a chance to meet you and talk to you, because I'm single and I know you're single. I would have wanted to be introduced to you even if I didn't know about your career."

"Well, is that supposed to be a compliment? Do I look like the attractive and subservient wife I sense you're looking for?"

She didn't understand why she had turned sarcastic. She feared, even as she spoke, that he would call her on her bitchy attitude and walk out. Indeed, she hated herself for being caustic, but something inside had taken control over her speech. She held her breath, waiting to see if Aharon would in fact leave, but he wore a smile as he contemplated how to respond to her questions. Well, she thought, he's not overly sensitive. She would have to control her evil impulse.

Aharon was cute, she'd decided two seconds after they sat in the wicker chairs arranged for them by Rabbi Beck. She silently berated her snideness and resolved to treat Aharon with the utmost respect.

"It's a compliment about how you look praying, because I can see glimpses of you when I'm on the *bimah*."

"And how do I look?" she asked, finally relaxing enough to smile.

"You look devoted to *Hashem* in a way I wish I could feel."

That this young man was making a major admission about a personal fault – a lack of feeling for *Hashem* – stopped Kayla from saying anything. They were hardly good enough friends that he should confess such a thing to her, yet his matter-of-fact honesty intrigued her. He waited for her response, and she was unsure what to say. It wouldn't do to make fun of his lack of faith; for all she knew, she was the only person who could urge Aharon to regain it. Well, he was dressed as a *Chasid*; he must have felt something for *Hashem* at some point.

"I don't know of any religion – well, except maybe for one – in which adherents are always in a prayerful mood."

"The one? The exception?"

And so Kayla, ignoring the subject of music altogether, recounted to Aharon the weird facts of her family's history, how her aunt was a nun at a Greek monastery, how this aunt, once known as Kal Covo, now known as Sister Theodora, might be just that person who could marshal the deepest feelings of love toward *Hashem* every time she wanted to pray. Well, not *Hashem* exactly, but the Christian version; still, prayer was prayer, wasn't it? Kayla went on for longer than she intended, as she turned to the history of her father during the Nazi occupation of Greece.

"Thank you for sharing so much with me. I ..."

But Aharon was interrupted by a polite knock on the door from the main part of the house. Rabbi Beck stood in the doorway.

"Still getting to know each other?"

Aharon looked at Kayla as if for guidance.

Wondering whether they had extended their stay beyond reason, Kayla said, "Well, it is late."

"May I see you again please?" asked Aharon as he stood. "Here, I mean …?"

"No problem with us, Kayla, if you want to."

Kayla paused. Did she? It wouldn't hurt, she concluded, and he was good-looking. "Next week then," she said. "Same time?"

"Same time, yes. Thank you, Kayla."

"But Aharon, next time you tell me more about yourself. And … we'll talk more about music, I promise."

Beating About the Bush

She learned a fair amount about Aharon from asking what she hoped were discreet questions at the *Chabad*. To get information, she had to share with the women her interest in Aharon. The women were generally not inclined toward gossip, *lashon hara* being terribly frowned upon by observant Jews, so Kayla had to be careful not to seem like she sought just negative information. No one would venture to tell her anything bad, unless Aharon was a known sex abuser, but she didn't feel this likely. She expected to hear only good things.

Kayla gathered that Aharon's family had always lived in the area, that his parents were furriers whose main store was in Newark. Aharon himself had been away for eight or ten years, and – most tantalizing – had studied a musical instrument or was very musical himself. Yes, although his family did not particularly value what Aharon could do musically – he played a stringed instrument, Kayla learned, but no one was sure which – they were pleased to have him home. Aharon was probably between jobs. That's how more than one person put it, a polite way of saying he was unemployed. His job teaching at *Chabad* was only temporary and part time. So, if you don't have a real job, you're not a great marriage prospect, thought Kayla, and she wondered now if she should be unhappy with Rabbi Beck for setting up their meeting. But, one confidant assured her, Aharon had "good prospects." He was interested in business. He was thought to be smart and ambitious. Hearing as much, Kayla duly presented herself at their second private meeting.

Aharon confirmed all Kayla had been told. He'd studied the cello, starting at age nine, he'd been in his school's orchestra, he got a music scholarship to Georgetown University, he'd obtained a Masters in Music Performance from Yale, he'd taught at Stonybrook for two years, but now he'd returned to his hometown and wanted to settle down. He had minored in Business Administration and was looking for the right situation, but did not want to go into his family's furrier business.

Kayla was fascinated. She and others at Bellington had taken a different approach to music. Music for Bellington students had been so important it blocked out attention to other disciplines entirely. Aharon focused on music, true, but had a more rounded education. Along with business courses, he told her with obvious pride, he'd taken courses in religion, Israeli politics, drama, and international relations.

"I never got a degree," she said wistfully.

"You didn't need one. I was at your concert in New Haven, by the way. Stunning. I've never heard that kind of ovation anywhere else. I tried to get in line to visit you, but you came out front to sign CDs for only a few minutes, and many of us were disappointed.

"Oh, dear. I'm so sorry, Aharon. If you want something signed, I'm happy to do it."

"Really? Great! But that night I just wanted to meet you, and it was public, and no one would say such a meeting was inappropriate. You left, making apologies, before I even got close."

She was hesitant to ask him about what symphonies he'd performed with or what classical recitals he'd given on his own. She didn't want to embarrass him. Perhaps he'd had none and he'd think she was trying to draw a comparison between their careers.

"Well, I'm here now." Attempting humor, she asked, "You didn't move back to West Orange only to meet me, did you?"

Aharon smiled, but didn't appear to realize Kayla had been joking. "No. Like I said, I had no idea. I just thought this was the place to settle down, near my folks, near the *Chabad* I knew. And, in DC, New Haven, Stonybrook … I never found an observant woman whom I wanted to spend a lot of time with."

She thought for a few seconds before continuing. "Do you buy into the idea that, if the marriage is good, then love will come along later?"

He chuckled. "If I thought love always comes along, I think I'd be naïve. Like Nick said at the end of *Gatsby*: Wouldn't it be pretty to think so? I'm a realist. A good marriage is made better by love, but if there's enough respect and caring and devotion to getting *Hashem*'s will done, then it can be good without romantic love." He sounded to Kayla as if he were trying to convince himself.

Kayla wasn't sure what response Aharon was hoping for, if any. She was just trying to get him to talk. Well, she'd gotten an answer and a not unexpected one. In *Chabad*, marrying was not about love, unless it was love for *Hashem* and a desire to do *Hashem*'s will, namely, be fruitful and multiply. Sadly, not everyone could do that. Some were destined never to marry. Her aunt was one, for example. But Kayla felt herself still in that category of woman, only twenty-six, where marriage might fulfill a great longing and need. But to marry without love? She didn't think she could do that.

"I don't know. How do you ever get to enough respect, I think you said, and …"

"Caring and devotion."

"… caring and devotion, without love behind it? Isn't love what makes one care and be devoted and have respect for the loved one?"

She'd thought Aharon would be ready with a retort, imagining that this was a conversation he'd had many times, if not with other women, then at least with himself. Yet, she appeared to have stumped him.

"I'll have to think about that one." And he did appear to think for a minute, while pouring himself another glass of iced tea, before continuing. Waiting, Kayla munched on the potato chips Miriam,

Rabbi Beck's wife, had set out. While she was on her third, Aharon finally continued. "We don't know what love is, do we?"

"I thought I knew once."

"Yes, you have a son. I've seen him at *Chabad*."

"I thought I loved his father, but ..." Kayla's silence conveyed as much as she could have said with words.

"That's why I don't put a lot of stock in love as a basis for a marriage. It can be so temporary, wouldn't you agree? And, in truth, what is it?"

"So you never were in love ...?"

She couldn't tell what lay behind his brief smile.

"Never in love, although I had a crush on a girl once, at Georgetown. But that went nowhere. She wasn't even Jewish."

"Did you ask her out?"

"No, never. I'm committed only to an observant Jewish relationship. That's why I'm here now, with you, exploring possibilities. Isn't that why we're both here?"

"I think, if August had loved me, I might never have become *Ba'alat T'shuva*. In a way, I'm lucky he was only using me. The terrible loneliness and fear I suffered when I realized he didn't care about me as he said helped lead me to *Chabad*. It was *Hashem*'s way."

Aharon looked at her intently, as if ready for her to continue revealing what had driven her to this group of *Chasidic* Jews. But Kayla's thought had drifted quickly, from August, to their concert tour, to the idea of musical collaboration generally. And that quickly caused her to remember what she'd promised. "Please tell me about the cello, Aharon, what you've done on it, what it's meant to you."

"Can I be honest with you?"

"I expect you to be honest, or there's no point in our talking."

"Agreed. So, I love the cello, and yet it's so frustrating."

"Because you haven't yet reached your potential?"

He frowned for an instant, then replaced the frown with a smile of self-recognition. "No. Because I have, unfortunately. Because I've gone far past my potential and I recognize – I've recognized for a long time

– that I don't have the great talent or the dogged perseverance to make performing a career. I decided when I was at Stonybrook that I would only teach cello, not perform professionally. Well, I admitted to myself I couldn't make it as a performer. So, I do teach, I have two students, but only two. I can do much more there for perfecting the world, for *Tikkun Olam*, for helping to guide young people toward *Hashem*, than I can do through performing."

"I thought I'd heard you were going into business somewhere."

"Well, that's what I imagined too. But I've been mulling it over. Business for my folks seems to be their life, but I don't want to worry constantly about dollars. So, now I've decided teaching Judaism is a better way to live. It doesn't pay a lot, but I can make do."

"Do you love teaching? Because I think you must love it to want to do it for a living."

"It too has its frustrations, just as anything else worth doing."

"Frustrations. Such as?"

"Unmotivated students, for one."

"It's the teacher's job to motivate them, like Herr Lindorf at Bellington motivated me. Your job – if you want to make it your life's work – is to guide your students toward *Hashem*."

"True, and it's a worthy undertaking. Worthy perhaps of a place in *ha'olam haba*. But still frustrating. Ha, listen to me complaining about my non-career, when you …"

The dismal look on her face, one she couldn't hide, caught him in confusion for a second. Then, he understood.

"I'm sorry, Kayla. That was thoughtless. You had to give up your career …"

"Please," she said, stopping him with a raise of her hand. "I know what I gave up. And I assume you know why. Let's stop beating about the bush, if you will. What do you think about … about connecting with someone who has schizophrenia? An illness that will never be cured?"

He reddened around the roots of his thick beard. "I don't know much about your illness, other than you stopped concertizing eight years ago because of … They called it mental exhaustion. At first, I thought you would just take a break and come back to the concert stage. But in the music circles at Yale, yes, schizophrenia was mentioned. I did want to broach the topic, but we don't have to do it now. Maybe, if we're still inclined to meet, we can …"

"No. Let's get it out now." She took a deep breath. "Okay. You heard 'mental exhaustion.' What a euphemism. I'm glad you'd heard about it, however, and still wanted to talk with me. If we decide we're attracted to each other …"

"Are we attracted to each other?"

She stared at him blankly.

"Let me rephrase that, Kayla. Yes, I am attracted to you. So, what I mean to ask is, is this mutual? Is it too soon to say?"

"Let me think." Okay, schizophrenia was out on the table. He'd known, or at least he'd heard the rumor. He still wanted to talk with her. He was still interested. And, she reminded herself once again, he is cute. But she would have to move this forward one tiny step at a time. "I would like to keep meeting. For now. Is that enough? I mean, it's not exactly what you said, but it's not the opposite either."

He smiled. "Do you think the rabbi and rebbetzin will go along? We might have to rent out their Florida room."

"Let's ask. Or maybe we can meet somewhere else."

Investigations

It was time, Kayla thought, to begin additional investigations. She was pretty sure one of her fellow piano students at Bellington had gotten a Ph.D. and joined the Georgetown School of Performing Arts faculty. She knew he'd arrived at Georgetown long after Aharon had left, but her friend was willing to inquire of old-timers. Only one, who'd conducted the school orchestra, remembered Aharon, and not well. But the report was encouraging. A "solid" student was the term that kept coming up. "Nothing bad, but nothing to write home about either." Well, that assessment was obviously not up to date. Aharon certainly had something to write home about, as he'd earn a master's degree from Yale.

But she was frustrated in her desire to learn more. Kayla had driven to Newark and wandered about his family's store for a few minutes, learning nothing other than what she'd already known. She could ask Rabbi Beck for further details about Aharon's family, and it probably wouldn't hurt to ask, but she didn't want to seem overly eager or suspicious. At some point, if Aharon wanted her to become his wife, she would have to learn more. She felt unfairly inhibited by the limitations imposed by strict Orthodox protocols on any courtship. Aharon had never even offered to shake her hand, apparently respecting her presumed desire not to be touched by a man except following a formal engagement.

The best way to get to know Aharon was to do so at her home, as long as Max would be there and cooperate. Max could be a jerk. She'd known for years, maybe even as far back as her early childhood, that Max cared about her deeply and would look after her. But Max also had had difficulty with her maturing into a woman, didn't like the publicity photos she was required to pose for, and had obviously been jealous when she became involved with August. It was part of the reason, she suspected, why Max had flattened August with a punch after learning she was pregnant. Although she was sure Max wouldn't have a similarly violent episode with Aharon, still, she'd have to consider Max's anticipated jealousy.

And what about Jackie? She had scarcely thought about what her having a boyfriend, a husband possibly, might mean for Jackie. All the more reason, though, to have Aharon over to the house soon. She had to learn if Aharon and Jackie were compatible. They had a common interest in music, which was probably good, although she couldn't imagine Jackie, with his clarinet, managing a duet with a cellist. Well, things could happen along those lines. There was some creative music still being composed for that combination. But Aharon was a teacher, and he was teaching music as well as Judaism, so she wondered if he might try to interfere with – in his view aid – Jackie's musical education. Jackie was not the seven-year-old one could pressure into practicing a different way. He was devoted to his clarinet, but insisted on doing everything as he saw fit. A smart Aharon would show interest, but not become oppressive. How was this to be arranged?

She broached the topic at dinner.

"So, guys, listen up," she started. "I've been meeting a man at Rabbi Beck's house to see if we're compatible."

"What?" they chorused.

"A *Chasid*, he goes to *Chabad* and has come back to this area, where his family lives. We're evaluating each other to see if we're a match."

Max was too shocked to comment immediately, but without hesitation Jackie asked, "*Ima*, what do you mean, a match?"

"Well, someday I might meet a man I want to marry. If I meet someone who is the right man for me and I am the right woman for him, then that would be a match." Kayla explained quickly how she knew Aharon, how Rabbi Beck had suggested they might want to meet, and how she had now met him twice privately. She also explained Aharon taught at the Chabad school and played the cello, making his connection to music another reason for her to be interested in him. "And so, the next step, if you're willing Max, is to have Aharon over here for dinner. We're only two miles from his apartment, so definitely we could do it on a *Shabbat*. He wouldn't mind the walk."

"I guess I'm …"

"Surprised?"

"At a loss for words? It's not that I don't want you to have whatever life you want. It's just … you haven't mentioned interest in men, as men, since we've lived together. So, surprised? A bit. But, good, let's have him over."

"*Ima*, you told me many times I was your only guy."

"And that's true, Jackie. You will always be my most special guy. But don't I also need someone about my age to be with me? Like, for company when you go off to college?" She thought for a second, concerned Jackie wasn't buying into her reasoning. "And maybe to help make a baby sister or brother for you, if *Hashem* wills?"

"You could do that?"

"It's possible."

"But why do you need *Moreh* Aharon for that?"

"Um … That's how *Hashem* has designed us human beings, that's how it's usually done."

"Well, maybe. A baby would be cool, but I'd have to think about it."

"We're nowhere near making such a decision yet, but is it okay if this new friend comes over? To meet you and Uncle Max?"

"Does he like jazz?"

"I haven't asked him yet."

"Ask him. Please."

"I will."

Three Young Mothers

It had been exceedingly warm for March, even late March. Some of the forecasts predicted temperatures as high as 80 degrees by mid-afternoon, and, although it didn't get quite that warm, still there were many out and about in Donaldson Park, sunbathing as it were after a long winter, when Sarah drove up to Helen's house, the house where Sarah had grown up. She had decided on a mid-afternoon arrival, to ensure she could talk to Helen alone, without Nicky's hovering.

Once in the house, Sarah spotted Helen rushing down the stairs to meet her. Before Sarah could say anything, Helen hugged her fiercely. Helen had been crying, and Sarah knew why. She'd said the purpose of her visit was to explain what Dr. Galvani, the oncologist, had just told her over the phone. No, Sarah had insisted, it would be much better for her to share everything in person with Helen, and she could be over in fifteen minutes. Helen knew then the news was bad, maybe the worst, and had been unable to hold back her tears.

After a minute, Sarah gently released herself from Helen's grasp. "It's as you've guessed, Mom. Not good. The scan lit up throughout my spine and pelvis, and there's ..." At this, Sarah broke down as well. "I thought I could do this ..."

"I know, darling. It's okay. Let it out." Helen led Sarah to the sofa, where they sat, and Sarah once again sought the comfort of her mother's embrace.

"Six months, tops," she finally said through her sobs. "But it could be much sooner. No way to know."

"I'm so sorry, love. I don't know what else to say. Just let me hold you."

That her daughter was going to die – and die soon – from this horrid disease was a reality now, no longer an abstract concept of statistics and probabilities. Ever since Sarah's cancer was discovered, throughout the trials of chemotherapy and radiation, Helen had tried to imagine how she would react if and when faced with news every parent fears the most. She thought she would be brave; after all, a social worker hears many sad stories throughout a career, loses clients to all manners of death – one had shockingly been murdered – and needs a thick skin. She would make sure she kept everything under control. But when the time came, as it had, Helen felt unable to be brave. Indeed, she felt exactly the opposite of brave; she had never felt more frightened in her life. She could not maintain the façade of control. Sarah was the one who clearly needed support, but Helen felt herself a victim too, a victim of cruel circumstances, albeit a manifestation of *Hashem*'s will. And she felt ashamed that, at this crucial moment, she was more concerned with herself than with Sarah. Yet, she could not in the instant stop worrying about her own mental health. Would she collapse at Sarah's funeral, making a fool of herself? How could she possibly be a substitute mother for her grandchildren when she was aging and they were in the prime of youth? How could she, as frail as she felt, possibly be a source of strength to them?

Even as Sarah forced herself to stop crying and blew her nose into tissues she'd taken from her bag, Helen's crying increased.

"This is going to be tough on you, Mom."

"Tough on everyone. Poor Jonah. The kids."

"I had to tell them over the phone. It couldn't wait. I have to get home now and face everyone in person. God, this is horrible."

"You just got here. Don't we need to talk? Talk more? Plan?"

"We'll have a chance. We'll have plenty of chances. Planning? I won't see Danny graduate from high school next year. How do you plan for that? I'm going to miss so much I wanted to see. That I was foolish enough to think I would see. And what are the kids going to do without their mother? There is a lot to talk about, but not right now. I just had to tell you in person."

"What can I do for you?"

"I don't know. Pray for a miracle, maybe. Pray, and never stop praying?"

As soon as Sarah had driven off, Helen called Nicky in his office and felt fortunate he was able to answer. She told the news as simply as she could. After all, she was not privy to any detail, but, then again, what details would have mattered one way or the other? As she spoke to Nicky, her voice sounded to her as if it were coming from a faraway place, flat, robotic.

Over the year Helen had been together with Nicky, and particularly since their wedding in the fall, Nicky had always expressed great admiration for Sarah, more so than he expressed for her other children. So the news was grim for Nicky as well. She wasn't surprised when he swore.

"*Gamóto!* This is terrible, Helen … I can cancel my last patient if you want?"

"No. Treat your patient. We can't have the medical world collapse because … because it's not foolproof. Because people die, will die, have …." She sobbed again, thinking of her older sister Catherine, who had died just the previous fall from breast cancer.

"Easy for me to say, Helen, but try to get hold of yourself. Pour yourself a shot of Jim Beam. A double, if you need it. I'll get home the usual time, depending on traffic."

She found the Jim Beam in the back of her liquor closet, poured about an inch, added two ice cubes, then tried to down most of it in one gulp. The surge of alcohol into her throat and esophagus brought about a coughing spell, and a small quantity of bourbon became airborne as droplets in Helen's kitchen. When the coughing stopped, Helen spilled out the rest of her drink. Bourbon had never been her favorite. That's what grief does to you, she thought. It makes you selfish. It makes you reckless and thoughtless.

Helen had turned on the house's air conditioning, and now she was cold, even though she wore a light sweater. She needed to get into the sun, she thought; she opened her front door, walked across Valentine Avenue, and into Donaldson Park. She kept walking without seeing much of what was going on around her, not the teenagers playing catch, not the pigeons pecking the ground for pieces of bread thrown by an older woman whom Helen did not recognize.

However, she couldn't help but notice three young mothers wheeling baby carriages. What have you done, she addressed these mothers in her mind, bringing new lives into this world when you're unable to protect them properly?

Magaritsa Soup

Max had to fly out of Newark on the coming Sunday. The war room needed to be set up properly for the two days of hearings on pretrial motions, he explained to Kayla and Jackie, and that was one of the many jobs of second chair. He had to make sure the computers were in their proper positions, working, he had to check all office supplies and purchase anything extra Phil might need – Phil was one of the name partners of his firm and the lead counsel – he had to supervise the associates who would prepare initial drafts of the last pretrial motions they would file on behalf of their client, and God knows what other tasks Max would have to perform. So, yes, if Aharon was going to come, it would be best this week. Aharon would be welcome for dinner on Wednesday, Max would be delighted to meet him, and, as protocol required, he would be "around," but he would surely not bother them or intrude in their conversations.

As it turned out, Kayla's fears of how Max might react to the news of her interest in Aharon were unfounded. Max was fully distracted by his own situation, the coming trial. He had not had an opportunity to consider the implications of Kayla getting involved with a potential marriage partner. His most important question for Kayla was whether she had taken his pile of shirts to the cleaners, as Max had politely asked. When he found out she had, he was satisfied and went to his room to decide which suits were appropriate for a courtroom. Phil had instructed him to wear only red ties.

Kayla reminded Jackie on the afternoon of Aharon's visit that her new friend was coming to have dinner with them. Jackie was indifferent.

"Okay, *Ima*. I've got to practice now. I'll come down for supper when you call."

When the doorbell rang, Kayla was surprised to see that Aharon had brought her a bouquet of Lily of the Valley.

"For you. I hope these are all right."

She smiled. "Of course. I don't think there is *halacha* prohibiting this. Thank you." At that moment, Max appeared beside her, stopped for a second as he took in the view of the bearded and mustached man wearing a dark suit and white shirt with no tie, *tzitzit* hanging down the sides of his pants, and a large black bowler hat, and then extended his hand.

"Hello, Aharon. I'm Max, Kayla's older brother."

"A pleasure to meet you, sir," responded Aharon, shaking Max's hand firmly.

As Aharon walked into the house, Kayla stepped back. Max glanced from one to the other. It looked as if they were maintaining at least four feet between them. "Well, please call me Max. I'll be around if you need me, Kayla."

Kayla led Aharon into the kitchen, where she had been finishing preparations for their meal. "So, you trust I fully observe *kashrut*?"

"I have no doubt. I'm not the kind of person who goes poking through a host's pantry to make sure everything has the proper *hechsher*, and our sages tell us not to fear without having a good reason to do so." He inhaled deeply, looking around. "What are you making?"

"You'll laugh."

"Maybe," he said with a smile.

"This is Greek magaritsa soup. It's better known as Greek Easter soup. Fully vegetarian."

"And how, might I ask, did you come to be making this? An old family recipe?"

"Indeed, I learned about it from my Aunt Kal, when she was visiting last year. She said she often made it at the monastery. So, I looked it up in the library and copied the recipe. It's got mushroom, leeks, eggs, couscous, dandelion greens ..."

"What?"

"Here, try some. And then there's a quiche. And I baked some bread today. Sourdough. This will be simple, as promised."

He sipped cautiously from the spoon she held out toward him. "Mm. Tasty. So, do we keep talking now about ... well, compatibility and the like?"

"Let's not, just right now. Let's just share dinner and you take time to talk to Jackie and Max. Then, we'll sit in my piano room. It will be a fine place to continue our conversation."

When Jackie came in, Kayla introduced him to Aharon as "my friend from *Chabad*." Aharon held out his hand. Jackie ignored the gesture, but said hello. He'd certainly seen *HaMoreh Aharon* at *Chabad*, chastising one of the older children in the hallway outside a classroom. About what, though, Jackie could not remember.

The dinner itself felt awkward to Kayla. Max wanted to talk about the upcoming trial – the plaintiff was a woman whose husband had allegedly been killed by their client's drugs – and wasn't particularly curious about Aharon's musical career or his teaching position at *Chabad* or his other prospects. Kayla wasn't surprised, at least at Max's lack of questions about music. Max had shown less interest in music over the years since Kayla had eclipsed him as a pianist. He might ask occasionally for her to play for him the prelude she'd composed for his fourteenth birthday, and he would from time to time sit at his computer with earphones on, listening to classical music, including her piano recordings and to recordings of her compositions, so he still had some connection, but not what it had once been. And when Aharon asked a few questions about the trial, Max's responses were polite, on the surface at least. Kayla could not point at anything concrete suggesting Max was hostile toward Aharon.

More problematically, Kayla felt the distinct lack of a quick connection between Aharon and Jackie. At most, they glanced at each other, then looked away. Did they see each other as threats? Since Jackie had already suffered so much at her hands, she couldn't bear the thought of hurting him again by involving herself with a man he was not comfortable with. Nor, however, did she like the idea that Jackie should have a veto over what might turn out to be something exceedingly good for her.

Max excused himself from their table before the rest began their *bentching*, the grace they recited after meals, the prayers thanking *Hashem* for His goodness. After *bentching*, Kayla sent Jackie to bed.

"But *Ima*, it's too early."

"Don't send him to bed yet, Kayla. I'd like to get to know him better."

"Well …"

"Jackie, I hear you play the clarinet. True?"

Jackie wasn't sure exactly how to respond. They had been warily looking at each other during supper. Jackie felt as if he were on display, the major purpose of this meal together to allow this *Moreh* Aharon to judge him. At the *Chabad* school, *Moreh* Aharon taught the sixth graders, those entering their final year of study before their *Bar Mitzvah*. Jackie dimly recalled hearing about his being a "very strict teacher" – Jackie wasn't sure what that meant, although it didn't sound good – but that was all.

"Yes, *Moreh* Aharon."

"I play a little music myself. On a cello." *Moreh* Aharon had smiled at him, finally. But in a second, *Moreh* Aharon turned away from him and back toward Uncle Max and was now asking his uncle one more thing about the trial. Jackie felt a flash of disappointment. He'd been readying himself for a series of questions, as many as Sister Theodora had asked him when they'd first met. *Moreh* Aharon would not judge him, though. In fact, *Moreh* Aharon seemed not even to care about him, preferring just grown-up talk. Jackie knew that Uncle Max was going to be away for two weeks during the summer because of a trial. As far as Jackie was concerned, he'd heard too much about the trial already. Uncle Max had tried to explain what would happen, but the trial just wasn't interesting. All Jackie wanted to do was to make *Moreh* Aharon turn back toward him and continue talking about music. Or about anything.

But he knew he'd be punished by *Ima* if he interrupted.

"You can go to bed now, Jackie."

"But *Ima*!"

"Or you can practice, if you want, but not for more than a half hour, and keep your door closed." He looked expectantly at their visitor, as if a word from Aharon might ward off Kayla's harsh decree.

Aharon smiled. "I would like to see Jackie's clarinet and hear him play, for a minute or so, if you don't mind, Kayla."

She laughed and nodded. "But certainly. Why else did I want you to come, Aharon? Jackie, wash your hands first."

A minute later, Jackie and Aharon were together in Jackie's bedroom, and Jackie was putting his clarinet together and moistening the reed. Aharon glanced at the papers on Jackie's desk – mostly Hebrew homework – and sat on the desk chair. Aliyah, Jackie's cat, ran under Jackie's bed, putting as much distance as she could between herself and Aharon.

"What will you play for me?" Aharon asked.

"How about 'When the Saints Go Marchin' In.' Have you heard of it?"

"Sure. A famous song. Go ahead."

Jackie played it through without a mistake. Then he closed his book. "I can play by ear, too. You know *Chag Purim*. They taught us at school to sing it, and then I figured out how to play on the clarinet without music." He played through the song perfectly, picking up the tempo toward the end and finishing with a flourish by adding an octave jump.

"Say! That's pretty good. You've got some talent there, young man."

"You think so? Thanks. So, are you going to marry *Ima*?"

Moreh Aharon laughed. "I don't know. Maybe? Would you like me to?"

"No." The answer came out before he even had time to think of what answer would be the best. Jackie turned away, embarrassed.

"No? That's it? No reason?"

"I mean maybe. But I have a father. His name is August Sorel. I don't see him anymore, though. But I have a father already." He had made it about as clear as he could. He wanted to say also that Uncle Max was already the man of the house and that the house didn't need more than one man, but thought to hold his tongue.

"Oh, I understand. Shouldn't be a problem, because marrying your *Ima* wouldn't make me your father. I wouldn't want to compete with anyone for that job. By the way, I know of your father's music. He's a famous violinist, most talented. Like I said, I play the cello, another stringed instrument. It's a lot harder to carry around than a violin, though."

"I know what a cello is." There was something he'd wanted to ask about this, now that *Moreh* Aharon had brought it up, but what was it? He thought for a few seconds before continuing. "Do you give concerts, like *Ima* used to on the piano?"

"No, but I still want to, someday. In an orchestra. Not as a soloist. Not like your *Ima* was. She was great, by the way. I'm sure you've listened to her CDs. She made them when she was only fifteen or sixteen."

Jackie had often listened to them, but he didn't want to admit having done so. "No."

"Really?"

"Well, maybe." Jackie felt bad for having lied, but picked up his clarinet from his bed and stood again, looking at the book on the music stand. "I guess I'll practice now, so good night."

"As you wish." Aharon walked out of the bedroom. When he had closed Jackie's door behind him, Aliyah ran out from under Jackie's bed and jumped up on it, making a soft spot for herself on Jackie's pillow.

——

He found Kayla wiping the last crumbs off the kitchen table. She smiled as he entered.

"How did it go?"

"I enjoyed listening to him play. He's practicing now."

"I mean, between the two of you."

"Um … he doesn't want us to get married. Says he already has a father."

"Oh dear." She sighed. "I'm sorry. I can't believe he would say that, but …"

"It's normal, I would guess."

"Rude."

"No. He has feelings. If you can … well, we'd have to deal with those feelings."

Kayla shook her head. "I don't know. Kids, I guess," as if that one word carried all the necessary meaning, forgetting she had the parenting experience and Aharon had none.

"Kids, yes. Jackie is a lovely boy. Smart, obviously, and I've heard that as well from Zvi. I'd like to get to know him more. Maybe follow up where we were tonight. Maybe take him to hear someone play the clarinet at a concert?"

"Do you think you could ever get to be real friends with each other? He seemed pretty quiet this evening. With you in particular."

"We weren't giving him many chances to speak."

"Maybe. But real friends? Yes? No?"

Aharon hesitated longer than Kayla would have liked. "Of course. It's clear he makes lots of friends in the school. I see him chatting with others in his class."

Kayla wondered. Jackie's teacher, *HaMoreh* Zvi, had expressed concern to her that Jackie often seemed standoffish with the other kids, and the only classmate about whom Jackie spoke frequently was Moshe, a boy of Ethiopian descent whose blackness was of a much deeper hue than Jackie's. But there had been few invitations to birthday parties. She had been worried about this and had meant to speak to Rabbi Beck, but hadn't done so yet. "Well, he might have a friend or two there, but that's not what I meant."

Aharon moistened his lips before responding. "I'm sure if there was a good reason for Jackie and me to become friends, we would easily do so. But will there be a good reason? That's the question."

"I don't know."

"So where do we go, the two of us?"

"We move to the piano room, sit, and talk."

Miracles Might Yet Occur

Despite her best efforts to avoid doing so, not wanting to be diverted from her ritual of prayer, Theodora continued to mull over Nicky's letter. For maybe the tenth time, she pulled the letter out of its envelope and reread it.

Sarah, Helen's daughter, desperately needed healing. Theodora recognized it was her solemn duty to pray fervently for the health of Helen's daughter. After much deliberation, she finally added to her daily prayers a plea for the intervention of the Theotokos to save Sarah's life. The Mother of God had saved Theodora's own life and brought her to the monastery. She had saved Nicky's life too, the life of a teenager who was not only not a Christian but who believed in no god at all. She would hear Theodora's appeal.

Yet, it was imperative for Theodora to moderate slightly the traditional prayer for healing, which assumed that the sick person was already one of the faithful. Helen's daughter was Jewish, and there were no traditional prayers by which Orthodox Christians could seek the help of a non-believer. Thus, Theodora prayed: "O Lord our God, the Physician of our souls and bodies, look down upon Sarah, daughter of Helen, who might yet become thy servant, and cure her of all infirmities of the flesh, in the Name of our Lord and Savior Jesus Christ, with Whom Thou art blessed, together with Thy Most Holy, Gracious, and Life-giving Spirit, always, now and forever, and unto ages of ages." Theodora did not seek permission from Abbess Zoe for this change, even though its execution took Theodora out of the Orthodox mainstream. As Theodora reasoned, even though Helen's daughter was Jewish, she could still eventually discover the joy and oneness of the Savior of All, Jesus Christ. And if, through Theodora's prayer and the intervention of the Theotokos, Sarah's life might be spared, who could deny the possibility she would conceive more children and start a line of new Orthodox Christians to serve God's will? And if, through Theodora's prayer, Sarah simply evaded the cancer eating at her and lived a few more years to give joy to her mother and husband and to nurture her children, that would by itself be a blessing.

Even after adjusting her daily prayers to accommodate Nicky's wishes, Theodora was still uneasy rereading his letter. It finally occurred to her that Nicky's casual mention of Jackie had caused this unease. "One thing he hasn't mentioned recently is how you thought he was Jesus. Just as well he forget that." Had Jackie forgotten? Theodora couldn't imagine that he had. Her beliefs about Jackie had led them to becoming close friends. He couldn't have forgotten, even if Theodora had later admitted to Jackie she'd been mistaken.

Theodora had not forgotten her deep feeling that Jackie was the Second Coming of Jesus Christ, although she and Abbess Zoe did not talk about it. Theodora was grateful to Zoe for not shaming her by reminding her of her error, but Theodora's mistake could not be forgotten, either. When Theodora confessed to the village priest upon returning from America, she did so with no detail, couching her admission of guilt as one of losing humility, of being presumptuous, of allowing the Devil to interfere with her right thinking. The formal forgiveness she received from the priest did little to quell her guilt. But the guilt was as much related to Theodora's feelings of inadequacy as of her mistake. She had been inadequate, she mused, because perhaps, had she not been so presumptuous, had she not insisted on visiting Jackie in America and throwing herself into his life, maybe the message in her dream would have come true. Maybe, without her having visited, Jackie would still have emerged as the Second Coming of Jesus.

Another deep layer of guilt afflicted Theodora. Abbess Fevronia had begged with her not to heed the Devil's message, supposedly delivered in the dream that Theodora thought had come from God Himself. Now, because of the enormous stress Theodora had caused Fevronia to suffer, Fevronia was dead, the dream was dead, and Jackie could not be Jesus.

Or maybe Jackie still could be. Maybe, if Nicky's family visited the monastery during the summer as Nicky had suggested, the divinity in Jackie Covo could be brought to light. The monastery was the place where she should have first met her great-nephew. She began to think of how such a visit, in the coming summer, might unfold and what miracles might yet occur. She'd grown close with Jackie over her couple of months in America. How much closer might they become if they could share the beauty of Theodora's church, of the nuns' singing of the Psalms, of the vineyards ripe with grapes, of the purple hills, of the glittering stream Microdermis, of the peaceful and beautiful place she called home?

On Notice

She thought Jackie had been asleep for an hour. After reading him his last bedtime story, Dr. Seuss's *Oh, The Places You'll Go*, Kayla had returned to her piano, once again trying out a variety of melodies for the possible first movement of a piano sonata. She had thrown out everything she'd been working on before and now wanted to model a sonata after Beethoven's Appassionata, any part of which she could hear clearly in her head whenever she wanted. It wouldn't do, though, to write in F-Minor. The associations with her favorite sonata needed to be less obvious, but certainly a minor key was required. C-Minor would too blatantly suggest the Fifth Symphony and the Pathetique Sonata. Finally, she decided to experiment in B-Minor, a key in which Beethoven had written little. She let her right hand wander over the keys, eliciting a melody close to but not exactly the mood she aimed for. For a second and third time, she repeated a sequence of notes, each time with substantial modifications. Closer, she felt. She was gradually approaching a melody that might do, when Max appeared at the door of the piano room.

"Kayla? I'm sorry to disturb you. Got a minute?"

She sighed and looked up with annoyance at her brother. "You broke my … I'm sorry. Let me just scribble a bit more." It took another minute for Kayla to write the melody she'd last played. She got most of it, but then lost her way near the end, as the developing music was modulating into D-major. "D-d-damn." Further annoyed with herself because of her stuttering, she put down her pencil with excessive force. "Well, what did you want, Max?"

"You can't hear it down here, obviously, but Jackie has been up, practicing. He's got his mute on his clarinet, trying not to give himself away, but I still hear him from my room, and he's keeping me up. I need my sleep. He should be sleeping too. Do you want me to go in and tell him to stop?"

"Sure. You didn't need to disturb me. Next time, just barge right into his room and shut him down when it's this late."

Max left, and Kayla looked again at the notes she'd written. Now, they didn't seem to make sense, but she tried playing them anyway and slowly regained the musical ideas she'd been constructing when she felt Max's eyes looking at her once more. She turned and glared at him.

"And this time?"

"I'm really sorry to bother you again, Kayla, but can we talk?"

She lowered the cover over the piano keys and swung her legs to the other side of the bench, thus facing him as he sat in one of the upholstered chairs. "Okay. Shoot."

"I hope you don't feel I'm butting into your business, but it's about Aharon. Aharon and you."

"It is my business." She paused for a second. "You've always had something to say about me and men I was interested in, about me and August, and before that Bryce, and now it continues."

"But …"

"I know you mean well. You want to protect me, always. That's it, isn't it? You want to protect me from Aharon? There's something about him you don't like? He's not good enough for me?"

"No. I wasn't going to say that."

"Then what?"

"He seems like a fine man. But, I'll admit, thinking about the possibility you might marry and move out, take Jackie with you, does make me wonder how I'll get along here, when the house is empty of everyone I love."

"So you're against my marrying because you'll be lonely?"

"No, I'm not against it. In principle. And Aharon is obviously a devout Jew, the kind of man you *should* marry, if you were going to marry. And I can't point at anything specific about Aharon, who as I say comes across well, on the surface at least, but something about him also seems a bit off."

Anger grew within her. Max was interfering with her life, with her free choices, and it was clearly based upon his own needs for companionship, despite his denials. But she needed to hear him out. He'd been right about August. Part of her anger was at herself, because she knew Max could see things about her that she couldn't see, because she was still so dependent upon him. "You speak in riddles, Max. You say Aharon is a fine man, yet off. Somehow. Go on. Let's get it out on the table."

Max reached out to take Kayla's hand, and she let him. "He's of course acting very nicely toward you, but I wonder whether, if you were to continue, make a commitment, actually marry him, whether his niceness is a façade. I'm not party to your private conversations, but when he was here for dinner … it seems like an act." He looked away for a second, as if regretting the conclusion to which he'd come. "I can't put it any better than that. Just a gut feeling. I wanted you to know."

"All right, Max. You've told me. Thank you. You're absolutely right that you haven't been party to most of our interactions. He's acting? That's utterly ridiculous. We all act, all the time, don't we?"

"But I mean …"

"You don't know what you mean." She sighed heavily. "It drives me bonkers you think me such a dunce, so naïve I'd involve myself with someone who's, I don't know, insincere, performing, hiding something."

"Kayla, please, I'm sorry …"

"B … b… but you've done a good job to put me on notice of how you feel about Aharon. Maybe time will prove you wrong."

"Just keep in mind what I've said, in case …"

"Enough. Keep in mind? I'll never be able to forget what you've just said."

They both rose, Max tightening his grip on Kayla's hand. "I love you, Kayla. I'm only trying to look out for your own best interests."

"Which happen to magically align with your own best interests."

"Which …"

"G….g…good night. I've had enough for now."

"I'm sorry I've upset you."

With that, Max released Kayla's hand and left the piano room. A minute later, Kayla gave up any hope of further composing, turned out the light, and retreated to her own bedroom.

A Notable Absence

Little by little – despite Max's ham-handed advice – the idea of marrying Aharon appealed more to Kayla. Even as she struggled to regain her momentum as a composer, sitting at her piano and trying out melodies only to discard them immediately, her thoughts constantly turned to the prospect of uniting with this man, who, after all, had been a serious musician. That Aharon was a cellist, had studied music formally, and was still teaching, was not the primary reason for Kayla's attraction, but a significant reason. If they married, there was a common background, a shared interest in something monumental in both their lives. It made sense that any future husband should be one with whom she could discuss at length her musical ideas.

If there was a primary reason, it was that her continued meetings with Aharon – all of which required her to imagine their having a life together – had deepened the sexual desire Kayla had for many years unsuccessfully tried to suppress. During their meetings, she operated on two separate planes of consciousness. On one, the face that Aharon could see, she listened carefully to his remarks, admirably kept up the conversation, adding bits of humor now and then, and presented as the chaste, observant *Ba'alat T'shuva* she'd been for years. On the other, however, she imagined what he would be like physically, how they might lovingly touch each other in bed, what terms of endearment he might whisper to her in a naked embrace. She could feel herself becoming excited on this level of consciousness but managed, or so she fervently hoped, to hide her arousal from Aharon. She would occasionally interrupt their conversations, get up to use the bathroom, and try to focus on any images that might tamp down her desire; often, for this purpose, she tried to visualize Sister Theodora at prayer.

And it had become a habit, after her meetings with Aharon concluded and she'd gone to bed, that she would allow the ideas of touch, attraction, intimacy, and even love, to have full reign over her body. Her hands were no longer hers, in her imagination, but Aharon's. She was no longer a single woman who lived with her brother, but a married woman entitled to enjoy what *Hashem* had made possible through His creation of male and female. When no one else was home, she'd listened occasionally to "Sexually Speaking" with Dr. Ruth on WYNY. Sex with oneself was natural, it was important, and it made a woman healthier mentally; Dr. Ruth assured her it was right "to make the best out of every day you have." If Dr. Ruth could say all this on the radio, if she could become a star by advocating a woman's right to self-gratification, then Kayla could learn and imitate.

The slight guilt she felt after masturbation was more than offset by the pleasure she now felt during the act. She'd done her research. There was no explicit rejection of female self-pleasure in Jewish literature, a notable absence given how much attention had been paid to the prohibition of male masturbation. She was not wasting seed; her eggs were as ready as ever to conceive, in the proper circumstances. And if, under Jewish law, it was a husband's obligation to satisfy his wife, then female sexual pleasure was a distinct good in *Hashem*'s view.

She thought it might be about time to say to Aharon she was ready to commit. Something held her back, however. She still had no clear idea of what marrying Aharon would mean for Jackie and Max. All she knew was that Max didn't trust Aharon. Well, Max wouldn't be marrying him. It would be her decision, and she knew how she felt, knew what she needed as a woman. She knew she didn't want to wake up alone in her bed for the rest of her life.

She would need to talk to Max and Jackie again, to further test the idea of changing her life so drastically. She would need to gather from them whether and to what extent they would be hurt. She would need to figure out whether she could endure this cost.

What If?

But had she understood? *Ima* hadn't punished him, she hadn't even raised her voice to chastise him, and yet he felt somehow punished. He felt as if everyone he knew kept watching and judging him, even though, when he looked at *Ima* or Uncle Max, they weren't watching him at all. They were purposely looking away an instant before he could meet their gaze. They would not want it to be obvious that he was punished. If he were punished, then they also were angry with Sister Theodora, who'd given him the icon, and she was a grownup they couldn't be angry at; she was a special person in their family, maybe the most special person because she had been in the *Shoah*.

Sister Theodora had told him about how the Theotokos had saved her life and saved the life of Grandpa. Jackie was supposed to be asleep, as was Sister Theodora. It was only a few days before she'd left to go back to Greece. He'd been lying in his bed, staring at the ceiling, waiting. Somehow, he'd known Sister Theodora would come to his room that night, although it had never happened before and she'd not said anything to him. So when he'd finished his clarinet practice, he lay under the covers, and when *Ima* poked her head into his room, as she did every night before going to her own bedroom, he'd feigned sleep. It was easy. Just lie quiet and breathe slowly, eyes closed. When he could hear his bedroom door clicking shut, he knew it would just be an hour or so before Sister Theodora visited. And then Sister

Theodora was there, as if no time had passed. She sat on the side of his bed, took his hands in hers, and described in great detail what had happened to her in the *Shoah*. As she did so, he sensed she was holding a lot back, that there were things so terrible in her story she didn't feel they could be revealed to a seven-year-old.

When she'd finished, he'd asked her to repeat parts of the story, which she did with no impatience. Nothing she said made sense from the perspective of his Jewish upbringing. His instinct was to tell her she was wrong again, just as he'd told her that he was just Jackie, not Jesus. But he checked his criticism. It would be unkind. She was their guest, and she was leaving soon, and he didn't want her to go away unhappy with him. And he saw her story as a gift; she was giving him a gift even greater than the icon.

"Tell me once more, Sister Theodora, about when you were locked in the closet. Was the … Theo …"

"The Theotokos?"

"Yes. It's a hard name for me to say. Was she really orange?"

Sister Theodora had smiled, then leaned forward to kiss him gently on his forehead. "She glowed orange. It was like an orange light. Like the sun, but not as hot."

"But warm?"

"Very warm, yes."

"Like you're warm? Like when you touch me, and it feels like you have a fever?"

"No. The Theotokos has all the warmth in the world, and I have just a little left over from Her. Does that make sense?"

He wasn't sure it made sense. The Theotokos had been the mother of the god Sister Theodora had told him about, of Jesus, who Theodora thought Jackie might secretly be. Jackie had convinced Theodora that her idea was wrong and, in fact, that it was scary for him to imagine being someone other than who he was. *Ima* wasn't a lady who shone with an orange light. *Ima* had been his mother since he was born; he had grown up as a tiny baby inside her belly. But Sister Theodora's story was captivating. She wouldn't lie to him. She'd been in a war.

She'd been shot at by enemy soldiers as she through the woods far from home. She'd saved Grandpa with the veil of the Theotokos. As incredible as were the events in Theodora's story, Jackie wanted to believe them.

Grandpa would have been blown up had it not been for her! A grenade had exploded in Grandpa's face! And, because of Sister Theodora and the orange-light lady, nothing had hurt him! Not even a scratch! It was a story Grandpa had told him, too, after he'd gotten home from his visit to Greece where he found Sister Theodora, who had been his baby sister. He had said it was as if the force from *Star Wars* had chosen him for protection at just the moment he needed it. But in Grandpa's telling, he didn't know then that his baby sister was protecting him; he hadn't been able to see her. He'd seen nothing, he said. He could not explain why the grenade hadn't killed him until he'd met Sister Theodora and heard her tale.

Sister Theodora was certain these things had happened exactly as she described them. She told him these were the workings of God on earth. After a while, with his hands clasped in her very warm hands, as if he'd held his hands too close to the *Shabbat* candles, he said he needed to go to sleep and would see her in the morning.

But even after she'd returned to her own room – since Abbess Fevronia had died, where Sister Theodora slept alone – he couldn't sleep. He'd taken the icon from the back corner of his drawer, turned on his little flashlight to see better, and thought.

What if?

Too Forward

After a few days of now surprisingly productive hard work, still immersed in the key of B-Minor, Kayla thought she had the rudimentary structure of the first movement of a piano sonata. She had not intentionally made the piece difficult to play, but as she reviewed what she'd written, she saw that it would be extremely demanding and would require a pianist of the highest caliber to perform it adequately. She herself could barely manage the pages she'd written at three-quarters time in the privacy of her own house. That aspect of her work-in-progress – its challenging nature – did not bother her in the least. Indeed, the piece's difficulty was a plus. Few virtuosos would attempt it; it would be a mark of honor to perform it flawlessly. Well, she was at an early stage and had no idea what her slow movement might be like, nor had she yet conceived the last movement, although she was thinking in terms of a fugue, one that might turn out to be even harder to play than the first movement.

Then she played again what she'd written, a bit faster, and was dissatisfied. She did not like the development section and explored on her keyboard how that might change. Once again, she felt stymied. No new ideas popped into her head. She shivered, suddenly cold. Her breathing came harder than it should have. Were these new side effects of the drugs she had to take? She had been stuttering more lately when under stress, all because of her meds. She wondered whether her meds would now also prevent her from composing as well as performing. No, she thought. That couldn't be it. She'd composed many excellent chamber pieces while still fully dependent on her meds for sanity. Something else was getting in the way.

Once more she played what she'd written, this time much slower, attempting to let each harmony and disharmony linger. She added a sustaining pedal as she felt her way through the music. The development section was still off. It seemed mechanical, almost perfunctory. Was this music truly coming from her heart, as she had hoped? Or was the music somehow faking an emotion? She tried to conjure images of the music, longing to see anything that called out to her as its inner essence, its soul, but came up empty. The only image flashing through her mind was Aharon. She had to stop, get up from the piano, find her water bottle, and take a long drink. She'd worked so hard that she'd been on the verge of dehydration.

Kayla sat once more and this time played what she had written at a tempo a bit slower than what she'd indicated on the music paper, but not as slow as the previous attempt. She tried to clear her mind of all images, just letting the music flow through her, just as it had long before, when she'd performed at Carnegie Hall. With some minor changes in the development, she thought it was not bad. So much like a combination of Beethoven and Schubert. She'd begun to smile at herself when, yet again, she stopped in the middle of a measure and covered her face with her hands. She could feel herself blush profusely. Another effect of the drugs? Maybe, but she'd suddenly seen a major problem with what she'd written. Her music sounded too much like Beethoven and Schubert. It was as if she'd brazenly stolen from them, even though she hadn't. She felt as if a pit had opened within her. Completely unoriginal music. A schoolgirl could do better if told to mimic the great classical composers. Could she have wasted so much time, just to come up with ... nothing? She slammed the cover over the keyboard.

Then she looked at her watch. She'd forgotten entirely that Aharon was to visit. She looked a mess, still wearing the sweatsuit with which she'd started the day. She hadn't even showered. But it was too late to call him off. He would already be on his way, perhaps only a few blocks from her house. Shit. Shit and double shit. She'd have to stop him at the door, make excuses, say she felt unwell – not quite a lie – and make another plan. And, yikes, Max wasn't even home to chaperone. He'd been required to stay late at the office once again by Phil, his demanding, unreasonable partner. Well, two reasons were better than one. And she had to put Jackie to bed. She would say she had to read him the bedtime story she'd promised. That was another reason to send Aharon home.

But when he came to the door, holding a bouquet of pansies, Kayla couldn't follow through with her plan. She smiled and invited him in.

"Sorry I look like this, Aharon. I just lost track of time."

He didn't seem to mind. He smiled and handed her the bouquet. "I'll wait while you dress."

"I'm dressed. Not like I wanted, surely, although this is modest enough by *Chabad* standards."

She took the bouquet, pulled an empty vase from inside her China cabinet, filled it with water in the kitchen, and inserted the pansies. Then, she led him to a living room chair and sat on the edge of the sofa. Had they reached out their hands toward each other, they would have barely been able to touch. Touch was exactly the thought intruding itself into Kayla's mind, though. Perhaps it was because she was clad in a sweat suit, attire which suggested pajamas, and the idea of pajamas suggested bed. The thought of bed – the thought of Aharon and herself lying together – led to wondering if Jackie had fallen asleep, waiting in vain for her to read to him, while she'd been composing. She excused herself, rushed up to find that Jackie was indeed asleep. She creeped closer to him to make sure he wasn't faking. When she gently rested her hand on his curly hair for a second, she was assured. He would sleep at least until six in the morning. She returned downstairs to find Aharon sitting just as she'd left him.

"Where's Max?" he asked, frowning. "He's supposed to be around."

"Unfortunately, he had to work this evening. With the trial coming, he's a slave to his boss."

"Then I'd better leave. If I stay, there'll be scandal." He rose and took a step toward the front door. Kayla rose quickly as well and blocked his way.

She put her arms around him. "Don't go yet," she murmured, only half aware she'd spoken. His arms found their way around her as well. She looked up to be kissed, and he likewise pressed his head downward toward hers. Their lips touched tentatively for a second, and then the kiss deepened. Kayla felt Aharon shudder suddenly as he tightened his grip, then he pushed himself away from her so forcefully that she half-fell back against the front door. The dark red blush that crossed Aharon's face before he could cover it with his hands told her all she needed to know about what had happened. He'd had an orgasm from their brief contact.

"Aharon … I'm sorry."

"I have to go. This is not what I expected, not what I wanted." He picked up a tissue from the box on a side table and wiped his forehead as if it were intolerably hot in the room.

"But ..."

He didn't turn back toward her as he stormed out of her house. He didn't bother to close her front door on the way. Kayla watched as he quickly backed out of her driveway.

Nothing was going right. The composition she was working on was worthless. She'd been too forward with Aharon, and he wouldn't want to see her again. She'd embarrassed him, offended him mightily by her advances. She was a worthless person who couldn't live up to her *Chabad* ideals when it most mattered. And she was sure her meds were doing things to her she didn't like. She was stuck with them, needing to keep taking them because she'd sworn a solemn oath to do so, but they were more a burden than a help. They had to be interfering with her judgment, her intelligence, her instincts toward the people closest to her, her creative side.

She grabbed at the vase, intending to throw the flowers in the trash. As she did so, she knocked the vase over and spilled its contents – pansies and water – on her living room rug.

Maybe it was time to give it all up.

Malachim

That was the last thought she remembered – the idea of giving it all up – before she finally fell into a fitful sleep. Then she'd had what she would later describe to Sister Theodora as a very weird dream.

In her dream, she'd been sleeping, naturally, in her own bed. It was near morning; she could tell by the light filtering through her closed eyelids. She'd tried to move her limbs, ready to start her day, but an awful weight kept her pressed into the mattress. To make matters worse, Max barged into her bedroom. She should have screamed. She should have ordered him out immediately. But just as her body was immobile, pushed by an unseen force, she also could not utter a syllable. She could only point, lifting her right arm with difficulty, extending her index finger, and grimacing. Her brother must have gotten the message, because he disappeared as suddenly as he had appeared.

With his absence, she could finally move. Whether she floated over to her closet or walked was unclear, but she willed herself there, reaching to the shelf where she kept a shoebox of odds and ends, brought it down to look through, and picked up the icon she'd confiscated from Jackie's room. Why hadn't she thrown this away? Why hadn't she mailed it back to Theodora? She had no personal use for it.

She was considering how she might best get rid of the icon when the man in the icon spoke to her. "Be strong" were the words Kayla heard, not once, but in a continuing echo. And then she heard a chorus of angels humming a melody. She looked down at Jesus again and could see he'd been crying. She thought she smelled roses, even though she could see none, and …

Kayla jumped up, now awake, remembering the instruction – "Be strong" – and the chorus singing one last chord in B-Minor, unmistakably B-Minor. She could still hear the triad of B, D, and F-sharp, but she heard also many subtle overtones. It was a complex sound, one which somehow moved her to feel great love. She could love nothing as much as she loved Jackie, but the love in her at this moment was a love for *Hashem* and for the universe *Hashem* had created. Of course, it could be only angels – *malachim* – who created a sound like that. It called to mind Bach's B-Minor Mass.

The melody of the *malachim* still lingered as well, and in the darkness, Kayla grabbed for the pencil and paper she kept on her night table. In a minute, she'd captured what she needed to capture, a melody, pure and sweet, subtle and dangerous, perhaps deadly, but a melody she could work with. This could be the theme for the slow movement of her sonata. But how could it be part of something that didn't exist? There was no longer a first movement to which she could link a second.

Her heartbeat slowed steadily as she worked until she'd forgotten her dream, but the scent of roses lingered around her.

Fireflies

And yet, their visits continued. They both decided, independently, not to comment on their kiss and on Aharon's reaction. Blotted entirely from their memories, it was as if the incident had never happened. They met now only at Rabbi Beck's house, where they both felt more comfortable. Until, three weeks after their first kiss, things changed again.

Kayla was shocked, but only at first, when she realized what Aharon was clumsily implying. He'd kept mentioning it was time they get to know each other even better, to make sure they were compatible for marriage. The continuation of their meetings was something she'd come to expect, though. Then he'd said something stupid about horses playing with each other in a field, stallions and mares "so to speak." Finally, and much to Aharon's embarrassment if one could judge from the redness of his face, she got the message. He was asking her apologetically if she would consent to premarital sex.

"But it would be a sin in the eyes of *Hashem*," she protested, without much conviction. If she had been offended by the suggestion, she realized, she would have stormed out of their meeting immediately, telling him not to bother calling her again. He must have sense that she would be at least marginally receptive.

He was honorable enough not to deny her accusation. "I thought you'd say that. And I won't argue the point with you. But there are sins, and there are *sins*. Marriage is a lifelong commitment. If for some reason we weren't compatible ..."

"If you ask me to sin, if that's what you want, then we're obviously not compatible."

Still, she sat, her behavior glaringly at odds with her words. Still, she looked at him as if she had expected that they would have this conversation, that they could patiently discuss the issue as friends, a *chavruta* interpreting a minor section of holy writings, trying, not necessarily to glean the meaning from a complicated sentence, but to envision ways around its directives.

Aharon took her hand lightly in his. "If we were meant to be together, Kayla, if it was *Hashem*'s will for us to find each other, as we have, and we've met often and found we enjoy each other's company, then how could it be any real sin in *Hashem*'s eyes that we experience our bodies together physically as well as sharing our minds?"

Kayla's instinct was to argue against Aharon's logic. She knew it was fallacious, diametrically opposed to the teaching of *Chabad* and the Torah. She sensed he was trying to confuse her and thus take advantage of her, and she feared that, if she gave in to his urging, he would have her, find her imperfect – in so many ways she knew she *was* imperfect – and then abandon her, leaving her in her shame. As she tried to formulate an absolute rejection of what he wanted, though, she felt herself giving way to the excitement the proposal engendered. Now it was her turn to avert her gaze as she blushed. She stood abruptly, pulled her hand free, and moved to the screened window of the rabbi's Florida room. Kayla looked out across the backyard, in which warm yellow dots lit and disappeared, the beating sexual signals of fireflies searching in the night for a mate.

He came up behind her and gently took her hand again. She turned to look at him, weighing whether she could, just this once, do what *Hashem* clearly did not want her to do.

"I don't know, Aharon. Talking is one thing. We can talk with strangers. Making love is for making babies only, within a marriage."

"If that's what you think, I respect that, but then why haven't you just walked out?" It was the question she was asking herself. "I think you see my wisdom, particularly when we can be sure to prevent conception, when that's not even a possibility."

"It's always a possibility, even if we were careful." As she spoke, she allowed her hand to remain in his and leaned against him gently, letting him feel the weight of her body.

"Look. We would do this the right way, when you're ritually clean. That by itself would mean we were abiding by *Hashem*'s will. We can do it only once, and then we will each make our own decision whether to marry or to separate."

"What if one time isn't enough to decide?" She surprised herself by asking and blushed in recognition of the direction in which the conversation was going, as if the *yetzer hara*, the evil inclination, had spoken and not she. Amazing herself yet more, she continued, "What if we decide ... we need to experiment more? Maybe practice?"

"We won't let it happen."

She put her arms around him and held her face up to be kissed. He obliged, but not with the kiss she hoped for. Not with the deep kiss she wanted. He kissed her gently and quickly, only on the lips, then abruptly turned away, ending the conversation and the connection between their bodies.

Twenty-Four Hours

She decided to tell Jackie, her father, and Helen at the same time, when they were most relaxed and, she hoped, most amenable to her suggestion. So it was at a *Shabbat* dinner she began, not sure whether she'd receive resistance or support.

"Dad, everyone … there's something we need to talk about."

"What?" asked Nicky, as everyone's eyes turned toward Kayla.

"I think it's time we did make a trip, together. To Greece. To visit Sister Theodora, as Jackie has been begging. The four of us."

"*Ima*, can I bring my clarinet?"

"Jackie," Nicky broke in, "you need to say *may* I bring my clarinet. It's *may* when you're asking for permission."

"Dad, maybe it's not the best time for a grammar lesson. But what do you think?"

"It's pretty obvious Jackie wants to go, and I would love to see Kal again. So … I'm all for it. I mean … yes, if Helen's amenable."

"What's amenable?" asked Jackie.

Helen smiled warmly at Jackie. "It means agreeable, Sweetie. If someone is amenable to an idea, it means they will go along with it. They agree." She turned then to her husband. "Yes, Nicky, I'm amenable, but for one major thing, which you seem to have forgotten. Sarah needs me around. I don't see how I can take off for Greece when she's so sick, when she's got so little time left." Even as she spoke, she felt a great dollop of fear pass through her. She shuddered, sure everyone could see.

Nicky bit his lip and lowered his head for an instant. "God, I'm so stupid. Obviously. But if you can't go, then neither can I. I would never abandon you."

"Jackie and I can't go by ourselves, obviously," observed Kayla. "The only word of Greek I know is *efcharisto*. You can't get by just saying 'thank you' constantly."

Nicky and Helen ate their baked chicken for a while in silence, while Kayla and Jackie picked at their roasted carrots and mushrooms and potatoes mashed in almond milk. The silence was awkward, quite unlike their usual *Shabbat* dinners. Helen felt a twinge of guilt. Her reservations about Sarah's health had immediately stopped the potential planning, but that wasn't what Helen really wanted. What she wanted was to be as far away as she could. With dread, she saw herself at Sarah's bedside while her daughter gasped for her last breath. Helen would be unhinged, she would scream, she would die at the same time. Didn't Nicky understand?

Helen took a deep breath. She needed to calm herself, she needed to start again. "Kayla … Why now this interest in going to Greece after all? Jackie's been talking about such a trip for a while, but you've resisted the idea. So, may I ask why the change?"

"It's a variety of reasons," Kayla said, after a brief pause. What should she tell them? Kayla wanted to be scrupulously honest, but did that mean sharing the last incident involving Aharon? Was his crude desire for extramarital sex even the main reason she'd been thinking about visiting Greece? For more time to think? For a place to hide?

"Will you share?" Helen pursued.

"Well, J… J.. Jackie's part of the reason. He's never been out of the country, and a trip abroad would be great for his education."

"You've known that all along, however, my darling daughter," observed Nicky drily.

"Right. So, I have felt for a while that I need a change of scenery. My work – my composing – has languished. It's like writer's b…block.

I've been struggling. Walking around the neighborhood has fallen short of its usual good effect on my creativity."

"That's all?"

"No, not everything." Kayla, until she spoke, had not clearly seen another intriguing reason for the trip. "I want to … how shall I say this? … be with Sister Theodora again and talk more with her and, maybe, just learn what it's like in the monastery. I want to get to know her as the person she is in her own world. Ever since you first told us about your visits there, Dad – you and Helen – I've been fascinated with this special place. How religion works there. What *Hashem* wants us to feel there. Is that curiosity? Maybe. There's nothing bad about that, is there?"

"Bad? Of course not, Kayla. But you're a devoted Jew. Why would you care about how it feels to be in a Christian monastery?" Nicky turned toward his wife, who looked exceedingly pale, then back at his daughter.

"She's your sister, Dad," Kayla said. "Somehow, her Christian faith saved your life. Otherwise, I wouldn't be here, would I? So I need to spend more time with her, more time to help me understand what this all means, where her power came from. Comes from."

"It's a lovely idea," agreed Helen. Nicky reached out to hold her hand as she spoke. A bit of color had come back into her cheeks. "Our visits to the monastery were too short last year, and it was all we could do to absorb Theodora's story and the fact your father was reuniting with his sister after forty-odd years. And, when they visited us in the fall, we were all mightily distracted. A longer visit to Greece would be blessed by *Hashem*. I'm so sorry that my family crisis might… prevent …" She turned to look at Nicky with a question in her voice.

"Maybe it doesn't have to prevent," said Nicky quietly.

"What do you mean?" asked Helen.

"Would Sarah come with us?"

"And leave her family when she's so sick? Hardly."

"Could they all come?"

"Nicky, are you entirely nuts? You must be."

"Dad," piped up Max. "You're getting obnoxious. Helen can't go, and you're trying to force her."

"No, just throwing out possibilities."

Everyone ate in silence for a full minute before Helen took up the thread again. "Look. I see this is important to you, Nicky. For you and for Kayla. I could go and try to stay in touch with Sarah by telephone every day, couldn't I?"

"Of course. We could arrange as much contact as you want, easily enough."

"And …. think carefully before you answer … if I needed to get home in a hurry? How long would it take?"

"If God .. if *Hashem* wanted it to happen, we'd get from the monastery to the airport in Thessaloniki in a few hours and then catch the next flight to Athens and then connect to one of the New York airports. You already know how long the flight is. Depending on the time of flights, connections, you might be home in, say, twenty-four hours from … from …"

"A call telling me she's died?"

"God forbid. But if there was a call from her that she needed you, we'd get on a plane together, as soon as humanly possible."

Helen closed her eyes and imagined herself taking a call from New Jersey at the monastery. It would be painful, but not nearly as painful as being there in the room with Sarah as she passed away. More likely than not, she would be back home from Greece before that sad moment. And perhaps, while at the monastery, while with Sister Theodora, Helen might be able to pray more effectively for the miracle Sarah needed. *Hashem* would hear Helen's prayer from anywhere, true enough, but what if the force of Helen's prayers could be magnified by starting their ascent to *Hashem* from the Holy Monastery of St. Vlassios?

"Give me a day to think about it and to talk to Jonah and Sarah. And the kids."

"You have as much time as you need. Talk to everyone."

Refua Shlema

When Abbess Zoe entered Theodora's cell after knocking and hearing no answer, Theodora was hardly surprised at the intrusion. A small part of her was aware of Zoe's presence, because no one else but her new Mother in Christ would have come in uninvited. The remaining part of Theodora's consciousness was immersed in prayer. Fully committing her soul, she repeated with whispers the Jesus Prayer: "Oh Lord Jesus Christ, please forgive me, a sinner."

As she prayed, she reviewed every aspect of her trip to America, where she felt she had most sinned. Guilt grabbed hold of her heart, the guilt of prolonging her absence from the monastery, where she was needed; the guilt surrounding Abbess Fevronia's death, for which she felt responsible; the guilt for her misguided approach to Jackie. And, as to Jackie, she began to regret leaving with him the icon of the Savior. She'd given it to Jackie in part as a remembrance of her visit and in part because she thought that, one day, he might need it. She'd done so while suppressing awareness that Kayla would consider the gift intolerably rude. At the time, the gift had seemed absolutely right and necessary. Only through reflection and prayer did Theodora regret her actions. She saw ultimately that Kayla would discover what she'd done and would hate her forever. It was one thing to have unbending faith, as Theodora did, but another thing entirely to try to indoctrinate a child being raised in a different tradition.

"Sister Theodora, I am sorry to interrupt your prayer, but you must come with me. Your brother from America is on the phone. It's long distance, and it's probably costing him very much to hold."

Theodora got up from the kneeling position she favored for prayer and felt Abbess Zoe's gentle hand on her arm, helping her.

"Nicky?" She was not expecting his call.

"Dr. Covo, yes."

"Did he sound okay? Is anything wrong?"

"He didn't say, my child. Do come."

They walked to Zoe's office in silence. Theodora imagined Nicky was calling with terrible news. It would have to be Sarah's death. Or had something happened to Kayla or Max? Or, equally horrible, Helen, so soon after they married? Or … no … it couldn't be Jackie. He still had his destiny to fulfill, the destiny she still hoped would save the world. By the time Theodora picked up the phone, her hand shook badly. They spoke in Greek.

"Nicky?"

"Kal. Are you well?"

"Am *I* well? Thanks be to Christ, yes, but you, your family …?"

"We're fine."

"Thank the Lord. I was so worried when I heard you were on the line."

"I'm sorry to have scared you. I'm calling because – well, maybe this will sound strange – but we, all of us, almost all of us, would like to visit you, sooner rather than later. I mentioned the idea in one of my letters. And I was hoping we could make arrangements."

So. Nicky was indeed following up on the idea that had troubled Theodora when she first considered it. She would have to think fast.

"Who is *almost all of us*?"

"Good question. Helen and I, Kayla and Jackie. Everyone but Max."

"Where would you stay?"

"Doesn't the monastery have extra rooms for visitors? I always thought monasteries had such accommodations."

"Such as we have here are only for women. We do have rooms where Helen and Kayla could stay together. They wouldn't think the rooms comfortable, though, just two cots, and the bathroom is down the hallway. And, I have to add, these rooms are typically for the faithful. So, I would have to ask Abbess Zoe for a blessing. You understand, I hope."

"Of course."

"It would be a kindness of Jesus Christ, Our Savior, to have you visiting me again." She wondered whether that was true. Nicky, yes, her beloved brother. Jackie, certainly, who could one day grow into Jesus. But Kayla? Helen? They were sweet and loving, but Jewish, and would they be happy at the monastery that was a monument to a faith they chose not to share? She would nonetheless ask Abbess Zoe for a blessing. If the blessing was received, then it was God's will.

"Where could Jackie and I stay?"

"The closest hotel is in Serres. The Siris is a hotel I've heard mentioned when a husband brings his wife to our monastery and he wants to remain in the area."

Naturally, a hotel. Where else? Then Nicky pondered whether Helen and Kayla would be willing or able to sleep in the same room. For that matter, would Helen be comfortable spending so much time away from him, particularly as he was the only one among the family able to converse in Greek? And would Kayla be comfortable not having Jackie with her?

"How far is the hotel from the monastery?"

"I've never been there, but I think … roughly fifteen kilometers. You'll have a car, I guess, so that's pretty close. But, Nicky, when would you come? And for how long? I need to know so I can ask Abbess Zoe."

"Honestly, Kayla's ready to go now. Would it be possible for us to come right after *Shavuot*? Pentecost, in your church. That way, Kayla and Helen won't have a problem traveling over a major holiday. Is it doable?"

There was a monthly calendar hanging on the wall in Zoe's office. Theodora turned a few pages to check. "June 2 is Pentecost Sunday. We'll be full of guests into that week. But the beginning of the next week might work. I would love to see you, to see all of you, particularly Jackie, but I will have to check, as I've said."

"Please do. I long to see you again, Kal. It was so good when you were here, our being together. Even with the problems surrounding Jackie. His spell, his premonition about Fevronia. To tell you the truth, the whole thing with Jackie scares me a bit, and I'm not easily scared. He is very much part of the instigator of this trip, he's been talking for weeks about visiting you, and now, suddenly, Kayla wants to go. Urgently, it seems. It's puzzling, but she says it has something to do with her music, her composing."

"I can sense all that from your voice. It's … I feel I could touch your hand through the phone and see all that's going on."

Could that be true? Clairvoyance was one of those magical attributes of some of her church's elders, Nicky had read, and he'd automatically dismissed the reality of such claims. They were just more imagined miracles to convince the gullible that they should believe what the church leaders wanted them to believe. And yet, he immediately chastened himself for the thought, recognizing how the magic of Kal's beliefs – he called it magic – had saved his life.

"You understand, then, how this trip is important for my family."

"I do, indeed. Well, we have a lot to talk about, don't we? Here's another option for you and Jackie, if you want to be much closer. Our friend Andros lives in Inousa and has an extra room. I don't recall if you met him when you were here, but his house is only a short walk from St. Vlassios. Maybe half an hour. It's hilly, but the hills are never an impediment to the villagers who visit the monastery, and some are in their upper years too, like you. We could look into that."

"Sounds good, if it's not an inconvenience for him. We didn't meet him on our last trip, but I remember Fevronia mentioning him. I would be happy to pay him what we would otherwise pay for a hotel, if that wouldn't be offensive."

"If he opens his house to you, which I'm sure he will, it's as a gift. You can bring him a present of some sort, but you're right, the suggestion that you pay him would be a bad insult. And, by the way, he speaks a bit of English, so it will be easier for Jackie."

"Got it. As for the walking … well, I could use the exercise. But one more thing. Does he like music?"

"Pardon?"

"Jackie would want to bring his clarinet and practice. That might be a deal breaker. So, when you talk to Andros, please ask him about that. If it's any problem, we'll stay at the hotel."

Theodora chuckled to herself. She understood that, at this time in his life, Jackie was most concerned about secular things, including his love for playing the clarinet. She'd heard enough of his practicing to last a lifetime and thought Andros would soon tire of it as well. But, on the other hand, Nicky was asking only for a short visit. "I'll talk to Andros, assuming first that Abbess Zoe gives us the blessing and we can find the room here for Helen and Kayla."

"Excellent."

"But I have a question, Nicky. I've been praying for Sarah. How is she?"

"Not well, I'm afraid, but she's a fighter. She's undergoing another round of chemotherapy, even though things look hopeless. Thank you for praying for her."

"To be honest, it's a challenge for me, as our prayers for healing assume the person we're praying for is a believer in Our Lord Jesus Christ. But I've found a work-around, so I'm happy to keep doing it."

"Thank you so much."

"For an atheist, Nicky, you put a large stock in prayer. I'm glad to know that about you."

"Well, I asked on behalf of Helen, but yes, maybe I'm softening a bit in my later years. Maybe even I've said a prayer myself for Sarah. Don't tell anyone. A prayer for *refua shlema*, if you remember your Hebrew."

Theodora wasn't sure she ever learned the Hebrew phrase. She could picture in her mind one day, or maybe it was many days, when someone, either Papa or Nicky, or maybe it had been both, had tried to teach her a few prayers. But she had no trace in her memory of how to say them or even what these prayers had been asking for. It had been another lifetime. She had been another person.

"No, I don't recall."

"Complete healing. *Refua shlema*."

"I will keep saying my prayers for her complete healing. *Refua shlema*. Please let Helen know that I am doing that for Sarah."

"Fine. I will."

"And I'll be in touch soon to let you know what Abbess Zoe says."

"I hope …" he started, but she had already hung up.

Stubbornness

Abbess Zoe's frown was palpable as she looked at Theodora from behind her desk. "Theodora, you know well that all four of them could easily stay at any hotel in Serres. The Siris is just one, but they're all relatively good, I've heard, they are fond of catering to tourists, they all have English-speaking staff, and we wouldn't have the problem of splitting up a husband from his wife, nor a mother from her son."

Theodora hoped it was a sign Zoe had not immediately rejected her request for a blessing. Theodora had grown accustomed to pressing on her superiors when necessary to get what she wanted – even though Zoe was ten years her junior, she was still a superior in the Church's eyes – and she was not about to back off without a sterner negative response. "Yes, I know that, my beloved Mother in Christ. How could I not? But they were most specific about the accommodations they wanted, and if we could let Dr. Covo's wife and daughter share a room here – just one cell – we would be remiss in denying them the opportunity. They are both religious. They would respect our traditions and our rules. You would enjoy speaking with them."

"Religious, but still deniers of Christ. How religious is that?"

Theodora ignored Zoe's question. "And as to the problem of separation, if it's anyone's problem, it's not ours. Jackie will always stay with my brother at night, and so Nicky will have company and won't miss his wife. Or won't miss her that much. And Kayla – I'd love her close by. I'd love both of them close by. They are exactly the type of devout women whom we always welcome here."

"Theodora, please. Don't insult my intelligence. You know we've never had non-believers occupy our cells."

"And perhaps it's time we made an exception. What do you think these Jewish women might do? Contaminate the cell with their breath? Expose the nuns to unholy thoughts?"

"Of course not. But every change in how we do things, even the slightest, risks calling into question our whole enterprise."

Theodora wanted to argue that Abbess Fevronia, were she still alive, would not only have given her blessing, but would have done so without hesitation. But explicitly raising the memory of St. Vlassios's previous abbess would insult Zoe, who was now in charge. It was her judgment only that mattered.

"Had things been done exactly as spelled out by our Fathers of the Church, I would never have been accepted as a nun here. I was a Jew by birth, living here for many years before my baptism."

"I know, but …"

"And, if I may say so, I would never have been saved by the Theotokos from the closet in which I'd been locked, where I should have died. There was no precedent for that either."

"Yes, I have heard your story and believe in what you say happened to you, but …"

"So maybe you feel my being here has caused more trouble than … than whatever good I've done for Christ, and the monastery itself, and those who come to me for confession."

So there it was. Theodora had laid down her marker. A rejection of the blessing Theodora had sought would implicitly mean that Zoe did not value her. If Theodora could be described by one trait above all others, it was her stubbornness. The automatic response to Theodora's stubbornness was for Zoe to be stubborn herself, but stubbornness was a trait Zoe was actively working to suppress. The confrontation now gave Zoe the opportunity to show flexibility.

Having thought this through for a minute, she was about to speak when Theodora requested permission to leave.

"No. Stay a bit longer, Theodora. When you put the matter as you have, as strongly as you have, you make me see how important this is to you. I don't mean to demean you or your presence here and, least of all, the miracle wrought by the Holy Theotokos and which you have shared with us."

"Well?"

"I can see what Abbess Fevronia meant about your persistence – all in the name of good things – when she spoke to me from America. I have to caution you about too much persistence against the thoughtful and loving advice of your superiors. But, putting that aside for a moment …"

"I was doing only what I felt the Lord God, Our Savior Jesus Christ, had commanded."

"I'm sure." Zoe's tone conveyed the sense she was anything but sure. "Abbess Fevronia – may she rest for all eternity with Our Lord – said quite plainly that the delay in your return from America, which went quite against her instincts, was due only to your persuasive powers. Do you know, Theodora, that being as stubborn as you are sometimes puts you at great risk of abandoning humility altogether? And do you realize that the more you talk the less humble you seem to be?"

"If I'm what you call stubborn, something I might call persuasive, it is only the will of Our Lord that puts the words in my mouth and the desire to speak in my heart. It is only the will of Our Lord that puts the emotion in my voice."

"Indeed. And somehow you know the Devil isn't masquerading as Our Lord, which the Devil will do to susceptible beings?"

"It is Jesus alone who fills my heart, Mother."

Zoe wanted to remind Theodora of how she'd been wrong in the past and could still be wrong. But she knew that, against Theodora's determination, she might be arguing all day. She might be arguing forever. Zoe sighed, thinking of how Fevronia must have felt when confronted with the same intransigence, the same utter conviction within Theodora that her instincts – her dreams and desires – must necessarily have been placed within her by God. But what else could one expect from a person who had such a direct and sustained encounter with the Holy Theotokos?

Above all other considerations, and the reason Zoe consented to grant the blessing, was that her curiosity had been prodded. What *would* it be like to have two mature religious Jewish women stay within the monastery for a week or so? What *might* Zoe learn from these women if they talked at length? And, unlikely though it seemed, wasn't there a possibility they might be persuaded to join the Church? Or at least one of them? Zoe did not see herself as proselytizing, nor did she think her other nuns would try to convert these two Jewish women, but if Dr. Covo's wife and daughter listened to the chanting, attended services during their visit, were exposed to the beauty of the Church, anything might happen. So, Zoe concluded that what Theodora now begged did not seem so unreasonable. And, if Theodora's family visited her at the monastery, wouldn't all still be within Zoe's supervision?

"All right, Theodora. Let me check our calendar." She picked up an appointment book and flipped a few pages. "Holy Pentecost is the second of June. We're booked through the third. But a room opens on June 4. We could offer it for ten days. If that's what you want, then I give you my blessing for Mrs. Covo and … uh …"

"Kayla Covo, Nicky's daughter."

"Yes. Kayla. You have my blessing for them to be your guests here then. I pray to Our Lord, Jesus Christ, that I am doing the right thing. You must make sure they abide by our rules."

Zoe had expected Theodora to smile, but she took the news without a change of expression, as if she'd been expecting more. The long silent seconds left a vacuum that Zoe felt obliged to fill. "I, too, would like this visit to take place. I'd like to meet your brother, who was saved by the Holy Theotokos. And … I would like to meet these devout women, perhaps to talk to them about Christ." Finally,

Theodora smiled; it seemed apparent that Zoe had said what Theodora hoped to hear. "And I'd like to meet this young boy, Jackie, whom you are so fond of, this young boy whom you mistook for the Second Coming of Our Lord. Is there anything else, then, Theodora? I too must pray."

Theodora resisted the urge to tell Zoe that perhaps she'd been right about Jackie, that Theodora's mistake had been in her approach to the Lord Inchoate and not in the rightness of her belief. But they didn't need to flesh out the matter then. Time in its full measure would show Zoe and the others the truth, maybe long after Theodora departed this world for eternity at the feet of the Lord Jesus Christ. Theodora had received the blessing she'd come for.

"Very well. Thank you. May Christ's light always shine upon you." With that, Theodora walked out of Zoe's office, forgetting to close the door behind her.

Dickhead

Barely ten minutes into his deposition, Nicky was both angry at himself for not having taken more time to prepare with Edelmann, angry at Edelmann for not having prepared him properly, and mostly angry at the plaintiffs' attorney, Mark Silber, who in Nicky's mind epitomized the worst of the legal profession. What galled Nicky more than anything was the sneering and disgusted tone that Silber affected. Every question was laden with the assumption Nicky had done something horribly wrong, knew he was wrong as he was doing it, wanted the patient to be harmed, and was now trying to hide his crime. Part of Nicky's brain understood the accusatory nature of the questioning was just Silber's technique to get under Nicky's skin and that Nicky needed to avoid taking the bait. But Nicky's emotional reaction to the lawsuit and the circumstances of the deposition overwhelmed the cautionary messages of his brain.

"Dr. Covo, don't you agree a physician has a responsibility to his patient and that patients can come to harm when the doctor refuses to abide by the reasonable expectations of his profession?"

He waited a second in the hope Edelmann would object, giving Nicky more time to think of a good answer, but Edelmann remained quiet, incongruously doodling on the yellow legal pad in front of him. Doodling with his eyes closed, as if he were thinking about Silber's question and perhaps even agreeing with its implications.

Edelmann had at least reminded Nicky as they made their way into the conference room for the deposition that he shouldn't answer a question he didn't understand. That was as good an answer as any. "I don't follow your question, as it seems to have two parts. Which do you want me to answer?"

"Answer the question as best you see fit."

"I can't answer it as you phrase it."

"You don't know whether a physician has a responsibility to his patient?"

Count to ten, slowly, Nicky said to himself. Take a deep breath. Let the air out deliberately. Think only of your breath.

"You've misstated me. I agree a physician has a responsibility to his patient, to act in accordance with the standard of care."

"What is the standard of care for a physician whose patient is suicidal?"

At this point, Edelmann objected, but without giving Nicky much guidance, asserting only that the question "lacked foundation." Nicky tried to remember whether Edelmann had prepared him for this kind of objection and, if so, what it meant. How was he supposed to respond? He grimaced as he tried to remember, but the effort was to no avail. He could feel himself sweating heavily. He asked for the question to be repeated.

Silber read from the notes in front of him. "I asked: 'What is the standard of care for a physician whose patient is suicidal?'"

"So, it's what a reasonable physician would do, not what a perfectly omniscient physician would do. They don't teach you in medical school how to read a patient's mind."

"What would a reasonable physician do?"

"Use reasonable care, not perfect care."

"What is reasonable care in that situation?"

"There's no one answer. It depends on the circumstances."

On and on it went. As each minute passed, Nicky felt himself growing more tired, as if he were a marathon runner trying to complete the last few miles with nothing left in the gas tank. He felt as if he were on trial for his life, as if his attorney had abandoned him. Just to relieve himself of the accumulating stress, he found himself more and more tempted to agree with Silber's accusations. Nicky felt tremendous relief when Edelmann finally stood up, said "we're done, you've had your two agreed hours," and pulled him out of the conference room. As he left, Nicky could hear Silber dictating an objection on the record about never having agreed to a time limit.

Nicky and his lawyer didn't speak again until they were in a cab.

"You did well. Mark was pissed as hell he couldn't get anything out of you."

"Where the fuck were you all morning? Did you make, what, two objections through the whole thing?"

"You wanted me to be more involved? Disruptive? It's not enough I ended the damn thing when you were ready to give up? I could see you were at the end of your rope."

"And maybe I wouldn't have been if you'd stuck up for me more," snarled Nicky, to which Edelmann did not respond. Nicky stared out the cab's window. He had hardly enough energy left to argue with his lawyer. Finally, he said, still looking away from Edelmann, "I thought you were supposed to defend me."

"I'm supposed to get the best result for my client, which is your med mal carrier. And part of that, frankly, is to watch you and see how you hold up under intense cross-examination. If I keep butting in, I'm never going to find out. And if you were about to say something stupid, well, I would have called a recess and had a stern talk with you. What we call woodshedding. Happily, that wasn't necessary."

"Woodshedding? And you wonder why people hate lawyers, even their own."

The taxi stopped at a light, and a swarm of pedestrians floated in front of them. For an instant, Nicky thought they were looking into the back of the taxi to discover why two well-dressed men were fighting with each other. Then the fear of being watched disappeared as suddenly as it had come.

"Doctors get sued a lot more than lawyers."

At last, Nicky turned to Edelmann, whose expression he couldn't parse. Had he been joking? Trying to get a further rise out of Nicky? "What happens now? In the case, I mean."

"That dickhead might just file a motion to compel."

"What's that?"

"He goes to the judge and cries that you wouldn't answer his questions. I think, frankly, you were answering adequately. He would complain we had no agreement to end the deposition after two hours, and he'd be right. Whatever he argues, he tries through this motion to get the judge to order you back for a continuation of the deposition."

"Fuck that."

"And, if he gets the order he wants, he can try to get costs awarded against us, including his attorney's fees."

"That never happens, does it?"

"Not as much as it should. But I don't think he'll bother filing a motion. He has to confer with me first under the local rules. Like I said, I think we can show you gave him as much as he was entitled to, if not more. And, if he files anyway, I don't think the judge would require you to go back. You've answered enough. Don't forget, you're a busy psychiatrist, with many sick people to see and heal. Two hours is more than reasonable. In fact, I'd be pleased if Silber did file a motion, just so I could beat him at it, and then we might get *our* costs. Judges don't like to have their time wasted with frivolous motions any more than doctors like to have their time wasted by sitting at depositions."

But Nicky had stopped listening. In the last fifteen seconds, he'd developed an intense headache, directly behind his eyes, nearly as bad as the cluster headaches he'd learned about in his residency. He put his head back and brought his hands over his closed eyes.

"Are you okay, Nicky?"

"Is anyone?"

Abandoning the Playing Field

Kayla had expected a telephone call from Aharon – either to apologize or press her again on the subject – the morning after their last meeting. She was both chagrined and relieved when her phone failed to ring.

On one hand, she worried that her decidedly negative response to him had been too negative, that he was about to or maybe already had lost interest. In many ways, Aharon would have been the perfect husband candidate, someone religious, like she was, and someone who appreciated not only classical music, but her very own brand of classical music. She might never have another chance to link up with such a desirable man. In this state of mind, her memory often brought her back to certain sexual moments with August. In the technical sense of being a lover, August had been amazing, or so she had thought then. The hope of returning to that sense of wonder – within the confines of a *halachically* correct marriage only – was why Kayla had agreed to meet with Aharon.

The converse was also true. If things were over with Aharon, there was still a good side. Marriage was too drastic a commitment. For starters, the upheaval in her life would be overwhelming for Jackie, who'd already suffered enough at her hands. Aharon and Jackie had gotten along all right the evening Aharon had come for dinner, but Kayla was sure that both were just playing roles, the roles they both knew Kayla wanted them to play. And, although Kayla didn't feel as if she owed anything to Max by way of maintaining their present living arrangement, Kayla's marrying anyone would remove both her and Jackie from Max's house, and she didn't want to hurt Max by leaving him. She might have already satisfied any type of sibling obligation by caring for Max for seven years, one might even call this a great *mitzvah* she had performed, but Max's need for this particular *mitzvah* hadn't ended and didn't seem it would ever. She felt the need to honor *Hashem* by taking care of her brother in a way no one else could.

Kayla sat at her piano after supper, playing haphazard melodies, barely thinking of the music, while she pondered her two opposing states of mind. The sound of Jackie's clarinet began to bother her, making it harder for her to think, so she shut the door. With the clarinet sounds blocked, Kayla decided to try to capture each of her two moods on the piano. To embody the sexual excitement she yearned for, she elected to play what she remembered of Bach's Chromatic Fantasy and Fugue in D-Minor. She couldn't remember when she'd learned it, but it easily floated back into her memory, as if she had just played it the day before. Playing at perhaps only a touch slower than performance speed, she didn't have to think about the playing at all. It came so naturally, as if Kayla herself had written the music. She even closed her eyes as she continued to play, imagining that she and Aharon had indeed married and were about to consummate their marriage on their wedding night.

In a trance, she had not heard the phone ring, nor had she heard Jackie knocking on the door. Only when she realized the door had been opened did she stop her playing abruptly and swung around to glare at the intruder.

"Jackie, haven't I told you …"

"It's the phone for you, *Ima*."

"Oh." She softened her tone immediately, aghast that she had been ready to lay into Jackie when all he'd done was what she'd asked him to do if he answered the phone himself. "I'm sorry, Jackie. I must not have heard it."

"It's *Moreh* Aharon. I told him you were busy, but he said it was important."

"That's fine, Jackie. You go back up to your room now, and thank you."

"Will you read to me tonight, *Ima*?"

"Happy to. Go find a few books and wait for me."

When she was sure Jackie was out of earshot, she picked up the receiver. "Aharon? Are you still there?"

"I'm here."

"I thought you might call this morning. Then, when you didn't, I expected you would never call." Now, why had she said that? Her emotions were too close to the surface. She needed better control.

"It's been less than a day since we saw each other. What's gotten into you?"

She wasn't sure what, if anything, had gotten into her. Nothing, she thought. She remained silent. In a second, Aharon continued as if he hadn't just asked a question.

"Here's what I've arranged. I booked a room in the Wilshire for tomorrow night. I'm assuming you can get away, right? Once Max is home from work? You can say you're going to *daven ma'ariv*? Your brother would never call the *Chabad* to check on you."

"What?" She had heard him clearly enough, but was astounded at his effrontery.

"I'll leave a note for you at the front desk with my room number."

"I haven't agreed to do this. It's against everything I believe. I thought I made this very clear last night, of all the …"

"Hold on. We don't have to do anything. We can decide just to talk."

"We can talk now, and this is absurd, Aharon."

"You wanted me to kiss you last night. That wasn't absurd, was it?"

"That's different. That was just a kiss, we weren't in a hotel room, and you were the one who pushed me away."

"Because we weren't in a hotel room. But you did want me to touch you. I know it." He paused for several seconds, and Kayla was sorely tempted to hang up but couldn't bring herself to do so. Aharon had sensed her desire. "All right, I'll be as honest with you as I can be. If you don't trust me enough to come to the hotel room, you don't trust me enough to be my wife, that's all there is to it, and we should stop all this nonsense about seeing each other. It's important for me ... to find out if we can be a functional human couple."

"How could we not be ... that way?"

"I have to spell it out for you?"

"Spell what out? You've completely lost me."

"Look. You've been up front with me about your illness. And the effect of medications. I don't want to marry someone unless I feel ..."

"You don't know what it would be like to make love to a woman with schizophrenia? That's what you're trying to tell me? May *Hashem* forgive you. You could never love anyone."

"You're misunderstanding, and I'm doing a poor job of explaining. I'm not worried about myself. Getting satisfaction ... performing, if you will. But you ..."

"You want to know if you can get me off? That's what this is about?"

"For a marriage to work, there has to be mutual satisfaction."

"If I were a person who used foul language, boy, would I love to use some now."

"Just say no, and we'll part as friends."

This would be the right time to slam down the receiver, she thought. But she continued to talk. "You have no ... no f-ing idea how obnoxious this is. I'd probably get more satisfaction from humping a tree than from you, Aharon."

"All right, then let's end this."

"No. Let's not." She startled herself by rejecting his suggestion so quickly.

"Let's not?"

Kayla thought for a few seconds. The constraints and customs of their brand of Judaism, the impenetrability of words, and his fears had thrown up multiple barriers between them, and there was only one way to tear it down, as full of risk as it might be.

"Max has been getting home at eight lately. He'll believe me when I tell him I want to go to *ma'ariv*. I don't want to lie to him, and haven't for years, but ... I should get to the Wilshire by eight-twenty or so."

She could hear his sigh of relief. "*Baruch Hashem.* Why this change in heart?"

"Your concern about mutual satisfaction is ridiculous or, let's say, would be if you knew me well. I guess that's your purpose. I'll come, but no promises. I still think this is wrong. But it would be a greater wrong, perhaps for both of us, to abandon the playing field."

"What?"

"It's a baseball term my father taught me. It means giving up. Walking off the field of play. It means that the umpire calls you out, even though you weren't actually put out during the play itself. Well, I've had to give up too much in my life already. You know that. But I had no choice in the matter."

"Your career."

"Here, at least I have a choice. Or will make one tomorrow night."

The Wilshire

Even as she got into her car, having put Jackie to bed early with a book and having made her excuses to Max, who had come home early after all – she would be late, she said, as she was meeting a friend for dinner after *ma'ariv* – her heartbeat rose to fever pitch. August had been her only previous lover, and that had been so long ago. As much as she hated August for having tried to steal Jackie from her, she still remembered the excitement of his touch. The prospect that she might soon once again enjoy sex made her giddy with desire. Her hands shook so badly she could hardly insert her key into the ignition. She knew she had to calm herself before trying to drive. She leaned her head against the steering wheel for a full minute before starting the car.

The drive to the Wilshire seemed to take much longer than usual, now that she was on the verge of much longed-for sex; every possible red light impeded her journey, and she pulled over twice to make sure she wasn't followed. The idea of impending sin contributed to, rather than interfered with, Kayla's desire. Her rabbi wouldn't know; no one from *Chabad* would know. Her father, brother, and son wouldn't know. It would be a delicious secret she kept with her fellow sinner, and the idea of shared responsibility made their assignation less of a sin and more an exploration of goodness. True, Aharon had assured her they might only talk, but she knew her body's desires; there would be no time for talking, no interest in talking, at least not at the beginning.

She parked herself in the hotel's lot, rather than dealing with the valet. She forced herself to walk deliberately into the hotel's plush lobby. Not hesitating, but not rushing, she approached the front desk. No one but the desk clerk was there, much to her relief. He was a middle-aged black man whom she interrupted reading a book. Without ceremony and with hardly a glance at her, the clerk handed her the envelope marked "K. Covo." Kayla found the women's restroom and entered a stall before tearing the open envelope. "Room 339" had been printed carefully on a folded piece of hotel stationery. She tore up the note and envelope and deposited them in the trash on the way out of the restroom. Then she washed her hands with soap and hot water for a full minute.

Kayla hesitated, but only for a second, as she faced the elevator bank. Yes, she could escape now, return to her usual routine life, maintain her strict Judaic observance, and say goodbye to Aharon forever. But, in her mind, she had already crossed the drawbridge, and the way back was, if not blocked, much harder than the way forward.

Kayla knocked softly on the door of Room 339, which Aharon opened immediately. He was wearing his usual white shirt, black slacks, and *tzitzis*. He pulled her into the room gently, pushed the door closed with his foot, and locked it. Then they embraced and kissed as if they had been doing so for years. They found the bed within seconds, Kayla taking the lead. She pushed Aharon onto the bed and climbed over him, hungry to feel his body against hers, desperate for a second kiss. As their tongues met again, Aharon shuddered unmistakably. It was over for him that quickly, and, as Kayla gasped in astonishment, he pushed her away and sat up.

"Aharon?" Her voice held the uncertainty of a question, not so much as to what had happened, but why. He had put his hands over his face. She watched him try to slow his breathing. Then he turned and buried his face in a pillow, which was still covered by the bedspread. "Aharon ... Are you all right?"

"I'm so sorry, Kayla."

"You came. You had an orgasm. That's nothing to be sorry about. Let's get undressed and hold each other."

He sat up quickly again. "No. It can't be."

She hoped she had misheard him. "What? You wanted me. I'm here for you to take. How can that *not be*?"

Aharon rolled out of the bed and straightened his clothes, then sat gingerly at the desk chair, his erection not fully subsided. Kayla repositioned herself to sit on the edge of the bed, close to where Aharon sat. The last vestiges of desire in her ebbed as quickly as her desire had grown a minute earlier.

"Talk to me. You came. That's part of what you wanted. So now that's it? You're done? Goodbye, Kayla?"

"No, it's not like that."

"Then how is it? What am I missing?"

"It's a message from *Hashem*. We are not meant to be together like man and wife. And we are not meant to sin."

"That sounds awfully like 'Goodbye, Kayla' to me. I'm not accepting that this is some message from *Hashem*. It's just … you were overexcited. You wanted me so much that my just being in the room with you drove you over the edge. It's a compliment to me. If it's a message, you're being told you *can* love me, as a husband should, and …"

"No. It's … this has happened before. Not only with you. I hoped that, somehow, I could master it."

"Master?" Kayla suddenly felt dirty. She saw quickly that she had been unfairly used, if this was all it came to, if all the weeks of meeting with him had been to set her up as the substrate of an experiment in which he gauged whether his issue with premature ejaculation somehow could be conquered. "This has all been about you and you alone, hasn't it? You were eager to turn me away from *Hashem* so you could work on your own problems with women." Her voice rose, in anger at herself more than at him. "How could I have been so stupid?"

Aharon did not answer. He would not look her in the eye. He looked down, instead, grabbing the *tzitzit* hanging on both sides of his pants. It looked to her as if he was whispering a prayer. For what? she wondered.

She did not want to cry in front of him but could not hold back. She would unfortunately have to give him the satisfaction, not only of humiliating her, but seeing her shameful tears. But he would not see her cry for long.

Kayla stormed out of the room.

The White Hotel

Nicky and Helen were packed and ready to take a cab from his Manhattan apartment to Kennedy, where they would meet up with Kayla and Jackie. While Nicky rummaged through his study for material to read on the long flight, Helen sat on their bed and stared at their suitcases.

It had been a bit more than a year since their last trip to Greece, and so much had changed. Helen tried to remember the woman she'd been then, what her life had been like, what she'd been thinking about, and it was hard to imagine. Hard to believe, in fact, all that had transpired. She had already grown very fond of Nicky and was excited to be traveling to Greece with him, but not ready for an intimate relationship, certainly not thinking of him as a possible second husband, and thus she feared what might happen during the trip – or what Nicky might want to happen. But she had pushed the fears aside. And then to think that, as they left for Greece, they did not know whether Nicky's sister still lived and, if she did, what it would be like to meet her as the mysterious Sister Theodora. Nor could they have conceived they would learn about a miracle that had saved the lives of both Theodora and Nicky. Most amazing was that Helen and Nicky had become lovers, despite her concerns. They had married in the fall. Those were the good things of the year.

But there had been bad, too. They'd almost lost Jackie twice, once by way of his muteness, which had scared the family as the harbinger of more serious psychiatric issues, and once in a custody fight with Jackie's father. And Helen's sister, Catherine, had died from breast cancer.

If Helen feared going to Greece the first time, her fear of a second trip was even more profound: her recognition that, at any moment, she might be called back to the deathbed of her daughter. She could have opted out of the trip, any loving mother would have done so, everyone would have understood, but Sarah had asked Helen to pray for a miracle and had assured Helen it was the right thing to go, to allow her prayer to rise to *Hashem* from a holy place. Sarah had assured Helen that she'd be fine and looking forward to Helen's return; Helen would be home soon enough. Her son-in-law, Jonah, and her grandchildren, Rivka, Danny, and Ezra, agreed as well, or so they said.

Helen allowed herself to be persuaded. Nicky had to go, and she had to be there with him and the rest of the family. Nicky was preoccupied, if not completely depressed, by the outrageous lawsuit, and he was still haunted by ghosts of the war. Maybe he could forget his troubles and expunge the remaining horrors by one more visit with his beloved sister. Kayla, too, had looked a wreck lately. Something had happened, Helen was sure, between Aharon and Kayla that made Kayla want to get away. And as Kayla's health went, so would Jackie's go. There was a lot at stake, and it would be an absence of only ten or eleven days.

It was the right decision, she kept telling herself, even knowing how hard it would be to leave her family, the family she'd created with David, *zichrono l'vracha*. What would David say? He'd probably tell her she worried too much. Support Nicky, he'd say. He's your husband. You chose well when you married him, so keep on being a good wife, he needs you. Our kids will be fine while you're away.

You'll see. And don't forget Nicky once saved my life when I was getting the shit beat out of me. So go. Be with him.

"Eureka! Helen, I found the book I'd been looking for. I'm going to read this on the plane."

Nicky's entry into the room broke her chain of thought. He was smiling, and it made her smile in concert.

"What book?"

"*The White Hotel*, by D.M. Thomas. A patient gave this to me years ago. He said I'd love it, as a psychiatrist, he emphasized. It's about Freud, but fictional. I read it a long time ago, and I wanted to reread it, but I've been distracted and haven't done so."

"Well, good. But don't you plan on sleeping on the plane?"

"Hmm. I'll try to read this first. And maybe it will put me to sleep. But maybe not. It's got a lot about sex."

"Well, I suppose that's to be expected, if it's about Freud. Even a fictional Freud."

"Here, listen to this. From a poem by his patient: 'I started having an affair with your son, on a train somewhere in a dark tunnel, his hand was underneath my dress between my thighs I could not breathe … I could not stop myself I was in flames from the first spreading of my thighs, no shame could make me push my dress down, thrust his hand …'"

"That's enough."

"Well …"

"Let me see that." She reached over, took the book from his hands, and began to read where he'd left off. "… the two, the three, fingers he jammed into …" Then she snapped it closed and handed it back. "Is most of it like that, *Hashem* forbid?"

"No.

"Obviously a book meant for men."

"Actually, no. This woman is a hero, if I recall."

"I'll bet. Well, whatever. If I were you, a book about Freud – about any psychiatrist – is the last thing I'd want to read now. But I can see how you might like it."

"I don't think Freud was ever sued. They didn't do much of that thing in Europe. But maybe it will also help me get my mind off, well, how litigious we are here. Fucking lawyers."

"That by itself would be a blessing."

Visions and Voices

The Final Word

Although Nicky considered it a touch too expensive to have everyone fly business class on the Emirates Airbus A300 nonstop from Kennedy to Athens, he had no interest in being crammed into an economy seat for the nine-hour flight and no interest having only himself and Helen fly in the more luxurious seats while Kayla and Jackie suffered in the back of the plane. It would be a bad start to their visit to have his group separated like that. So he sprang for business class for all and refused Kayla's offer to pay half the fare.

At the airport, Jackie was sullen and, Nicky thought, rather unreasonable. First, it was a trip to the nearby men's room that Nicky had insisted they take; Nicky almost had to drag Jackie, who claimed loudly that he did not "have to go." Then, inside the men's room, Jackie refused to use the available urinal and instead demanded to use one of the stalls, which were occupied. Nicky kept looking at his watch, not wanting to miss the call for early boarding. Finally, having waited an extra few minutes until he could use a stall, Jackie needed to go back to the men's room as soon as the two returned to where Kayla and Helen were sitting. "I couldn't go before," he explained. Yet again they had to wait for a stall. This time, as they exited, passengers were boarding, and Kayla and Helen were waving at them to hurry.

"Kids," observed Helen as she took the window seat next to Nicky, nodding toward Jackie across the aisle.

"What about kids?" asked Nicky, accepting a cup of orange juice from the flight attendant and handing it to his wife.

Helen took a sip before continuing. "Well, for one thing, we expect them to act as adults all the time, particularly when we're in a hurry. We forget they're just kids. And, for another, they're funny. You can never figure out what new thing they're going to come up with. Jackie's a lot like Ezra."

"Your grandson is only four. I expect more from Jackie than from a four-year-old." Another flight attendant handed Nicky a plastic cup filled with ice and the small bottle of Maker's Mark he'd asked for.

"Oh, of course. Jackie's much more mature, agreed. But he's acting his age today. I think they're alike because they're, well, cute ..."

"All of your grandkids are cute," he said happily, after downing half of his bourbon in one swallow. "They've got your genes, right?"

"Ezra and Jackie are cute in the same way. You know, when we get the families together, Jackie likes to play with Ezra, likes to teach him things, and Ezra loves the attention. But not only are they cute, they're both unpredictable."

"Like all kids."

"Well, like most. Some kids are just little clones of their parents and not particularly interesting. But that doesn't apply to Jackie or Ezra."

"By the way, what's happening with Aliyah when Max has to leave for Chicago and everyone else is gone?"

"Don't you know? She's staying with Sarah and company. Ezra promised to feed her."

"Cool. You'd think my family has enough to worry about without a cat, but maybe she'll provide some distraction."

"I hope she's not a burden. Mostly she stays out of sight." He paused for a second. "You know, Helen, I wish I could predict how Jackie will be on this trip. He's got quite an imagination. I'm going to spend a lot of time managing him on my own and ..."

"Look … during the day, you'll both come to the monastery, and he'll be under Kayla's care when you'd rather be doing something else, and I'd be happy to look after him too, so it won't be all on you."

"We'll see."

After putting his drink into the cup holder, Nicky opened his briefcase to withdraw *The White Hotel*. He turned, not to its beginning, but to a point about four-fifths toward the end.

"You're not reading it from the beginning?" asked Helen.

"I will. It's just that the conversation about Jackie reminded me – I don't know how I'd forgotten – there's a young boy about his age that's a main character in the next-to-last chapter. 'The Sleeping Carriage.' I wanted to remind myself of his name. Here. Right. He's Kolya. Sounds a little like Kayla, at that. Odd coincidence."

"What about Kolya? Why is he so interesting to you?"

Nicky thought for a few seconds before answering. "I think you should read this book yourself, Helen. There's a lot here that's hard to explain. But … Kolya is an orphan, Jewish, and he's with his step-mom, who's Christian – well, she was the one writing the poem you read the other night – and they're both …" He stopped then, in thought.

"Both what? Come on. The mystery is driving me crazy."

"Both on their way to be murdered at Babi Yar. Machine-gunned."

"Babi Yar? The book is about Babi Yar?"

"In part."

"That's what you wanted to read on the way to Europe? A book to remind you of our greatest disaster? Sometimes I wonder about you, my love. All the time, in fact."

"I don't want to spoil it for you, if you ever want to read it. The book is about discovering those events in our lives that we hide from consciousness, which is one reason it intrigues me. That's why Freud plays such a big role. Anything about Freud makes me think about why I wanted to become a psychiatrist. I mean, I read about Freud's patients – fictional or not – and I think about mine. And Babi Yar, as horrible as it is, is not the final word of *The White Hotel*. I'll give it to you when I'm done."

"You ordered a kosher meal for me, right?"

"I always do."

"I *will* sleep after we eat, and if you have nightmares …," she said, pointing at *The White Hotel*, "don't wake me up for comfort."

"I won't."

They returned what was left of their beverages to the flight attendant making his way up the aisle with a plastic garbage bag. The usual announcement explained takeoff was imminent. Helen looked over to see Kayla reading to Jackie, but from what book she could not say. Then she turned toward their window as the flight attendants took their seats and strapped in. In seconds, the plane accelerated down the runway. Nicky watched Helen watch the tarmac speed by. When she turned back toward him, they were already above the clouds. "Not the final word, you say?" as she pointed toward his book.

"No."

"Well, maybe I'll read it. Someday. I want to read the rest of the sexy poem."

"It's a doozy."

Behind a Tree

On the first morning in Greece, following breakfast at the monastery, Jackie asked *Ima* if he could go back to Andros's house with him and practice his clarinet. *Ima* turned to Grandpa with a questioning look, and, after a brief exchange in Greek between Grandpa and Andros, the grown-ups agreed. Andros smiled at him, said something Jackie didn't understand, and took his hand. Jackie felt he was more than old enough to follow Andros without having to be led by the hand, but he didn't put up a fight. It was not the time to be difficult. Happily for Jackie, Andros dropped his hand when they were outside.

As they walked down the dirt road toward his house, Andros began a conversation. "So, Jackie, you are wanting to play the *clarineto*?"

"Clarinet. *Ima* told me it's important to practice every day."

"You are loving much your *mitera*? Your mother, better to say, yes?"

It seemed an odd question. Why would anyone wonder about that? But *Ima* had warned him to be polite, particularly to the man who was sharing his house with him and Grandpa. "I love her, of course. How do you say that in Greek?"

"I love her?"

"Yes, but in Greek. How do you say it?"

"*Tin agapo.* You are wanting to learn Greek?"

"Sister Theodora taught me a bit, like I helped teach her English. She's an aunt. A great aunt. And also she is Grandpa's sister. Did you know that?"

"*Nai*. I know that."

They continued their walk, quietly, as Jackie thought about other words he might want to know in Greek. He knew "god" was "*theos*," that Jesus – a most important person to Sister Theodora – "*Eee-sus*," and music was "*moosiki*." Now he'd learned the Greek for "clarinet." Really, he thought, a lot of Greek words were like English. He was about to ask about the Greek word for "jazz," when Andros began again.

"Sister Theodora is very good, *nai*?"

"She is nice to me."

"She will be a saint."

He'd heard the word before, but wasn't sure what it meant. Somebody important to Jesus, he thought. "What is a saint?"

"We say *agios*."

"But what *is* a saint? What *is agios*?"

"Come sit with me on … there, the tree that has fall down." Andros took his hand again and led him gently off the road to the large log lying on its side. "I will to explain."

"You are tired?" Jackie asked.

"No, not tired. *Ochi kourasmenos*. But better to sit and talk than to walk and talk. *Nai*?"

"*Nai*."

They sat. Andros took out his pipe, filled and lit it, and smoked, while Jackie just watched him, waiting. Jackie liked the smell, which reminded him of the campfires Uncle Max and *Ima* had made when they'd camped the previous summer. He thought perhaps, when he was a man, he would smoke a pipe too. He would also wear a cap like Andros was wearing, black wool, pulled down over his forehead at a jaunty angle.

"So, *agios*. You want to know?"

Jackie nodded, now unsure it was the right thing to do. He wondered what *Ima* would say if she found out. Probably she'd be unhappy with him, because he was asking a question having to do with Christians, not Jews.

"*Agios*. A saint is one who is most holy. One who is closest to God. You know of God, *nai?*"

"There is one God, but we call God *Hashem*."

"One God, yes, but God has three … how do we say? … three faces. *Tria prosopa*."

The conversation was making Jackie uncomfortable. He didn't want to argue with Andros. He was only a boy and, at best, could only repeat things Rabbi Beck and *Ima* had taught him. He could not compete by himself with a grown-up who wanted to tell him Christian things. Yet, he wanted to know about saints, because Sister Theodora would be one, and he loved her, and he wanted to feel confident that being a saint would be good for her.

"So Sister Theodora is close to God and so she's a saint?"

"Not yet. A saint must to have done miracles. Sister Theodora has done miracles, but a person can't be a saint until after they have died. A long time after. And there must be a relic of the body, and it too must show miracles. Someday – I won't still be here – someday she will … maybe my children and grandchildren will know her as a saint."

Jackie knew the word, but miracles were things that saved Jews. *Nes gadol haya sham,* he recalled. A great miracle happened there: the Chanukah miracle. There were others Rabbi Beck had taught him about. But now it turned out miracles were Christian, too. "What is a miracle of a saint?"

Andros puffed on his pipe for a full minute. Was he thinking of how to explain in English something hard to explain? Or was he debating whether to continue the talk? Or was he just daydreaming? Jackie realized he needed to pee. He hoped the talk would end soon, so they could get back to Andros's house, the bathroom, and then his clarinet.

"Miracle, you ask. In Greek, *thavma*."

"*Thavma*. Okay, but …"

"A miracle is something that should not to happen, could not possibly to happen, but it does, and it shows God has done it. And is something good."

"And Sister Theodora has done a miracle?"

"Many. It is proven. Your grandfather is one."

The story about how Sister Theodora had saved Grandpa when he was a young man was always told with an air of mystery. Jackie had assumed Sister Theodora had a superpower, like Superman, which he was allowed to watch on Sunday mornings. But he wasn't sure he'd heard the word "miracle" as part of Grandpa's story.

"You say it could not happen, but *Hashem* has done it?"

"Yes, through Sister Theodora. So do you see?"

He thought he saw. The grenade should have blown Grandpa to pieces, but hadn't, and that was because of Sister Theodora, still a little girl, and because of the woman Christians called the Mother of God. Jackie accepted the truth of the story, so he could now understand what the word "miracle" meant. Something happened that couldn't happen. Just like when the Jews celebrated Chanukah, when the oil burned for eight days although there was enough oil for only one day. He then recalled Rabbi Beck's teaching about another miracle, the burning bush, which was not consumed by the fire. And *Hashem* had spoken to *Moshe Rabbenu* there. So those were more *nesim*, other miracles. But *Moshe* wasn't a saint. Jews didn't have saints. Only Christians. There was a lot to think about, but, as Jackie thought, the urgency of his physical condition grew intensely. He stood quickly.

"I have to pee. Can we go faster to your house?"

Andros laughed. "Sure. Or you can do it here in the woods. *Ouro*, we say. Behind a tree."

Jackie weighed the options. Someone from the monastery might walk along and see him. He would prefer Andros's bathroom. "*Ochi*. Your house now. Please. Right away."

Promises

Nicky had asked if it would be permissible for him to visit her in her cell. He had made just such a visit the year before, when he confessed his horrendous sins. His sister Kal, now Sister Theodora, had listened patiently and, when he paused, encouraged him to go on. So she knew about his adultery with a patient while married to Adel, about the girl in the yellow smock whom he inadvertently killed during the war, about his being pursued by a ghost of one of his former comrades among the partisans, about his having lost his belief in God. All she had done at the end of his confession – when, exhausted, he could think of nothing else to add – was to hold his hands in a warm grasp and bring them to her lips for the merest touch of a kiss.

It was the warmth of her touch he remembered most about the visit to her cell. He felt, not only the warmth from her hands, but also the warmth of her entire body. He wondered whether it had been an illusion. Yet, even while he doubted his senses, he longed to feel that warmth again. It reminded him of how he'd held Kal as a newborn, of how he – the big brother – had loved to sing her lullabies, of how the mere fact of her being alive made his life immeasurably better.

But Sister Theodora told him with unfeigned sorrow that it could not be. Abbess Zoe was now in charge. She had decreed that Theodora could speak with male visitors only in the church itself. Propriety would no longer countenance private visits in her cell with any male, whether with one of the faithful members of the Church or with one of her own family. So they sat on one of the pews a few minutes after the *Orthros* service, which Nicky had watched from the rear. They spoke in Greek.

"It is so good to see you again," she began.

"Likewise."

"I have a lot I'm sorry about, Nicky," Theodora continued. "I feel, when we visited you in America last year, I was not as present with you as I wanted to be. I wish we had talked more."

"You came to visit us with a lot of things on your mind, particularly about Jackie."

"Yes, very true. I still think he's special. I think he's … amazing, a gift from God, but not in the exact way I had imagined."

Nicky smiled. "I'm his grandfather. I believe the same, but I'm biased too." He paused for a second. "And then … well, Abbess Fevronia dying like that, out of the blue. I don't think you were conscious of the stress her dying caused you, but I could see it. I could feel it. Your being a nun, having so much faith in God, doesn't exempt you from feeling grief, of needing to grieve."

Theodora picked an imaginary piece of lint from her black cassock. Then she looked up at her brother again. "And feeling guilt, because, if I'd acted differently, then Fevronia would still be with us. How could I have treated her with so much resistance? So much stubbornness?"

"You can't blame yourself for her death. She had a heart attack. A myocardial infarction, to be technical about it. It's so common, even among women. Adel, for example, may she rest in peace, gone in an instant. Helen's mother, too. I mean … people die. All the time. At the worst times. I understand why you feel guilty, we call it survivor's guilt in our profession, but you must see it's not rational. To feel guilty makes no sense, it's not logical."

"I always listen to confessions of those who feel much guilt. I often tell them what you have just told me. And you too, Nicky. The message applies to you. I know how guilty you still feel about what happened in the war. The guilt weighs you down more than any other person I've known."

Nicky couldn't bring himself to deny what Theodora had just said. But he felt the urge still to draw a distinction. "Pulling the trigger of an automatic pistol when you don't know what you're shooting at is one thing. I should have been more careful, and, yes, I still feel acute pain when I remember those moments. The little girl in the yellow smock … her blood. The way she looked at me as the light passed out of her eyes. But just being with someone when she dies of a heart attack – as you with Fevronia – is something else entirely."

"There's no difference before God. We both acted in ways we thought were right, and the consequences were what they were." She sighed deeply. "So there's more on your mind now, I know. Let me look deeply into you as we sit." She took his hands in hers, and Nicky once again felt her uncanny warmth. She closed her eyes, as if concentrating on what her hands could see that her eyes could not. The rational part of his brain told Nicky that this purported clairvoyance was a hoax, yet the part of him that loved his sister insisted he must trust her; she above all others could understand him and explain him to himself. He wasn't sure what he needed from her, just that he needed something basic and primal, something only she could give.

After a minute, she released his hands and looked down, eyes still closed.

"What do you see, Kal?" he asked.

She lifted her head, opened her eyes, and gazed into his own. He had the odd sensation she could see the many folds and valleys of his brain. "Someone accuses you, and it troubles you greatly."

He wasn't surprised she knew without his having told her. "Well, yes. I am both accused and troubled. You're right."

"Please to go on. I am here for you."

"A person died, and I am blamed for his death."

"I see this person was a man, a patient. Someone who was sick."

"Yes. He killed himself, this young man, and his family says now, in court, that I should have prevented that."

"And you worry the family is right."

It was not a question, but a statement. He had indeed been tearing himself apart about the possibility, ever since he'd read the complaint. Kal had sensed it immediately, as if he had clearly written the details of his fear on his face.

"Yes. I don't remember this patient, but the chart says I saw him in a hospital and I signed off on his discharge. He was a disturbed patient who had made suicide threats. I allowed him to leave the hospital."

"In America, everyone expects doctors to see into the future and be perfect."

Again, it was not a question so much as a statement. What did Theodora possibly know about litigation in the United States? She had never been involved in litigation. Yet, her observation was spot on, spoken without the slightest doubt.

"*Nai.* Exactly. Patients expect their doctors to be ... superhuman. Families of patients are the same. And there are tens of thousands of lawyers who encourage such expectations and make promises of ... oh, I don't know ... you listen to the advertisements ... promises of 'getting them the money they deserve' and such. It's all nonsense, but those are the conditions under which we practice medicine in the United States, the constant threat of lawyers suing us for bad outcomes, regardless of fault."

"No one can prevent what God has decreed. And so this adds to the guilt you already carry. I wish I could make this burden easier for you, Nicky."

He stood, pulled her up alongside him, and hugged her strongly, wishing as he did so that Papa and Mama were there watching them from some alternative dimension, happy beyond all measure to see two of their children united, caring for each other. Theodora returned the embrace with equal fervor. It was a long minute before they separated.

"You have done something for me, Kal. By letting me talk to you."

She lifted on her toes and kissed him on the cheek. "You're the only one in the world I will let call me Kal. And the only one in the world whom I would allow to hug me so tightly and for so long."

Vespinis Erminevo

Lunch on the first day of their visit was wrapping up. The three nuns who had been singing Psalms from a dais in the corner of the dining room had just finished with what Kayla assumed were the final blessings, similar to *bentching*, in which those who had eaten praised *Hashem* for having provided sustenance. The other nuns, including Sister Theodora, sat at their tables quietly, heads bowed, while the singers left. The monastery's guests – Nicky, Jackie, and Andros among them, at a table across the room – respectfully followed suit. When the singers were gone, the remaining nuns stood and began silently collecting the plates, utensils, and serving bowls. Kayla rose to help, but a nun behind her gently took her by the arm, said *"Ochi!"* This was obviously a job only the nuns could do, assumed Kayla, as it must also have religious significance. She resumed her seat. When the nuns had cleared the tables, they opened the doors to the dining room. Most of the guests then departed to resume their activities.

Kayla remained, however, saying to Helen in a low voice that she wanted to talk with Sister Theodora alone and would meet Helen later in their room.

Helen considered this with a look of concern. "Is everything all right?"

"Yes. Everything is okay, but, if you don't mind, I have unfinished business stemming from their visit. A bone to pick, if you will. I'll tell you about it later."

Kayla was pretty sure Theodora had gone into the kitchen. She would catch her on the way out. Five minutes passed as other nuns exited the kitchen and wiped down the tables. Kayla was impatiently on the verge of entering the kitchen herself – dismissing concerns that this might violate the rules – when Theodora emerged. She seemed startled to see Kayla still there, approaching her.

"Sister Theodora, we need to talk, please." Kayla pulled chairs from the nearest table, making clear where and when their conversation should occur. Theodora recovered her usual look of equanimity and sat, smiling.

"Yes. We will talk."

Kayla thought for a minute before beginning, contemplating how she might express herself in English simple enough for Theodora, who was not fluent. "You need to know how upset I have been, upset about what you gave to Jackie."

"What I gave?"

"The icon. The picture of Jesus. I found it hidden in Jackie's underwear drawer."

For a second, Theodora's face reddened. She closed her eyes, took a deep breath, then looked directly at Kayla. In her left hand, Theodora fingered her prayer beads, which had suddenly appeared from a pocket of her cassock.

"It was a gift of love, Kayla. I did not mean to harm you or Jackie. But I can see from how you talk about this that you believe I did wrong."

"I don't mean to be difficult, but this gift has troubled me. I need to tell you, to get this off my chest: Jackie is Jewish, and he should not have an icon of a different faith." Helen saw Theodora listening carefully. "He's young. He's been through a lot – with me, with his father – and I don't want him to be confused because you think he's Jesus or should become Jesus or has been Jesus. So, yes, to be quite honest, I do think you did wrong, and I'm sorry I have to say this to you – you have been through much pain yourself – but you must never do anything like that again."

Looking down at the floor now, Theodora prayed, "Lord Jesus Christ, please forgive me, a sinner." Then she added, looking again at Kayla as if the world was about to end, "I am so sorry. I wanted to give Jackie something to remember our time together. He was so good to me. He was patient. He answered my questions. He helped me with my English. He gave me his little model piano, the one he'd made himself, and I wanted to give him something in return."

"I see that."

"And I learned …" Theodora struggled to find the right words. "Kayla … I learned … I was wrong about what God was telling me, about Jackie. I mis …"

"Mistook? Misinterpreted?"

"Ah. *Nai*. Misinterpreted. *Vespinis erminevo*. I failed. I sinned. I missed the mark. I prayed the icon would mean a lot to Jackie, and now I see I made all worse, all terrible, with my gift. A gift like that should go only to a Christian boy. Please to forgive me, Kayla."

"I do forgive you," Kayla said immediately, realizing as she did so how important it was for her to let Theodora start fresh, even more important than chastising Theodora for violating Kayla's trust. The women rose and hugged. Both were crying, Theodora from guilt and Kayla with relief that Theodora understood, that they had a clean slate. "I took it away from him, Theodora. I brought it back here, to the monastery, to return to you. It's with my other things, in the dormitory. Shall I get it now?"

"Let's go together. And we can to talk more?"

But for a while, as they made their way, side by side, they were silent. Finally, Theodora asked the question pressing most on her mind. "When you took it away from Jackie, what did the poor boy say?"

"Not much. He was sad, he was terribly worried about my anger, but he saw my point. You can't be Jewish and venerate Jesus at the same time."

Kayla worried Helen might be in their room; she wasn't quite ready to tell Helen about the icon. But the room was empty. Kayla walked to her bed, pulled a small cloth bag from the suitcase resting on it, and handed the bag to Theodora.

Theodora checked to see that the icon was inside and nodded, smiling again. "You have … fixed this, the wrong I have done to you. Thank you. This, the icon, this picture of my Lord, is not for you and Jackie. I understand. You have a different faith."

"I'm glad we see eye to eye." Kayla noted the look of confusion on Theodora's face. "Which means I'm glad we understand each other."

"But, Kayla, please to see also … someone can be Jewish and love this as well," indicating the bag in her hand.

Two Staves

It was completely unexpected, and yet somehow Kayla knew it would happen. A sixth sense? A premonition? A dream provoked by her schizophrenia? It didn't matter. She knew he would call. When Abbess Zoe took her aside on the first evening of their visit and spoke softly to her as they entered the dining room for supper, Kayla knew what the message would be even before she heard Zoe's words.

"A gentleman from America was on the telephone for you and says he will to call back after our meal hour. You come to my office later?"

"A gentleman?"

Zoe unfolded a small piece of paper. "Ααρών. Aron, like the brother of Moses. I assume you know him?"

Kayla nodded, thanked the abbess, and moved to the table where she saw Helen waiting for supper to be served. Now, with conversation prohibited, with the only sound the mournful singing of three nuns, Kayla mulled over what exactly she should expect Aharon to say. She assumed he would start with an apology. But could Aharon possibly understand the great damage he had caused her? To have been treated as little more than … what had he treated her like? Little more than a guinea pig. But, no, a pig was at least alive. Aharon would have treated a pig with more respect. To be treated as something less than alive, as little more than a convenient test tube, a horrible metaphor, even if apt. To be treated as little more than a sick sodden handkerchief. More appropriate. Yet, she supposed she would have to take his call, loath as she was to have more contact with him.

She picked at her food with little appetite and returned Helen's smile with a weak one of her own. Helen gently squeezed Kayla's wrist for a second. Kayla wondered how she could explain to Helen what had happened with Aharon. It would have to start with her own mortifying confession of how she had desired him. She would have to come clean and confess her willful disobedience of a key tenet of her faith.

Outside the dining room, after the meal and prayers had been concluded, Kayla whispered to Helen, "I have a phone call coming. The abbess told me before our dinner. So I'll see you later."

Helen looked at her skeptically, wondering. First, it had been Kayla's urgent need to speak with Sister Theodora alone. Now this call. Impulsively, Helen leaned into Kayla for a brief hug, kissing her on the cheek, then departed toward the dormitory. In seconds, Zoe approached and asked Kayla to follow. Grimly, Kayla let Zoe lead the way to her office.

At first, they sat quietly, waiting for the phone to ring. Kayla was mesmerized by the sight of the Jesus hanging from a cross affixed to the wall. As she studied the statuette, Kayla could feel Zoe's eyes on her. She knew she was being judged; she worried the abbess was sorry she had ever allowed Kayla and her family to become guests of the monastery. The silence was maddening, and finally Kayla, looking away from the crucifix and back at Zoe, had no choice but to fill the silence with what she hoped was a plausible explanation.

"You see, he's a friend. Or was a friend. Aharon, I mean." Zoe waited, as if Kayla needed to say something more. Well, there was obviously more. Kayla continued, "I thought at one time, perhaps … Aharon and I might marry. Our rabbi was trying to encourage a match." Kayla cringed internally as she heard herself speak, knowing she sounded like she hiding her own responsibility, blaming someone else for the situation she was now in.

"Do you want to talk about it?"

"Aharon wasn't who I thought he was, Abbess Zoe. He was ..." She was about to call him a monster when the phone rang, unexpectedly loud. It was an alarm accusing her of *lashon hara. Hashem* had sent a warning that she should not speak ill of anyone, even of Aharon.

Zoe answered. "Yes ... she is here ... please to wait." With that, Zoe handed Kayla the receiver, reaching across her desk to do so, and left the office. Kayla took a deep breath and prayed silently that the call would be short. She waited for what seemed like an unnaturally long time before he spoke.

"Are you there, Kayla? Are you free to speak?"

"I'm here. Alone in the abbess's office, if that's what you're asking."

"There's no .... party line?"

Why won't he get to the point? Why this great concern for secrecy? She glanced at the door. Zoe had left it ajar by about an inch. Conceivably, Zoe could be trying to listen from the hallway, but that seemed unlikely. Nor would Abbess Fevronia have eavesdropped. This wasn't the conduct one would expect from those who had devoted their lives to prayer.

"We're alone," she said, in what she hoped was a let's-get-this-over-quickly tone.

"Then I need to beg your forgiveness, Kayla. I should have called to ask you to forgive me long before this. I'm so sorry for my behavior. This has been bothering me immensely since ... since the Wilshire ... and I couldn't live with myself any longer without saying that to you. I hope, I pray, you will forgive me."

Let him roast in his own juices, she thought. She counted slowly to five before responding. "I forgive you," she said laconically, then stopped. What else was there to say? Was he expecting her to promise to call him as soon as she returned from Greece?

"Will you find it in your heart ever to meet with me again?" he asked. "Only at Rabbi Beck's house?"

As she held the receiver in her left hand, she drummed the fingers of her right hand on Zoe's desk, and they played, seemingly of their own accord, a familiar melody in B-Minor, the simple and sad melody of Chopin's Prelude No. 6. She'd been hearing the melody in her mind and playing the piece completely through on the imaginary piano always in front of her. She thought that this music, written by a genius, might be a good starting point.

"Hang on."

Lying on Zoe's desk was a month-by-month calendar. Kayla picked it up, saw that the back of January was a color picture of a church, but the sky was whitish blue and would serve as an adequate background. With a ballpoint pen picked up from Zoe's desk, Kayla rapidly drew two staves, then filled in notes of a melody, a simple inversion of Chopin's. The two sharp signs could wait, the measure breaks could wait, even the time signature and time values of the notes could wait. Was this the melody to help her break through to a new composition? Was it too simple? Too derivative?

"Are you there?" asked Aharon after more than a minute. "This is torture for me."

"Yes. Here … just … okay."

"I asked you, Kayla, if we could meet again. You said you forgive me. Does that mean … you and I … could still talk about the possibility of a future? Together? Could we start fresh?"

Getting into a long conversation with Aharon was the last thing Kayla wanted. She urgently needed to go find real staff paper and elaborate upon the melody that had been coaxed out of her, as it were, through the magic of her favorite Romantic composer. Strangely, she also felt an overwhelming urge to cry. She thought she'd cried enough since the sorry episode at the Wilshire already. And now to cry again? For what? She didn't know, but tears spilled down her cheek. She wiped them away with the back of her hand. She had spoken words of forgiveness – had meant them – but did that mean she would be able to start over, as he had asked?

"I have to go, Aharon. I'll think about it and decide when I come back. Not now. And maybe not even when I come back. Maybe never."

"But Kayla …"

She didn't hear whatever Aharon was going to say, because she'd hung up, with much more force than necessary.

Kayla tore off the January page, folded it, and stuck it in her purse. Rather than leaving Zoe's office immediately, though, as Kayla knew she should have, she sat again and put her head down on the desk next to the telephone. In this position, she allowed herself the luxury of sobbing. She had wanted Aharon so badly. She had desperately craved – there was no other apt expression – the physical experience of Aharon promised by marriage. But now, even with his apology, she saw that a loving relationship was a hopeless fantasy. He had too many problems, too many by far. To link herself to him was to accept his problems as her own, to make them her life's work, and she felt she had little strength for that purpose. She had more than enough of her own worries: Jackie, Max, her music, staying on her meds, keeping off weight. Her own life, as complicated as it was, required every ounce of her energy. A union with Aharon would mean subordinating everything she cared about – and for what good?

She must have drifted off to sleep, but then felt a warm touch on her arm. Startled, she tried to stand, but her legs were pools of Jello. She could not lift herself from the chair.

"Kayla? What's wrong? Are you ill?" asked Theodora, who stood next to her. As Kayla tried to rise again, Theodora grabbed her under a shoulder to steady her. Kayla, through the cotton of her blouse, felt Theodora's unnatural heat. They faced each other, Kayla now leaning on the edge of Zoe's desk.

"I think I'm all right," she said, feeling anything but.

"Abbess Zoe said I am to find you here, she said you might want … support. That your friend Aharon called and that the news could not be good. You look not well. *Ochi kala.*"

"He did call." Kayla wanted very much to explain everything to Theodora, who still held her in a strong grip. But how to start? What specifically to say?

Theodora understood a lot without Kayla having to say anything. "You thought of him as a husband."

Kayla wiped away the rest of her tears with a tissue she'd taken from her purse. "How did you know? Did Nicky say something?"

Theodora released her grip. "No. I could see it in you. I could feel it. And then Abbess Zoe told me what you had told her. Do you want to walk with me outside? Before it gets dark? So we might to talk?"

Kayla nodded and found her legs, which moments earlier had not been capable of movement, had renewed strength. She followed Theodora out of the building and then around toward the vineyard. The midsummer sun cast long evening shadows, and the day was still warm. How Theodora managed the heat in her long black cassock was a mystery to Kayla, but apparently the sun had little effect on her aunt, the source of an even stronger heat. Kayla thought for a minute she was being led into the vineyard itself, but instead Theodora pointed up the path toward the winery. They walked in silence, Kayla willing to let Theodora guide her. It turned out that Theodora's destination was the last bench at the top. There they sat quietly, catching their breath, watching the shadows lengthen, noticing how the green of the pine trees and the vineyards faded to gray, and listening to the faint songs of grackles. A solitary yellow bird flashed past them like a streak of butter spread on bread.

"What was that?"

"A serin, I think. They're common around here."

Kayla felt clammy with perspiration, but the mild discomfort did nothing to interfere with the joy enveloping her as she gazed across the valley toward the distant hills. Finally, she broke the silence, in a voice barely above a whisper. "It's beautiful here, Theodora."

"I know."

"Cooler by a few degrees," Kayla continued. "But mostly it's beautiful because of the quiet."

Theodora nodded, and another half minute passed before she spoke. "It is one of my favorite spots. I expect always to see God here."

"Is it not strange, though? Should you not find your God in your church? In your prayer service? In the Psalms?"

"The prayer is with me, in me. If I am here, so is prayer. The mountains, the sky, all is part of the prayer."

Kayla thought about that with a tinge of regret and self-pity. When had Kayla herself believed the world around her was a prayer? Once, Kayla had found the universe in a Central Park tulip. But had she ever found the strength of Theodora's prayer? What is prayer, anyway? An offering to *Hashem*, a feeling of being at one with *Hashem*, a desire to share the love of *Hashem* with all who could hear. The times in Kayla's life when she had most felt prayer encompassing her, although she wouldn't have called it such at the time, was when she performed. Beethoven, the Appassionata in particular, was nothing but a prayer to *Hashem*, and it was a prayer she had shared with so many in her audiences, but for such a short time, before her gift had been stripped away. When would she ever experience that kind of prayer again? She knew the answer was never, despite her having found solace in *Chabad* and its ways.

"You are thinking about your music, Kayla."

She was startled. The way Theodora could read her mind bordered on an invasion of privacy. "How can you tell?"

Theodora smiled warmly and pointed. "I see your fingers moving. This is not … *mantiki kanotika* … wait." She pulled the well-worn paperback dictionary from the pocket of her cassock. "This is not … clairvoyance. I'm just watching you."

Kayla was painfully aware she could never stop her fingers from moving if she was hearing in her mind any piece of music. Every twitch of her fingers was brought about by the uncontrollable firing of synapses in her brain. She took a deep breath, then let it out slowly.

"You're good. Observant. You actually see people. You see what makes them move, what makes them human."

"So … the call. Aharon? Do you want to tell me? I am not to be *kritis* … I will not to judge."

Kayla took a deep breath. There was an overwhelming goodness in Theodora, which made Kayla trust her completely and want to share everything. She'd known that Theodora often heard confessions. Was Kayla about to confess? Did it mean that Kayla felt guilt and had to relieve herself of it in the succoring presence of her aunt?

"I will tell you."

"*Nai* …"

"I was meeting Aharon, talking, over a few weeks. About ourselves and our lives. The point was to see if we could be a husband and wife. This is how we do it in Orthodox Judaism. In *Chabad*."

Theodora allowed her thoughts to drift momentarily to her early childhood. She couldn't remember any weddings or any engagements in her Sephardic family or in her neighborhood at large. She had no idea how men and women found each other. She didn't even remember any stories of how her own Papa and Mama had met.

"Please to go on."

"Yes. Well, I don't know how to say this." Kayla now was the one to reach and take Theodora's hand, a gesture she hoped would not be seen as too forward. "But … my body wanted him. I was … I hadn't had a man since August, Jackie's father, you know …."

"You wanted sex. *Φύλο* (*Fylo*). It is natural for a woman to want. I have heard many women over the years to say this and to think it is a sin."

Kayla kicked herself mentally for having been afraid to mention sex to Theodora. A nun who hears confessions must hear about women's desires. The faithful women who came to Theodora would necessarily express their anxieties about their bodily urges. Many of them, too, would feel guilty. Now seeing it clearly, it made sense to Kayla. It gave her more confidence to speak about her own travails.

"I did more than want him, though."

"*Nai?*" Theodora's tone reflected infinite patience. Kayla could explain, if she wanted, or she could end the conversation there.

Theodora's demeanor – even her allowing Kayla to hold her hand – encouraged Kayla to believe she had control of the situation.

"I was ready to commit the sin of having sex with him, a sin because we weren't married." She paused, wondering what else to add. "I met him in a hotel room, I am sorry to say."

"Tell me more then, if you want." Theodora's demeanor revealed to Kayla once again her simple curiosity, openness to listen, acceptance of Kayla's humanity. She gently squeezed Kayla's hand.

"We didn't. Have sex, I mean. I left soon after I entered his room, but he made me feel … used. I knew I had done wrong in *Hashem*'s eyes, even though … I didn't give myself to him."

"Our desires can be as wrong as our actions."

"I suppose that's why I felt so cheap. I still feel cheap."

"But God was there to stop you from doing the wrong thing. God was present there for you, I am certain. You left when you did because God was there with you, ready to forgive you."

Kayla wondered whether that was true. Was it really *Hashem* who caused Aharon's excitement and inability to control his body's reaction? Or was it just a random event, of no greater significance than a stray meteorite burning up in earth's atmosphere?

"Theodora … I've never talked about this with anyone. My poor mother wouldn't have understood … or maybe she would have understood all too well, but …"

"But?"

"I have to try at least to satisfy myself. You understand?"

"Of course."

"I have to imagine some man – maybe not Aharon ever again – but I have to pretend inside my head that someone is with me. And the pleasure I feel then I know is wrong, or maybe it's not wrong, I'm never sure, but either way I am … I am too weak to resist."

"God gives us the means to resist sin."

"So this is a sin?"

"We regard it as such. Our Holy Fathers have said so."

"The Torah says nothing about this. Directly. At least for women. I hope it is not a sin for Jewish women, because, if it is, I don't think I could stop."

"You should stop doing what you feel is wrong in the eyes of God." But Theodora's words were full of kindness. The warmth of her loving advice mirrored the warmth of her body, which spread from Theodora to Kayla when they embraced. Theodora wouldn't tell Kayla it was wrong for Kayla, only that Kayla had to be the one to decide if giving herself the pleasure she so desperately needed was a sin according to *Hashem*'s law.

Kayla couldn't help but wonder whether Theodora had ever indulged, but knew that asking such a question would be the ultimate rudeness. Perhaps she had, perhaps not. Maybe it was one of the things for which Theodora always sought forgiveness.

Kadosh

By the third day of their visit, they had established their routine. Grandpa would wake him, he would say *kalimera* to Andros, wash up, and eat a small breakfast of Post Honey Bunches with milk while Grandpa and Andros chatted in Greek. He wished they spoke in English, but understood that Greek was much more comfortable for Andros. Jackie himself could catch only an occasional *nai* or *ochi*, but he felt a special friendship engulfed the two men. A newspaper would be open on the table, with photographs of soccer players in action, so perhaps it was soccer they talked about amiably. That must be the meaning of *podospiro*. Later, the three would walk to the monastery, a pleasant enough task in the cool, early morning air, shaded as they were by the tall pine trees.

At the monastery, there was a stone bench where they met *Ima*, Helen, and Sister Theodora. At home, he would have expected Grandpa and Helen to hug and kiss. He had often seen them embrace when they stayed overnight at his house. At the monastery, however, they merely smiled at each other and held hands. *Ima* would wrap him in a hug much too long for a seven-year-old boy, and within seconds he would struggle to escape. What he wanted more than anything was to talk to Sister Theodora. He was still trying to teach her English, and she was learning quickly. They would go off for a walk around the church by themselves, leaving the others at the bench, and then they would meet again for breakfast, his second.

On these walks, they would remain quiet until Sister Theodora began a conversation. She would talk about the beauty of the mountains or how pleasant the air was. Or she would mention how much she missed Abbess Fevronia. Jackie, although wanting to talk, had little to say, other than to agree with Theodora about the mountains being pretty. He'd wanted to talk about the icon *Ima* had taken from him, but knew this was not a safe topic. *Ima* would find out, and he would be in trouble again. More than anything, he wanted to avoid displeasing *Ima*.

In the dining room, Jackie would not be very hungry, but would take a boiled potato or a hard-boiled egg onto his plate to be polite. If an egg, he would carefully cut into it, pushing away the yolk, which he detested. The white parts were good, though. If there was fruit juice, he would have a small glass. If there was no fruit juice, he would content himself with water. At all meals, he had to be absolutely quiet while the nuns sang a prayer. It wasn't singing so much as chanting, with little melody he could recall. Jackie felt he could easily duplicate their chant on his clarinet and wanted to try, probably in the woods behind Andros's house, where he wouldn't bother anyone. And when the nuns weren't singing, he still couldn't talk, even to the person next to him. At most, he could whisper something like "please pass the water," but the Christians at his table didn't even whisper. They simply pointed at what they needed, and the object was silently passed to them.

As he began his walk with Sister Theodora one bright morning, maybe the fourth day of their visit, she led him, not completely around the back of the church, but straight out into the vineyard.

"Come with me, Jackie. I want to show you something." He hesitated, looking over his shoulder to where he could just see the other grown-ups chatting. "*Enain taxi,* it's okay. They know you're safe with me." To confirm, she waved at *Ima*, who waved back, signaling yes, it was fine.

He followed Sister Theodora between the rows of grape vines. No longer in the shade of the trees, he perspired quickly from the sun's heat. How hot Sister Theodora must have felt in her black cassock! But she seemed unaffected, and he had to walk fast to keep up. The flies constantly buzzing around his face added to his annoyance. Just when he was about to complain and ask if they could return to the church, they got to the end of the vineyard. Jackie looked out over a gently sloping meadow bordered by a small brook. He could now hear the faint gurgling of water, and the air was cooler, a gentle breeze touching his face and arms, even though he was still in the sun. Oddly, the flies relented their attack. Jackie glanced at Theodora, who crossed herself and murmured a prayer.

"Is this what you wanted to show me?" asked Jackie.

"We are getting there. This brook is the Microdermis. Please to come with me, Jackie."

He hesitated, worrying now whether he should have walked off with Theodora. She took his hand lightly though, and he at once felt its reassuring warmth. She led him toward the brook. About halfway to the water, she stopped and pointed at the ground. He looked to see what she was pointing at, but initially saw nothing but grass. Theodora knelt and pushed grass to the side, and then he noticed the small flat marker. It was a disk, perhaps six inches across. There was Greek writing on it. He could make out what seemed to be an "H," but all the rest was beyond his grasp.

"What is it?"

Theodora stood up, but continued to look at the ground at Jackie's feet. "Here is where we buried Abbess Fevronia. That's what those two words say: 'Abbess Fevronia,' but in our language, with our letters."

He stepped quickly away from the marker, as if it might explode any second. Theodora took his hand again, but this time the warmth of her touch was not comforting. For an instant, she seemed like an ice monster he'd had a bad dream about. He pulled his hand from hers and looked back in the church's direction, but was suddenly scared to realize it was no longer visible.

Theodora did not seem to notice how unsettled Jackie had become. "Do you want to pray? Here is where I pray often to the Lord Jesus." She smiled at him, that gentle, warm smile he loved so much. Did he still love her smile? He wanted to, badly. Obviously, she thought he *should* want to pray, but he was too surprised by what he'd just learned – about Abbess Fevronia's body lying underneath them – to consider praying.

He shook his head. "*Ochi.*"

"The Abbess's brother also rests here. His name was Silenos. Other holy men lie here too, in their big grave. They are called monks. *Kayoleroi.* And the ground is … *eiros* … sacred, I think. Yes, sacred. Holy."

"*Kadosh.*" The Hebrew word popped out before he could consider whether he wanted to say it. "*Kadosh* is holy."

"Will you pray with me, please?"

"No. I prayed already this morning. I say it every morning: *Modeh Ani l'fanecha* … It means I thank *Hashem* for letting me wake up again, returning me to life."

"*Nai.*" She nodded and dropped his hand. Then she knelt, crossed herself once more, and bowed her head to touch the ground. He heard her faintly praying in Greek and knew she was seeking *Hashem's* forgiveness.

The Beautiful Woman

Sister Theodora prayed for a long time. While he waited for her to finish, trying to be patient, Jackie felt again the sun's strength on the back of his neck; the flies returned too. The gurgling of the brook reminded him there was water nearby. He touched Theodora lightly on the shoulder, but she seemed not to notice. Saying nothing, he quietly walked off toward the Microdermis.

It had rained the night before, and he had to walk across a short muddy area to reach the water. He wondered whether he should keep his shoes on and let them get muddy or whether he should go barefoot, but, either way, he had to reach the water. He was thirsty and wanted to grab a handful or two to his mouth. He thought it must be clean enough, because animals would be happy to drink the water. There had to be animals around him, squirrels at least, but they all were hiding. Maybe they were afraid of the humans nearby. Maybe they watched from up in the trees. He could hear bird songs reaching him from somewhere.

He opted to take off his shoes and socks. The mud felt cool on his bare feet, and that in itself was rewarding, taking his mind off the heat and the bothersome flies. At the water's edge, he was fascinated by a large rock in the middle of the stream; water splashed and sprayed over it and the reflections of the sunlight through the water sparkled like burning orange jewels. Not caring about his pants getting muddy, he knelt, bringing his face as close to the water as he could, and scooped some into his mouth. It tasted funny, but good. He was still thirsty, though; one hand couldn't bring up much water. He scooped up a bit more.

Then he looked again at the spray of water over the rock and saw the face of a young woman staring at him from the reflected sunlight. He stared, transfixed. She was very beautiful. *Ima* was beautiful, of course, but this woman was younger than *Ima* and even more beautiful. The sun now no longer seemed to warm him; the warmth throughout his body came from this woman. He knew she wanted to speak to him.

"Jackie. Come with me."

The sunlight woman didn't speak, although he'd thought that she might. Instead, the words had come from behind him, as he felt a light touch on his shoulder. He turned to see Sister Theodora walking down to the water too. She had finished her prayer and was watching Jackie with what he felt was concern.

"There's a woman there, Sister Theodora." He knew she could see for herself, but he was too excited not to announce his discovery.

"Where?"

"In the water …" He looked back again and saw only the simple spray of droplets bouncing above the rock. He no longer saw the bright spectacle of reflected sunlight. "But she was there!"

"Who was there, my child?"

"I don't know who she was. But she looked at me. She knew me. She wanted to talk to me."

Theodora helped him to his feet and put her arms around him, hugging him tightly.

"Was it your mother? Your … *Ima*? The woman you thought you saw?"

"No. She was more beautiful than *Ima*. And younger. Didn't you see her?"

After a few seconds, Jackie understood he wouldn't get an answer. Sister Theodora didn't want to say what she had seen. But he knew she must have seen the beautiful woman. There was no way Sister Theodora could have missed the beautiful woman in the water, with the orange sparkling around her face.

"We need to go back to the church, Jackie. We've been away too long. They will worry. Πάμε! (*pabe*) Let's go." Her voice did not allow for any disagreement.

He had no choice but to follow her back through the vineyard. It was a good thing she was there to show him the way, because without her leading him he would surely have gotten lost. All the vines, every row, looked the same. Trusting her to get him back to the rest of his family, he paid little attention to the route. He kept his eyes set simply on the bottom of Theodora's cassock as, with each step, it swept over the dirt and stones between the rows. He could sense the grapes swelling in the heat of the day as they walked past.

From somewhere, he heard again the chanting of the nuns that created the mood for every meal. His fingers imagined covering and uncovering the holes of the clarinet as he breathed life into it.

For Her Peace

Theodora wasn't surprised when Helen asked if they could talk privately. She had been expecting Helen to approach her immediately upon the beginning of the family's visit, but it wasn't until the fifth day that her sister-in-law gently placed a hand on Theodora's arm as they walked silently from the dining room and nodded toward the corner of the vestibule. The look on Helen's pale face was pained and pinched, as if she hadn't slept the night before. Theodora knew the cots were not designed for comfort, but understood that more than loss of sleep afflicted Helen. Theodora smiled briefly in encouragement, but Helen had turned away, heading toward a small bench. Theodora followed, offering a silent prayer to Christ she would be able to assist Helen in whatever Helen asked.

After they sat, Helen took Theodora's hands in her own, and they were very warm, as Helen expected. "I hate to trouble you, Sister Theodora, but there is something important I hope you will do for me."

"In honor of the Holy Theotokos, I shall always be your servant."

"I ask you then to help me pray for my daughter, Sarah. We'll be leaving here in a week or so, and I will return to her side. But the cancer … you know the word?"

"Cancer, yes. It is a terrible illness."

"The cancer has spread throughout her body. It is only a matter of time. We don't know how much time she has left. I fear not much. She will die soon, prayer or no prayer. I tried to pray for a miracle, but I know it is *Hashem*'s will … she will not be long for this world. Yet, I don't want her to suffer, and I want her to have time to say goodbye to her family and …"

"But … should I not continue to pray for her to get better? To be healed? Nicky has asked me."

"Nicky asked you? To pray for her healing?"

"Yes."

Helen stopped to consider. That was not what she was asking Theodora. She thought she had been clear. Maybe it was the language barrier. And yet, recognizing the futility of her deepest desire, Helen wanted Sarah to overcome her cancer. What mother wouldn't want that for a beloved child? *Hashem* was All-Powerful and could save one from death. It was part of Helen's daily prayers. In *Atah Gibor* – You are Powerful – one referred to *Hashem* as *M'chaye Matim* – Who Brings Life to the Dead. If *Hashem* could do that, *Hashem* could stop cancer from killing Sarah. So perhaps Theodora knew after all what Helen wanted from *Hashem*. But no one could live forever, and *Kohelet* reminded everyone of the sad fact there was *Et La-Mut* – a time to die. As holy as Theodora was, as full of miracles as she had proven herself, she could not alter *Hashem*'s judgment of when each person must die. She could not prevent the inevitable tragedy of Helen grieving after the death of her daughter.

"No, Theodora, I'm not asking you to pray for Sarah to live, although that's what I desperately want. That's one reason I came to the monastery, in fact, to pray for her being saved by a miracle. But it is *Hashem*'s will taking Sarah from us, and we are powerless to pray for something other than *Hashem*'s will. It is *Hashem*'s decree I must mourn for my child … as Jacob mourned for Joseph when he believed Joseph had been torn apart by an animal. What I ask – even though I have no right to ask – but I ask you to pray for her peace, to let her leave this world calmly, not in fear, to leave this world feeling the love of her family around her."

Theodora removed her hands from Helen's and held her closely for a long minute. Had it not been for Helen, Theodora knew she would never have been reunited with Nicky. When she met the two of them for the first time in Abbess Fevronia's office, she could sense immediately Helen was the more stable of the two, that it was Helen's strength even more than Nicky's that had brought them so far. As she washed Nicky's feet – not yet realizing who he was – she sensed his despair, fragility, and fear, emotions she didn't understand at the time. As she washed Helen's feet – aware only that Helen was a close companion of Nicky – she could sense love, excitement, and a strong commitment to God. Yes, it was certain Nicky would not have been there had it not been for this woman. Thus, Theodora owed everything to Helen, without whom Theodora would never have reawakened to her Jewish roots. It was a debt she could never fully repay.

Theodora released Helen from their embrace. "I shall do as you wish, Helen. I shall pray as you ask on behalf of Sarah and the rest of your family. I shall pray for Sarah's peace and for the opportunity to have her family with her when God calls."

"Thank you." Helen leaned over and kissed Theodora lightly on the side of her head, touching her lips only to the material of Theodora's black veil. "I thank you so much, with all my heart."

"But I am a sinner, Helen, and I must always seek forgiveness from Christ, in all my prayers. You understand?"

"Yes. You must always be yourself as you pray."

Theodora nodded ever so slightly. Having promised, it was urgent she return to her cell and begin praying the right way for the things Helen longed for. But she wondered whether God – who knew she was a sinner – would heed her prayer.

Outrageously High

Nicky had briefly put the lawsuit out of his mind. It was with dismay, then, that he took a call in Abbess Zoe's office he'd been told was urgent. It was his damn lawyer, Edelmann. Well, not *his* lawyer, but his damn insurance company's lawyer. What could have been so urgent it needed his attention while in Greece? What couldn't have waited until he returned?

"Nicky. Glad they tracked you down. Two things. I found the article you and Waller wrote. I'm not sure if it's important, but I'll have my secretary fax it to you at the monastery."

"What's it about?"

"Of all things … the standard of care with suicidal patients. It seems the two of you shared a patient once, one who tried to kill himself. Or herself, I should say. Anyway, get back to me after you read it."

"What was the patient's name?"

"Greta S is the name used in the article. Ring any bells?"

"What bells?"

"Do you remember her or the case?"

Nicky looked up and his eyes fastened on the crucifix hanging on the wall. It was a sculpture that had bothered him intensely when he'd first seen it a year earlier, a look of pure anguish on the face of the man nailed to the cross. "I don't have a clue."

"Well, it may not matter as things stand. We have an offer of settlement."

"For what amount?"

"Five hundred thousand dollars. The policy limit."

"No."

"No?"

"No. I won't settle. I did nothing wrong."

"You don't understand, Nicky. Freedom Financial wants to take the settlement, but you have to agree. They're tired of paying my bills on what they think is a sure loser. If you pass up on the settlement offer, and you go to trial, you're on the hook for any verdict amount over five hundred thousand. It would be foolish for you to take such a risk."

"And if I take the settlement, Freedom is going to drop me anyway. And without insurance I can't practice, can I?"

"Well, technically, you can be self-insured. But I wouldn't advise it."

"I'm not ready to be pushed into retirement by a shitty lawsuit, most of all when I'm not guilty. Not like this. So isn't the only practical thing for me to do – if I want to keep practicing for a while – to fight for a defense verdict?"

"And what will you do if you lose and if the verdict against you is, say, two million? You got that much extra cash lying around?"

The question brought Nicky up short. Two million would wipe out his life savings. He wanted most of his estate to go to his three grandchildren. Edelmann was right: it was a lot to risk. Yet, he couldn't see his way to settling for five hundred thousand dollars on specious allegations. He was nearing retirement, but didn't want to leave the profession with a dark cloud over his head. He was an innocent doctor who had always worked his hardest to help his patients, including the patients – like Yahon – he encountered briefly in the hospital.

"Look," Nicky replied. "There's got to be another way. If anyone did something wrong, it was Waller. Make Waller or his estate pay everything. How do we do that?"

For long seconds, there was no response on the telephone. Nicky could hear another conversation going on in the far background. Then Edelmann spoke to him again. "Waller's family feels they need to protect his reputation, which, as far as we know has been good. He'd never been accused of any wrongdoing either, never any improprieties suggested by anyone, except in this case."

"So?"

"But they'd like the case to go away too. They don't want a trial. The estate is worth about ten million, or so I gather from hints offered by the estate's lawyer. Plaintiffs' demand against the Waller estate is in the neighborhood of five million. A lot of money for Waller's heirs to lose."

"What does that have to do with me?"

"I don't know yet, but do you think you'd be willing to testify against Waller? I mean, to say something helping the plaintiffs' case? Something to induce them to go after the estate only and leave you out of it. Like a plea deal? You get off with what you would call a nuisance settlement. Ten thousand dollars, say, just to make the annoyance go away."

"I've already testified I don't remember this case."

"Right. Hmm. Something might pop into your mind, though, as you mull this over. It's happened before. Deposition transcripts have been amended when necessary."

"Are you asking me to lie? To make something up?"

"No. Not at all. I'm offended ..."

"Cut the crap. That's exactly what you're doing."

Edelmann's tone changed quickly, from indignation to exasperation. "Look, Nicky. Litigation stinks. Any lawyer can allege anything, complete bullshit, and get away with it. It's a shakedown. People settle to avoid the worst outcomes, and you can settle within coverage limits, and yet you say no, no way. Nor are you willing to point a finger at Waller, you're too good for that. You're too honorable. Frankly, you're crazy to keep up this moral shit. What am I supposed to do to help you, huh? You're asking me to be creative in a system that's weighted heavily against you, and you're not giving me any help, nothing to work with. And all I'm doing is exploring the possibilities on your behalf."

"Exploring, sure."

"All right." Now Edelmann's tone was resigned, his deep sigh easily audible across the miles. "We're not making much progress on this call. Probably a bad idea for me to disturb your vacation. For now, I'll tell plaintiffs' lawyer we're taking the settlement offer under advisement, not rejecting it, but complaining it's outrageously high, given your tiny alleged involvement in what they say happened."

"Brilliant strategy, counsel."

"Read the case report, please. And, if you have any ideas, or even if you don't, call me back. Or I'll see you as soon as you get home. We'll keep thinking this through."

"We're thinking this through? That's what we're doing?"

"In the meantime, Nicky, enjoy whatever time you have left in Greece."

I Want It To End

The next morning, cloudy and chilly for June, Abbess Zoe intercepted Nicky and Jackie as they walked up the stony path to the church. She had in her hand a large envelope on which she had printed "Δρ. Covo" with a thick black marker.

"This came for you overnight. I found it on my fax machine this morning."

"Thank you, Abbess Zoe." He was anxious to peruse the case report Edelmann had promised, but Jackie had to be dealt with first.

As if reading his mind, Zoe asked, "Do you want me to take Master Jackie to his mother? I have to go that way." She pointed to the envelope. "This must be important."

"Yes, please take him to Kayla."

"Yes?"

He did not want to explain to Zoe why the fax might be important, despite her curiosity. Were all abbesses so nosy about things obviously none of their business? Yet, some response seemed necessary for the sake of politeness. He tried to smile. "Just some legal trouble back home. A hazard of being a doctor. Getting sued, I mean."

"I see." Now Zoe looked away, elevating her sight toward what seemed to be a few dark clouds gathering on the western horizon. "Looks like rain. By this afternoon, if not sooner," she said, as if they had been discussing nothing but the weather.

"Jackie, please go with Abbess Zoe and track down *Ima*," Nicky directed. "I will ... I will meet her outside the dining room. I want to talk to her."

"But Grand Pa," Jackie protested, emphasizing the syllables separately to display his displeasure at being sent away. "I want to stay with you. I want to see what's in there," he continued, pointing to the envelope.

"This is private, Jackie. I will be along soon. Now go with the abbess."

"Yes, come along, young man." She held out her hand, and Jackie reluctantly took it. "I'll teach you a word or two of Greek along the way. I'm happy you're trying to learn. Right now, we're walking on a path. In Greek, we call this *monopati*. Can you say that?"

As Abbess Zoe led him away, Jackie repeated "*monopati*." Nicky thought Jackie's accent – no doubt related to the genetic material Nicky had passed along through Kayla – wasn't half bad.

Nicky sat on the nearest bench, ignoring that the seat was still wet with dew. He pulled out a two-page case report entitled "Suicide in the Elderly: Suicidal Ideation and Attempt in 72-Year-Old Woman." Jonathan Waller was indeed the senior author and one Nikolas Covo, reflecting the long-abandoned spelling of his first name, was the junior author. The report had been published in 1960 in the *American Journal of Aging*. Nicky read with great interest, not remembering the case. The woman had been Waller's regular patient, although Nicky had apparently met with her twice while Waller was on vacation. She'd been desperately ill with uterine cancer and had begged both doctors, in her words, to "put her out of her misery." That's exactly how the report had been written, using the patient's euphemism for assisted suicide. Then the woman had tried to kill herself with an overdose of pain-killing drugs, but her attempt failed when she was discovered by her husband, who quickly called in the emergency. Waller and Nicky had talked to the woman at the hospital, together. Obviously, they had intended at the time to publish a report. The woman berated them for forcing her into this situation when they could have done the job –

ended her painful life – with expertise. In discussing the case, the authors forcefully rejected the idea that doctors should ever consider assisted suicide and cautioned medical professionals to "take seriously" all patient threats of suicide, including requests for assistance in committing that act. They emphasized the likelihood that even patients who had sought a doctor's help in ending their own lives would ultimately take matters into their own hands.

Nicky tried to bring up a mental image of the patient, but could see nothing. The article described her as Greta S, but Nicky didn't think knowing her entire name would have helped him remember. So, what was he supposed to do now? What memory about Waller was this report supposed to trigger? He couldn't see anything obvious. Two psychiatrists shared a problematic patient, interviewed her in the hospital following a suicide attempt, and used that event as the basis of an insignificant case report. The report's publication seemed a miracle, given that the message to the medical profession was obvious. Nicky easily saw why he'd never added this inconsequential piece of writing to his *curriculum vitae*.

But here it was, in front of him, so he reread it. The language now seemed stilted. It was only a case report, not a scientific study, it had not seemed terribly important when published, and it wasn't surprising Nicky had forgotten about it. The only things the case report showed were facts not in dispute anyway: Waller had been the senior psychiatrist, Nicky had helped him out in his absence, and they had collaborated on one inconsequential publication.

Nicky was about to replace the fax into the envelope and toss it all into the trash when he read it once more. The words "put her out of her misery" seemed to jump out at him. Hadn't he often heard such an appeal from suicidal patients? Many times. Then, had Shimon Yahon asked Nicky to be put out of his misery? There was nothing in Yahon's chart to that effect, but the possibility that Yahon had done so now nagged at Nicky's mind. It started with the name Yahon. The familiarity of the Sephardic name and the fact he'd known a Yahon family in Salonika must have caused Nicky to pay particular attention at the hospital. He'd been likely thinking of asking the young patient about relatives, about his connection to Salonika, about the war. Yes, he would have wanted to chat with the patient, even though, in the middle of a busy shift, it would have been hard to find time. But he must have found a few minutes. And now, in Greece, Nicky remembered something incredibly strange at the time he'd heard it but something he must have suppressed. There was no known connection to the Yahons of Salonika, but the patient, having become less agitated and apparently trusting Nicky, had indeed said something about Waller. How did it go?

Taking a deep breath, Nicky closed his eyes, the better to replay the scene in his head. *The ER is noisy. Nurses and doctors are running around. Doctors are being paged. A patient or two is groaning. And Shimon Yahon says, maybe, "Don't let Dr. Waller near me. I'm through with him. I want it to end."* Three short sentences, and now it seemed Nicky could hear them faintly, whispering in the back of his mind. He'd dismissed them at the time as the ravings of a disturbed patient, yet, Nicky now thought, being disturbed didn't mean a patient couldn't also be speaking the truth. Yahon had been calming down during their short conversation. But what had he meant? It could have been anything. It might have been simply that Yahon didn't want Waller to continue as his psychiatrist. Nothing more serious, what hundreds of psychiatric patients say when they want to make a change. Or, obviously, maybe Yahon's statements meant he feared Waller and wanted out of an *improper* relationship.

Was this the brilliant insight that Edelmann had hoped reading the case report might generate? Nicky worried his subconscious mind was making it all up as a way of getting out of the lawsuit cheaply. He couldn't possibly testify to these new recollections unless he was one hundred percent sure. But how could he be sure after so many years?

He decided he'd been confabulating. The conversation he imagined had never happened. He had never even spent a few extra minutes talking to Shimon Yahon. Or, if he had, there was no true recollection of what they'd discussed. He could not make up a story just for the convenience of his lawyer.

He walked back across the monastery grounds, looking for Helen. By the time he found her, he'd forgotten what he'd wanted to talk about.

The Joy of Playing

Not even a postcard, he thought, and she's been gone a week. His sister goes halfway around the world, he's in the most God-awful litigation of his life, he can hardly breathe because of the pressure, his intestines are ready to explode, and she can't even think to keep in touch with him? Just minimally?

It was one of a long list of things on Max's mind, but, in terms of his overall life, the upcoming trial was the worst catastrophe. Phil had been impossible to work for. He sent emails at all hours and expected answers, or so it seemed, within minutes. And, when they were together – in the war room discussing strategy, in a conference room after prepping a witness, even at dinner, with associates, paralegals, and technical staff unavoidably listening in – Phil had nothing good to say about Max's work product or work ethic. And it was so unfair. Max felt he could take constructive criticism well, if given properly, but Phil's criticisms were not constructive. "Why the fuck did you pick this asshole as our main expert?" was one of Phil's common complaints, overlooking the inconvenient fact that it had been Phil himself who selected the expert, contrary to Max's advice.

He thought about trying to reach Kayla at the monastery, but the time difference made it harder and there was the constant slew of work thrown at him. And what would he have said? That he was miserable? Was sick to death with being a trial lawyer? Wanted to murder Phil? Kayla had her own issues to deal with. Although he would have welcomed her comforting words – she would have urged Max to trust in *Hashem* even though he wasn't a believer – he would have had to return immediately to the fight, to dodging not only the enemy's rockets but the bayonet of his commanding officer.

He wondered whether he was truly sorry about having chosen law as his career or whether it was only one bad case and a terrible arrangement with a stressed-out boss. If the latter, then he knew the case would end soon enough and, as to the partner, he could always find another law firm in New York which would value what he brought to the table. All he had to do was grit his teeth and fight through the experience, giving his best, and when it was over he could say goodbye to Phil forever. On the other hand, maybe the law had been a bad career for him. When he'd decided on becoming a lawyer, the choice seemed so obvious to Max, who constantly saw things from a legal point of view, who intuitively understood who could be trusted and who couldn't. But the positives might not be enough to outweigh the toll that the adversary system – with its inevitable battle fatigue – played on his psyche. He knew the toll on his health was inevitable when he was eating so poorly, not exercising, and not sleeping well.

What was the point? Who was he trying to impress by holding the title "lawyer"? His father? For all Max knew, his father was still miffed that Max had had to take the lead in proving that Kayla's managers at Bellington were stealing money from her. His kids? Joseph and Rosina didn't particularly care what he did; they were barely interested in talking with him during his weekly call to Seattle. He thought often that the occupation he would have much preferred was that of concert pianist, but the genes for such a career didn't fall his way, and he had long before lost what had once been the joy of playing for audiences and for himself. So "lawyer" had for years been the profession he would point to with pride, but had it really been a wise decision? How could any normal human endure the chaotic world he now inhabited?

There was no way, in the middle of trial preparation, to decide on a new career track or – staying with the law – a new place to practice. The only thing was to work and survive, to ignore Phil's rants, to bolster the morale of the rest of the troops.

If there was a God after all, maybe He was punishing Max for having disbelieved.

With Great Longing

"I just got off the phone," Helen told Nicky seconds after they ran into each other at the bottom of the path to the winery. "It doesn't sound good. Maybe we should go home now."

"Who did you talk to? What did they say?" He took her hand, and then they hugged, to the apparent embarrassment of two nuns who were on their way up the hill. The nuns turned their faces away.

By unspoken agreement, Nicky and Helen walked toward the church's western side, which was hidden from the winery path and also the closest area to give respite from the broiling sun. They sat close together on the sole bench there.

"All right. Share with me whatever news you got."

"First, I talked to Jonah, then Danny wanted to say hello, then Sarah. Everything was fine, they said, but I could hear in their voices everything was not fine. How could things be fine? They were hiding something, some turn for the worse, I fear."

"You asked them?"

"They denied anything more had happened. I know they were lying."

"But ... they weren't asking you to come back early?"

"Not in so many words."

"They obviously want you to enjoy the full time here, without making yourself crazy by worrying. If they needed you back, they would have told you so. And, anyway, we'll be back soon enough."

"But they wanted to make sure they knew exactly when we were coming back. Yet, they had the information already, from our itinerary. It's a long five days from now …"

"Of course, it's …"

"It's a long time. Anything might happen. It sounds like it's happening already." Helen brushed away tears with the back of her hand.

"I was going to say it's just a few days, not forever, but, regardless of our plans, I'll go back with you today, Helen. I don't care about extra airline charges. Just say the word."

Helen forced a smile through her tears. "That's just like you. The Nicky I love. You're putting other people's needs above your own. But what you need to know is that I'm not ready though because …"

"I have reason to go back early too. About the lawsuit. Perhaps I can deal with it better back in New York."

She shook her head, annoyed at the interruption. Nicky seemed not to have heard her begin an explanation about why it wasn't time yet to leave. "No, please … you're not understanding me. Just … can I talk for a bit?"

He felt chastened. Whatever Nicky did to accommodate Helen, it always seemed to be the wrong thing. How could he love this woman so much and yet somehow never see her clearly? "Go ahead. I'll keep my mouth shut."

"All right," she sighed. "It's like this. Call it the social worker in me, but I can see no one is ready to leave here, not even you. And why should we be ready? The things that are supposed to happen haven't happened yet, for anyone." Helen looked away.

"Wait a minute. The things? That are supposed to happen? Now you're scaring me." He gently but firmly turned Helen's face around again so they could look directly at each other. "Can you tell me more about these … things?"

"Nothing specific. I wish I could give you specifics. I wish I could talk to you rationally about this, but I can't. You should know, though … I've been praying since we got here. Praying for Sarah, most of all, praying for a miracle that will never happen, but also praying for everyone else. I believe *Hashem* led us all here together, the four of us, at this exact time, for a reason. A reason only *Hashem* understands."

Nicky wanted to argue that there was no God and that Helen was deceiving herself. But he knew, on this point more than on any other, he needed to stifle his impulse. "Go on, please," he managed to say calmly.

"The ridiculous lawsuit, for the first thing, since it's the top thing on your mind. I've been praying that it be *Hashem*'s will for this to end quickly and I trust *Hashem* hears our prayers."

"Your prayers."

"Fine. My prayers." She closed her eyes with the pain of trying to understand how Nicky could be so obstinate. "I feel *Hashem* might hear *my* prayers better from here than from New Jersey. And *Hashem* will find a way to end this agony for you."

"Yes, I see," he said mechanically, unhappy he was having to hear such nonsense from his wife. His training as a psychiatrist was telling him strongly that Helen was lying. But why would she lie to him?

"And you're not ready to go back, because going back would only put you closer to the pain of the lawsuit. Just the physical distance is helping you relax a bit. You need to keep taking advantage of the time away from that problem, to forget about it for as long as possible."

"I'm hardly relaxed here, and I'm unlikely to forget what's going on, especially when I get faxes from Edelmann and appeals from him to remember what I don't remember. Edelmann doesn't want to let me forget the case. He wants me to lie. But go on, please. This can't all me about me."

"It's not all about you. Whoever said it was? But you're part of us. If your dumb lawyer wants you to lie, can't you resist him even better from here? And you're not ready to leave for other reasons, too, maybe more important reasons."

"Such as?"

"You need to spend more time with your sister. You still need to spend time with her as Kal, not Theodora, for a while longer."

"And how do you know that?"

"I can see it in your face. In your body language. I know you well. When you and she are talking, or even if you're not talking, when you're in the same room, I can sense your need. At the morning service, where Kal was bowing and crossing herself and kissing the icons and singing along *sotto voce* with the other nuns, I could see you looking at her with great longing. As if you wanted to reach out, that precise second, and take hold of her, in a nice way, certainly, but you couldn't. You weren't ready, or she wasn't ready. That's what I saw. In a few more days, the two of you might be ready once more to be loving siblings. I want you to have that embrace."

"We have hugged each other."

"Then you need more of the same. And there's something more to happen between you."

She was right, he thought. It had been only the previous morning, when Nicky and Helen had stood at the back of the church during the service. He could recall the few seconds when he'd looked at Kal doing exactly what Helen had described. At that instant, he *did* want to hold Kal closely again and tell her how much he loved her and to tell her he fully understood why she had chosen the life she'd chosen and that it was all right. Why hadn't he done so yet? He hadn't availed himself of the chances he'd already had. And Helen had seen it all and understood that a main purpose of the trip for Nicky hadn't yet been accomplished.

"Even if you're right," he said firmly, "none of that's as important as your being home with Sarah and Jonah and the kids, all of whom need you very much."

"Let me finish, Nicky. It's you and Kal, and then there's Kayla. You've been forgetting about your daughter. I've been thinking a lot about Kayla and praying for her too. Something is troubling her, something making it so important for her to come to Greece. I mean, for a religious Jew, it seemed strange she so much wanted to visit the monastery, but she did. Why? I don't know. Just … she still needs to be here. Maybe, as with you, she needs to be here to talk to Kal, or maybe it's to watch Kal. Or maybe to pray like I've been praying. I don't know." She waited a second, then continued. "This doesn't make sense, you're about to tell me."

"I'm not saying that."

"But you're thinking it."

Nicky shook his head. "I wasn't thinking that. I *was* thinking you and I could go home now, and Kayla could stay here with Jackie. I'm sure the abbess would allow Jackie to take your place in the room you're sharing with Kayla."

"If you and I went back today, Kayla would surely follow. To support me, if for no other reason. She would naturally conclude that Sarah was at imminent risk of dying …"

"Which she might be …"

"Which my family has assured us otherwise. So Kayla and Jackie would go back with us, and I can't have that happen because – well, what I feel is yet to come, what must come, for Jackie …" As she brought Nicky's grandson into the argument, her logic sounded off, even to herself. She recognized briefly that she was afraid to go back and face her dying daughter. Then the part of her mind needing to shield her from the most unpleasant of truths kicked in and suppressed the thought.

"Jackie? What about him?"

Helen continued without hesitation, as sure of herself now as she'd been unsure just seconds earlier. "I don't know if he'll ever see Kal again, after this trip. Whether any of us will. But Jackie in particular loves your sister so much, although he couldn't possibly put it into words. I can see he does. And so I conclude he should be able to stay the full measure of time we planned out."

"A few days one way or the other won't make a difference. He could adjust to leaving a bit early. Kids are resilient."

"Yeah, sure."

"Well, they are."

"I've had more kids as clients than you've had as patients. I know what I'm talking about."

"This is not a contest about who has more experience."

"Listen. Jackie's so close to Theodora. In a way, Theodora might be like the loving grandmother he never had a chance to know. And maybe – please don't think I'm nuts – he's looking to her for some kind of spiritual guidance."

"But he's Jewish." Now Nicky was certain Helen had slipped a gear. Somehow, the stress of being away from her family had unbalanced her thinking. "Nuts" was exactly the term popping into his brain, and he had to be careful not to say it out loud. He pressed into service all of his training as a non-judgmental psychiatrist in order to restrain himself. "He's Jewish," was all he could muster.

"Yes, indeed, he will always be Jewish and he's not giving that up, stubborn as he is. And I'm not saying he should, *Hashem* forbid. But there's something intangible …? Is that the right word? Something intangible he needs to get from Kal, and he hasn't got it yet, and I want him to get it. Before he leaves." She paused again. "Or …"

"Or what?"

"Kal needs to get something even more important from him."

Count to ten, Nicky thought. Keep your face calm, neutral. Don't laugh. Don't smile as if you'd heard something completely goofy. He hoped he was doing a decent job of controlling his demeanor. "As I said, he can stay with Kayla."

"Who won't stay, if you and I return. And, just as importantly, we need to be here too, for everything to work out the way it's supposed to. I sense it is *Hashem*'s will."

"Pray tell … how do you know all this?" He could no longer keep severe skepticism out of his voice. At the same time, he could no longer hide from the fact it was futile to try to convince Helen they should return at once to her family. He'd lost. Helen was formidable when she had set her mind on a particular course of action. He asked himself once again why all the important women in his life – Helen, Kayla, and

Kal most of all – were as stubborn as they were. As stubborn, in fact, as he was.

"It's the strangest thing, Nicky. It has to do with my being close to Kal, with my being at this monastery, with my being in Greece with you again. Where we became lovers." She paused, then leaned in to Nicky for what ended up a long kiss. She hoped her affections could distract Nicky from the force of his logic. When they broke, she asked, "Do you follow?"

"Not really, I'm afraid."

"I feel I see things. My eyes have opened up in a way that perhaps they never have before. There is more that must happen. It's something about being in this beautiful place, with its tragic history, but still beautiful, where I love to listen to the nuns sing, to watch them in their devotions, to look at the mountains, all of it."

"You see things. Because you're here, your eyes are opened. You love the nuns in their devotion. Fine. I will accept that, because ..." And here he stopped, wondering what else to say.

"Because you're humoring me?" continued Helen after a couple of seconds.

What should he say? Because why? He needed to strip skepticism out of his voice again and respond as the husband – not the psychiatrist – whom Helen deserved. "No, because I love you and trust you. But Helen ..."

"Yes?"

"I hope that staying here doesn't turn out to be a big mistake."

"You and me both."

Talking to Nicky had helped to lighten Helen's soul. She could continue her prayers for a miracle and would not have to immediately go back to confront the impending tragedy in her family.

Lying Outright

Later, Nicky surprised himself by approaching Zoe after the *Ennate Ora* service and asking if they could speak privately in her office. Zoe appeared unsurprised by the request, as if nothing was more common than a male Jewish visitor needing to consult with her.

Once he sat in a chair before Zoe's desk, he glanced around and took a deep breath. The office was so familiar to him, the place where Abbess Fevronia – *zichrona l'vracha* [of blessed memory] – had reunited him and Kal more than a year earlier. It had been where he and Helen and Fevronia listened in wonder as Kal told her incredible but true story about being saved by the Theotokos, about both of them saving Nicky from certain death. It had been where Fevronia recorded Kal's story about the miracle and where Nicky had signed an affidavit affirming his role in it as the one who was saved. He could close his eyes from anywhere in the world and still clearly see the office in which he now sat and the pathetic statuette of the crucified Jesus hanging from the wall.

"Yes, so Dr. Covo. What is on your mind?"

"The fax you gave me. You read it?"

"It looked like a published article and, yes, I saw it pertained to a suicide attempt and you were an author. I hope you don't mind I read that much."

"Not at all."

"But the trouble back in America?"

"We are so litigious. We, as a country, I mean."

"Litigious?"

"*Litiyous.*"

"Ah, yes, I have got it. So you have been sued?"

"Yes. A patient killed himself. Some patient I'd seen in a hospital and released. And now his family blames me."

"Suicide is a great sin in our Church."

"And also under Jewish law. I studied Talmud for a long time and this I remember well, even though I tried to kill myself. Twice."

Zoe thought for a few seconds. It would not be proper at this point to admonish the monastery's guest about his suicide attempts. If she had any responsibility to Nicky, it was to maintain a neutral bearing and listen. "I am glad for the sake of Theodora and for the sake of your wife and children that you failed in this. But where does it say in your Bible, the Jewish Bible, that you should not kill yourself? I'm curious."

"*B'reshit.* Genesis, that is. I forget the verse exactly, but something to the effect of ..." He paused, considering. "*V'ach et dimchem nafshotachem edrosh* ... which means 'I, God, will take account of the blood of your souls.' And the rabbis said that means don't kill yourself. Our rabbis, I'm sure you know, made our religion what it is today."

"Genesis, you say?" Zoe scribbled a note on the July page of her desk calendar.

"Somewhere in the Noah story, if you want to look it up."

"I will. I'm sure what is happening to you is unjust and unfair. I hope you can get rid of this ... how shall I say? ... unpleasantness?"

"This might be the sorry end of my career. And maybe I should just give up, have it over with, settle. Cave in to their demands."

"But you don't want to. I can see that. You're not ready."

"No. I don't suppose I am ready, just yet, to give up."

"How can I help you, Dr. Covo? You're hardly here to confess. And you're hardly here to ask what our Church teaches about dealing with false ... *ischirisme*?"

"Allegations."

"Thank you. So. You're not asking me what our Church says about false allegations. Or lies, perhaps is a better term."

"But perhaps I am. If someone is lying against one, in a way that will hurt badly if left unchecked, is it ever right to lie in response? If lying is the only option? Now it's my turn to be curious. About what your Church says."

"Why ask when you well know the answer? It would be the same in Judaism, I suppose, as in the Orthodox Church. It's never right. How do you say in English? The end doesn't ..."

"Justify"

"Justify the means."

"In Jewish law, though, the rabbis permit lying if necessary to save a life."

"Hmm." She frowned briefly before returning her face to neutral. "Not so for us. If the life must be lost, then it must be lost, and the soul will live for eternity with our Lord Jesus Christ. And thus I must to conclude Judaism is different in an important way. Maybe I'm not particularly surprised, but please to tell me, Dr. Covo. In your situation, is a life truly to be saved?"

"My career perhaps?"

She shook her head, but gently, with the tiniest bit of a smile. "A career is not a life, I'm afraid."

"My ability to help others in need."

She shrugged. "As I say, a career, even one as honorable as yours, even the career of a life-saving doctor, is not itself a life. This seems obvious, if you will please to allow me the privilege of saying so honestly. It's not a matter for dispute. Or at least not a matter for dispute among reasonable people."

"I don't know."

"And the Talmud? You said you studied."

He nodded. "Very much against lying, and the exceptions – those I remember – don't apply here. We could start a new chapter."

"Excuse me?"

"Sorry … I suppose I'm daydreaming out loud."

Abbess Zoe sighed, rather more heavily than seemed necessary to Nicky. "So have I answered your question?" She glanced down at her desk, at what Nicky presumed was the paperwork he had interrupted.

"In this lawsuit against me, I will tell the truth."

"Well, I'm happy to hear that."

"But my lawyer might try to use the truth in a way implying something that never happened."

"If you are asking for guidance from me, Dr. Covo, …"

"I just …"

"If you are asking for guidance, as I say, the answer must be no. You must not allow your lawyer to use your true words in a way to create a falsehood. That would be as bad – if you want the view of our Church – as bad as lying outright yourself. And I would guess the Talmud would say so too."

"You are correct." He admired the quickness of Abbess Zoe's mind and the firmness of her answers. "The Talmud. Yes. When I was young, just fourteen, I pretended for a while that I was a Talmudic scholar. I thought for a while I might want to be such a scholar for my life's work, as strange as that sounds."

"I understand it's complicated. But if God …"

"I don't believe there is a God, Abbess Zoe, I'm sorry to say, sorry because I don't mean to offend you."

She smiled. "No offense taken. Many of our neighbors would probably share your opinion, although admitting it openly would embarrass them. Whether or not they believe in the Lord, they still come to our Divine Liturgy and kiss and bow before the icons." She stood and extended her hand toward Nicky, maintaining the smile, but more rigidly, it seemed to Nicky, as if she had plastered it to her face.

"You have been too kind to allow me to talk with you here and use your valuable time. You have been very helpful." Nicky took her hand gently and bowed, suddenly unsure of the proper etiquette.

"Dr. Covo, you have given *me* the blessing of being particularly useful this morning. May the Lord shine his face on you today and always."

Struggle

Max's breakfasts now consisted of two antacid tablets washed down by warm milk. The combination did little to ease the pain in his belly. The discomfort reminded him of when he was eight, still performing, trying to meet everyone's high expectations for him as a pianist, fighting off the nervous anticipation of stepping out on the stage. Remarkably, it had been twenty years since he'd last had such pains, and he'd forgotten about them. But, as the trial began, he realized that the body never forgets.

Jury selection was ridiculous, with the judge intent on accepting virtually anyone who walked into the courtroom and was too stupid to come up with a good excuse for not serving. The only potential juror who seemed halfway decent from a defense perspective was, incredibly, the general counsel of McDonalds. The plaintiff's attorney, Gerald Bradworth, immediately moved for his dismissal on the grounds he was "incredibly unlikely to be fair and impartial in a product liability case." Phil objected vehemently at the bench, but Judge Sharon Metcalf, who smiled at him as if to say she wasn't putting up with any of his defense shenanigans, granted plaintiff's motion to strike the juror. Metcalf would not even allow the prospective juror to be questioned as to his ability to be fair.

Phil was apoplectic and turned to stare at Max as if this had all been Max's fault. It seemed that Phil even blamed Max for their client having been sued. The rest of the jury selection, completed in less than an hour, resulted in an eight-person panel, all of whom looked like they'd love nothing better than to put the squeeze on the defendant.

And then things got worse.

The plaintiff herself, Anita Lodge – whose husband had allegedly died from Maripulol – was the first witness, and was soon being led by her attorney to testify about what her husband had said to her just before his unexpected loss of consciousness. Phil objected that the proposed testimony was blatantly hearsay; after all, the deceased was not available for cross-examination. Metcalf sent the jury out of the courtroom so they would not hear the argument, and Phil patiently explained the hearsay rule to the judge. He even handed her the trial brief Max had written, anticipating this issue. Metcalf put the trial brief aside without reading it, took off her glasses, cleared her throat, and asked Phil whether he was quite through.

"I've made my argument, Your Honor. It's hearsay, pure and simple."

"Well, sir, was it hearsay then or hearsay now?" The question made absolutely no sense. Max could tell Phil was stunned by the judge's stupidity, even though they'd already heard from many other lawyers that she lacked the basic intelligence required of a judge. Max and Phil had unfortunately discounted what they'd heard about her deficiencies. Now, Max wondered how she had secured her appointment to a lifetime position as a federal judge, how the Senate had seen fit to confirm her, and how a federal judge who'd been on the bench for years could not even understand the hearsay rule.

"It was a statement then, Your Honor, but it's hearsay now when it's being offered into evidence in a court of law, a court in which the Federal Rules of Evidence apply." Max marveled that Phil could respond as calmly as he did.

"Objection overruled." Well, so much for that. No reasoning, typical of trial judges with no idea of what they're doing. "Bring the jury back in," Metcalf barked at the U.S. Marshal, who jumped as if struck with a whip. When the jury reentered, looking around at everyone to figure out what had happened, Metcalf said in a pleasant voice, "You may continue, Mr. Bradworth, as you were before." And so Anita Lodge's attorney resumed his highly prejudicial line of questioning. There was no other evidence that the deceased Mr. Lodge had taken the Maripulol at the key time.

Max thought Phil should have objected more, as the testimony continued, to preserve the record for appeal, but Phil remained silent. Indeed, his demeanor was remarkably calm, as if the plaintiff's testimony, his objection, the jury's temporary exclusion from the courtroom, and the judge's smiling reaction when the testimony resumed were all part of Phil's plan. As if, indeed, the harmful evidence helped the defense case.

And suddenly Max realized the pain in his intestines had disappeared. He was caught up in the struggle and intrigue of the trial. He knew how much his client relied upon Phil (and him, by extension) to navigate a crazy legal system. How do you win a case with a judge who doesn't even understand the hearsay rule and who could not care less about having an impartial jury? How do you make the worst jury see it's all a game to drag dollars out of a deep pocket? He took a deep breath, resolved to stay alert, anticipate Phil's every need, and work through the night, if necessary, on an additional batch of motions. There was plenty of caffeine in the war room to keep him awake. They had lost the morning's battles, but he would do something, he vowed, to help his client win the war.

Trust *Hashem*

After performing the *Havdalah* service in their cell room, saying farewell to *Shabbat*, the women said goodnight to each other, and Helen was quickly asleep. Kayla could not drift off, however, in part because of Helen's light snoring. But it was much more than snoring that kept Kayla awake. The situation with Aharon weighed heavily on her mind, as she struggled to form a clear mental picture of what had happened and whether she could, after all, have a permanent relationship with him. When she stopped thinking about Aharon, thoughts that always returned to her own unfilled sexual needs, it was only because the lingering fear about her inability to create new music pushed the other thoughts away.

She checked her watch; it was just past midnight. Giving up on sleep, she decided a walk would do her good. She quietly slipped on a pair of jeans and a sweatshirt – clothes she hadn't intended to wear in public – and donned her sneakers and windbreaker. In seconds, Kayla was in the dimly lit hallway, holding her breath as she pulled the door to their room closed. Then she waited a bit more, listening carefully, and didn't move until she was fairly sure Helen hadn't stirred. Kayla didn't want to discuss with Helen why she was finding it difficult to sleep.

Kayla walked down the hallway, intending to exit the building and make her way toward the winery, when she was startled passing

Theodora's cell. In the half-opened doorway, in the flickering light from Theodora's lampada, there stood her aunt.

"Oh, excuse me!"

"I'm the one who's disturbed you, it seems," Theodora said softly, smiling. "You are still up? So late? Or maybe you are up so early?"

"Couldn't sleep." Kayla glanced at her wrist to look at the time again, but she'd forgotten to put on her watch. She shrugged. "And you as well?"

"I have not yet tried to sleep." Theodora stepped out into the hallway next to Kayla, pulled her door closed, and looked both ways before continuing. "If you are planning on a walk, I wonder if you would like to come with me. I often go out at this hour, when I feel my prayer for the day is completed, but before sleep. *Nai?*"

"Yes. That would be nice."

Without further words, Theodora led the way out of the building. Outside, they were freer to speak normally, but still kept their voices low. The night was overcast, and Kayla shivered a bit in the chill, even with her windbreaker. The clouds smelled of impending rain, and Kayla wouldn't have been surprised if a light mist began to seep from the sky, but precipitation held off.

"Where do you like to go?" asked Kayla, as she stuck her hands awkwardly into her windbreaker's pockets.

"All over. During the day, I might go into the fields or the vineyards or walk all the way down the road to Andros's house and back. Tonight, let's just sit on a bench and enjoy the quiet ... unless you want very much to walk."

"No. A bench will be fine. I didn't realize how cold it would be, so I don't think I want to stay out long."

They found the nearest bench and sat facing in the direction of the mountains. But the clouds, the surreal fog, whatever burden the sky carried, blocked their view.

"I'm glad we stumbled on each other tonight, Theodora, because..."

"Stumbled?" Theodora turned a confused face toward her companion. "I am without my dictionary."

"Sorry. I'm glad we ran into … no … I'm glad we met each other, even at this strange hour."

"Ah. So am I. Then you want to talk. You want to tell me some trouble in your life, *nai*?"

It suddenly occurred to Kayla that *Hashem* had planned their meeting, because, as she sat with Theodora, it was precisely to Theodora, and to Theodora alone, she felt she could reveal the things that were gnawing at her. Theodora would not judge. Kayla thought for a few more seconds, then began. "The first trouble is about Aharon."

"Yes, we spoke of him and your desire. There's more to say, isn't there?"

Was there more? She tried to play back in her mind their prior conversation and the thoughts that had helped to keep her awake on this night. What she felt would be difficult to articulate. But she was going to try. "I can't marry him, and I can't carry on any further relationship with him."

"*Ochi?*"

She shook her head. "I don't love him. Wanting someone sexually …" Kayla stopped to check if Theodora knew the word; Theodora nodded and waited for more. "To want sex and love are two different things. I don't want to be alone, but the desire not to be alone is not love."

"*Ochi*. It is not."

Theodora took hold of Kayla's hands and could feel Kayla tense up; her hands felt as cold to Theodora as the snow she occasionally brushed from her own hands during a winter snowfall, when she often walked outdoors without the benefit of gloves. The connection between their hands, as Theodora willed her own warmth to flow into Kayla, told Theodora more about Kayla than words could have. The women remained locked in this silent pose for a minute before

Theodora spoke. "This is more than about Aharon. I see as well it's about your brother."

Theodora's gentle, almost sweet, way of stating facts forestalled any possibility of Kayla disagreeing. Kayla's tension eased; she could stay for years in Theodora's grip.

"Max?"

"You found, where you now live, a solid place in God's world. You have found warmth and … how do you say? … stability with Max that you longed for, that you prayed for but never fully received in the home your parents made. All this is obvious to me when I hold your hands." She paused; she tightened her grasp on Kayla's hands for a second. They no longer seemed cold. "You don't need me to tell you this, but, since you want me to, I will. You came to the monastery to visit me, you came here because you trust me, and I will tell you everything."

Kayla knew that Theodora had spoken with wisdom. Her heartbeat ticked up from *adagio* to *andante.* "That is … why I came."

"You are already well loved where you've made your home. In Max's home. With Max. By Max. No one ever wants to leave the special place where they're cared for and loved. Some, sadly … some can't stay in the home they love. Life doesn't let them enjoy such … enjoy such …"

Kayla waited for a second, but Theodora faltered, struggling for the right word.

"Pleasure?" Kaya offered.

"It's more than a pleasure. If you grow up in a solid home … you find yourself supported by people who love you, for who you are, and that is the best home to be in. It's where you are now, Kayla, with Max."

"But I dreamed once, not long ago, about Max ordering me out of the house. Permanently."

"Did you leave the house? Either in your dream or upon waking?"

"Of course not."

Theodora nodded knowingly. "Dreams can lie. You think you understand a dream, but you are lying to yourself. I learned this, as you say, the hard way."

"And then I dreamed Max barged into my bedroom at night. It was so scary."

"In your dream, did he hurt you? Or try to? Did he even touch you?"

"No."

"I am not an interpreter of dreams, not like Joseph, but the meaning of both dreams together is plain. You are not threatened. You are where you should be."

"But …"

"*Ochi*. No 'but.' Please just to listen, because I can see everything so clearly. I can see every part of your soul."

Kayla knew what Theodora said was true. She could feel Theodora reaching into her depths, where all the joys, fears, and frustrations of her life lay in plain view to Theodora's gaze. "What do you see then?"

"You have what many people never have."

"But Max isn't a husband and never can play that role for me."

"No, he could not. Still, right now, you desperately need him. You don't quite realize that, but you must. And perhaps, someday, you will give up what you have now with Max – what you and Jackie both have – either because … because life will happen or you will find a man you love as a husband, but the time hasn't come. You've been trying to force it, you can see for yourself, and part of the reason you haven't come to love Aharon is that you love Max and what you have together with him. And the home Max helps make for Jackie. Your dreams are meant to tell you *not* to be afraid to stay."

Everything Theodora said made sense to Kayla. She *had* been trying to force things. She had nearly lost her virtue hoping that, by doing so, she could pave the way to a permanent relationship with a man who wasn't her brother.

"So, then, should I break off with Aharon?"

Theodora smiled. "You have to make the choice on your own. It's your decision. It's your … how do you say?... it's your call. All I can do is see the larger truth, the one that's always been … in front of you. There's a way to say that in English … always been …?"

"Staring me in the face."

"*Nai*. Such a direct way to put it. True."

"Do you think, Theodora, I will find the right man? The man for whom it would make sense to … to leave Max? To take Jackie from the only home he's known?"

Theodora finally withdrew her hands from Kayla's. "The Lord Jesus Christ, my Creator, has not given me the power to see into the future. Not yet, anyway." Here, Theodora exhaled heavily, as if she'd been holding her breath throughout the conversation, just waiting for the moment she had to make sure Kayla knew of the limitations of her clairvoyance. Kayla's face turned crestfallen until Theodora spoke again. "But … speaking as your aunt … who loves you … I do think it will happen. It might be in ten years. It might be more. Jackie will grow up. He will be off to university. He will seek his freedom, his own meanings. Until then, I will say this about your finding the right man: let it happen when it happens. Be open to the chance. When you find the man who should be your husband, you will know. Until then, live and enjoy your life with Max; the love you have for each other, as brother and sister, is right. It's what God wants.

"Is it right?"

"*Nai*. Without question. And trust God. I know you love God, as I do.

"Trust *Hashem*," said Kayla thoughtfully, absorbing everything Theodora had revealed.

"Yes, trust *Hashem*."

They sat quietly together for another few minutes. Amazingly, the weather seemed to improve. The clouds which had at first hung low had lightened and lifted slightly. Kayla thought she could see the faintest outline of the mountains.

"You know," said Kayla. "I think it will be a fine day tomorrow. No rain after all."

A New Creativity

Theodora looked up quickly, as if she saw something flying by. She took a deep breath, then turned to look at Kayla again. "I don't think it will be a fine day at all, and I know the Lord will show us what the day will bring when He is ready. But ..."

"But what?

"But what about the other thing that's troubling you? I know there's more. I felt it strongly, but ... in your heart ... wherever it is I see what others can't see ... there seemed a dark curtain. Something behind it. I know it has to do with your music. But that's all I know."

"Of course, Theodora, you're right about that too. I am having serious problems creating new music. It's hard to describe, impossible perhaps to explain to someone who is not an artist or a composer." As Kayla spoke, Theodora's smile faded for a moment. "I'm sorry. I shouldn't have said that. I know ..."

"*Ochi*. You are right. I have no musical skill. I have never created music as you have. Although, when I was a girl, before the war, I had hoped to be an artist. I could draw then."

"It's ..."

"But it's not about me."

"I'm sorry ..."

"Because it's about you, Kayla, and you don't understand what I *do* know that can help you." Theodora once more took Kayla's hands. "Here … please to stand up, so I can hug you. So I can see better."

They stood, facing each other, and Theodora embraced Kayla; Kayla could not help but to return the hug, with as much strength as she could. It was no longer the chill of night in the mountains that Kayla felt. It was Theodora's strange warmth, every cell in Theodora's body burning with its own special light, reaching into her as if they were gamma rays her skin could not resist. Nothing could be hidden from the onslaught.

Kayla was unable to guess how long the hug lasted. If pressed, she would have said for hours. In those minutes, Kayla knew why she had so desperately wanted to come to the monastery. It was to have just such a union with her aunt. When they broke, the disconnection felt like an electric shock. They sat again, and once more Theodora took Kayla's hands. And waited for Kayla to begin.

Finally, a minute having passed, Kayla said, "I know how much you want to help me, Theodora, and I know you believe you can. But isn't my problem – the composing – something I need to figure out by myself? Even if you *were* musical?"

"I will tell you what I have seen inside you. I have seen much there, just now, as we held each other. Then you can tell me if I am wrong. Although, through the grace of Our Lord Jesus Christ, I know I am not wrong."

Theodora thought for a few seconds before continuing. When she did, it was with her usual calm voice, a voice holding no uncertainty, not the tiniest seed of doubt.

"There are many reasons, just now, you feel not able to compose. I will tell you."

"Yes, please."

"First, and maybe the biggest reason, is that you long to perform again. For the public, in front of many people. The people, the fans, who loved to hear you play. You still see them, in your mind, in your heart, when you try to compose. Now, I can see it in you clearly, as surely you can see me sitting next to you."

"But …"

"No, wait. I must finish. Second, your faith in God … in *Hashem* … has been challenged. Because I see, when it was strongest, it was easy for you to create new music. But you have doubt. Your strong Jewish faith that you had found and the … how do you say? … that word again … not to move, to be firm? Stab—something?"

"Stable? Stability?"

"Yes." Theodora released Kayla's hands and held her own hands together, fingers interlocked, as if she were going to pray. "You thought all was stable in your faith, but then there was trouble with Jackie and his father. You feared you would lose him. You could not understand how *Hashem* might let that to occur, to lose your dear son. And your stable … stability … begins to fall. I mean …. Excuse me … begins to fail. If you are not safe from that, then how is your God protecting you and what is the point of making new music? This is what you are asking yourself. To almost lose Jackie is getting in the way. And you are blaming *Hashem*."

Kayla nibbled briefly on her right thumbnail as she thought, uncertain, yet troubled. She was deeply unsettled by the truth in Theodora's observations. "There were many artists whose lives were in turmoil. And they still created great art. Chopin, for one. Mozart, fighting poverty."

"Perhaps. But they are not you, Kayla. What you need is not what they needed. And so, I sense also a third reason. I feel you have come here to St. Vlassios to hear our music and to be … inspired by it. Or to be …" Theodora's voice faltered. She shook her head slightly, then glanced over to the nearby pines, through which now crept a fine mist that had made its way across the valley. She shivered. "To be inspired by this place. I have finished now what I needed to say. I have told you the truth, as the Good Lord Jesus Christ has allowed me to see it in you."

"Am I to respond?"

"Only if it pleases you."

"I will think about what you have told me, Theodora. Do I wish again to perform? I know I cannot, at the level required to be a concert pianist. To play for the public. But I've known for years. It hasn't stopped me from composing. It was my main motivation to compose. And yet …"

"Yes?"

"And yet, maybe I have missed that more lately, being on the stage and being loved by my fans, being loved for what I could bring to them through my music."

Theodora nodded. "That's what I see. And, I know you were brilliant. Your father played one of your CDs for me when I visited. Even for someone as … not trained in music as I am, I could tell you were great, a miracle."

"You are too kind."

"Don't be modest, Kayla. I saw what a holy gift God gave to you."

"Maybe. But you say I have doubted *Hashem*? I didn't think so, and the idea is terrible to me, yet, as you said it just now, it seemed real. I could feel you inside of me, touching that doubt. It hurt. But why would it make composing so hard? I don't know how this doubt connects with my problem creating."

"You have heard what I know, and what I know comes from God. It is not I who sees these things, but the God who created you, who knows you best. Please to not forget that. You will find answers inside yourself, if you trust in God."

Kayla sighed, nodding, immersed in thankfulness that she should be so close to this woman, who believed so deeply in *Hashem*. She would have loved Theodora even if the nun did not have the uncanny ability to understand and interpret the life of another human being, but she loved Theodora even more, given that she was helping Kayla discover everything Kayla had hidden inside herself. "And, as to inspiration, you're right there too. You've hit the nail on the head."

"I did what?" Theodora leaned forward, with a puzzled expression, to make sure she heard correctly.

"It means you're exactly right. I did want inspiration, and I thought coming here would be the answer."

Relaxed, now that she understood Kayla's metaphor, Theodora eased herself back. "It is the answer. Or it can still be. Here, Kayla, you can still become as close to God as you truly want. As close to God as you dare. As close to *Hashem*, as Jewish people say."

Kayla chuckled. "Even though the monastery is beautiful, I haven't felt nearly enough inspiration yet. Just a few ideas. I'm not sure they will work out. In many ways, I still feel as stuck as ever."

"You have not given yourself time. And … do you like our chanting of the Psalms?"

"It's beautiful. I wish I could sing as well."

"Is that not … to inspire you?"

"Should it? It's your ceremony, not mine. No disrespect intended. Yes, it's very beautiful, very moving in fact, but it hasn't given me any great ideas."

"I don't think the point is the melody. Or the … musical value. I'm not sure what you call that. Harmony? I believe what you can learn here is the spiritual value. The spirit. The soul. The breath of life. Is not your *Hashem* the same as the Father we worship here?"

"I … well, maybe?"

"There I must to tell you that God is everywhere the same. God's spirit is close to everyone if they are to reach out. God the Creator is the force who creates your music through you, when you write it, as much as when you play it for others. So, please come again to our Orthros service tomorrow and listen carefully to our singing. But please to feel it. Melody? If that makes you happy. You may have with you a pencil and paper to write whatever our music does to your heart. You will find more than what you think, if you open to God's message and love. If you think of the chanting as pointing to that side of God's soul that we poor humans can feel."

Kayla thought for a long minute, then said, "We share the Psalms, for sure."

"We do."

"They are as important to you as they are to us."

"*Nai.*"

"And they are so much about music, too. They were written to be sung. '*Shiru l'Adonoi shir chadash* … sing to the Lord a new song. *Zamru l'Adonoi b'chinor; b'chinor b'kol zimra.* Play to the Lord with a harp, with a harp and a voice of song.'"

Theodora immediately felt the seeds of a new creativity sprouting in the depths of Kayla's soul.

"That's what I've been trying to tell you."

Our Human Instinct

Kayla awoke slowly, forgetting for a few moments where she was. Then it came back to her: the monastery. Nearing the end of their visit. Three more nights and that would be it.

She saw it was only 4:05 am. It had been only about three hours since she'd returned to the room after talking to Theodora. She should have been tired, she thought, but felt strangely energized. Music was on her mind, the music she'd been unable to conjure for months. She needed to do something about music immediately. Yet, it was too early to rise. She still didn't want to wake Helen.

But when Kayla turned over, away from the wall, she saw that Helen was not on her cot. Perhaps the bathroom? Kayla pushed herself up and reached over to flip the light switch. The overhead fixture poured its unsettling yellow glow into the room.

Kayla had folded into her handbag the notes she'd jotted down following a dream, during which she heard the singing of an angelic chorus. On Friday, the day after, she'd been scared to look at these notes, fearing they would be gibberish and she would be no closer than ever to breaking through her composer's block. On *Shabbat*, she decided she had to look at the notes regardless of her fear, if only to put that misery behind her. But, on *Shabbat*, even just looking at the notes struck her as work, which she would never do on the holy day of rest. She would be too tempted to pick up a pencil. The rabbis had warned against doing anything, no matter how innocent, that might inadvertently lead to work. So Kayla forced aside the urge.

Now, in the early morning hours of Sunday, she reached into her bag again, carefully unfolded the pages, and spread them on the cot beside her. Ah, yes, B-Minor. The key once again called to mind Bach's Mass in B-Minor, a masterpiece and leagues greater than anything Kayla could ever hope to write. Here, in her notes, there was hardly anything worth keeping, just a few fragments that might, in time, have merit. Kayla tried to imagine how such fragments might be turned into real music, music to captivate a performer and an audience alike. She closed her eyes, wanting to see herself playing the music not yet composed. All she saw was dark purple shapes dancing on the inside of her eyelids.

This is all wrong, she thought. Music, like love, can't be forced. It wasn't like throwing a bunch of words onto a piece of paper and endlessly rearranging them until a story emerged or a legal brief formed or what have you. Music wasn't at all like writing. Beautiful new music had to envelop the composer in its entirety, all at once, so strongly and so convincingly that it would be all one could do to get the notes on paper before the vision faded. That's how it had always been for her. Now, however, she'd been waiting for months for such inspiration, without even a glimmer. In the past, particularly in the chamber music that had won accolades, she'd taken everything for granted, and the muse never failed. How had it ever been possible? It seemed like a dream in which a completely different, more deserving, more talented woman had been rewarded. What had changed? A gear had slipped somewhere, but Kayla could not say where or what its particular function had been.

She lay back on the cot, closed her eyes, and placed the pages across her belly. Taking deep breaths and letting the air out slowly, she tried to relax every muscle. She would meditate, allow any emergent thoughts to cross her mind and disappear. She wouldn't try to put it all together. That might be a later task. But for now she would just look at the ideas as they filtered into and out of her consciousness.

There was a flower, brilliant red and white. She could hear children singing playfully in the background. Then suddenly she saw a man's unnaturally white face, a face she recognized from her past, a face that had profoundly scared her during her performing career, but she willed her heartbeat to remain slow, exhaled, drew in another large breath, and the face faded. It didn't disappear, though; it seemed to change slowly into Max's face, then into her father's, and only once she was sure it *was* her father's face did it finally disappear. And, without warning, August's face now filled the purple stage. Was his look a sneer or a smile? She decided it had to be both, and then it too faded, and in its space she saw Jackie's face. Or maybe August's face had become Jackie's. It didn't matter. Kayla's heart swelled with the great love she felt for her son. Her breath deepened. She could feel herself smiling gently, and then without a further thought she fell asleep again.

Kayla wasn't sure how long she'd dozed. A few minutes? An hour? She'd left the light on, and the room was slightly brighter as the Sunday dawn neared. Helen had just come into the room and closed the door.

"Kayla? You're awake now?"

"Good morning." She yawned, covering her open mouth with her hands. "What time is it?"

"About five. What's all the paper on you?"

Grabbing her notes, Kayla sat and faced Helen, now sitting on the opposite cot. Kayla resisted the silly urge to hide her notes under her pillow. Instead, she handed them to Helen. "Looking at these and thinking about music. About composing. There's not much there, I'm afraid."

Helen glanced at the staff papers in her hand. "I'm not musical, as you know." She handed them back. "You're composing in your sleep?"

Kayla smiled and scratched behind one ear. Then she yawned again and stretched. Finally, she responded. "Hardly composing in my sleep, although it would be great if I could. Think how much I could've written by now. I've been having trouble doing anything creative lately. And I hoped coming here, to the monastery, you know, a quiet place, would give me a boost, but it hasn't worked out either. I've talked to Theodora about it. But ... but where have you been so late at night or ... well ... so early in the morning?"

Helen unzipped her light jacket. "Sitting on a bench, trying to watch the stars. Watching the sky be grim. The sky seems angry. It's probably angry at me. Does that make sense? I went outside because I couldn't sleep. You're aware you snore, right?"

"I'm sorry if my snoring kept you up. You snore too, but not too bad."

"I do? I didn't think so. But, anyway, you haven't been keeping me up with that noise until last night. In truth, I think I just wanted to be outside for a while. How can an angry sky be so beautiful? It's so dark here, as compared to the city. When it's clear, you can see so many stars, although now it's getting cloudy. Do you want to come out for a while?"

Within two minutes, the women sat on the nearest stone bench. Dawn came early in the middle of June, and, with the light and the clouds, no stars were visible. The clouds seemed to be building in the west and marching toward the monastery. The air had a biting chill, much colder than earlier. As Kayla scanned the sky, she breathed deeply, still refreshed from her few hours of sleep.

"Oh, clouds or no clouds, this is lovely, Helen. I don't feel it's angry at all. Just ... a sky."

Helen frowned for a second, then let her face relax as she turned to face Kayla. "May I please ask a personal question?"

Kayla suddenly felt uneasy, in part because of the clouds and Helen's dark characterization of their emotion, but also because of Helen's clear intent to delve into her life. She thought it had to be about Aharon, whom she hadn't mentioned to Helen since before they'd left for Greece. It must have become obvious to Helen, if not everyone, that something had happened between them. Kayla was still trying to digest everything Theodora had said to her and wasn't ready to talk to anyone else. "Well …"

"I wanted to ask about music, but if you'd rather not …"

Kayla felt a smidgen of relief, even though she had no great desire to discuss music with Helen either. But, at this point, the topic offered itself as something other than Aharon. "No, no. It's perfectly fine. Ask away."

"Why do you want to compose?"

It was such a strange question. The answer should have been obvious, yet it wasn't. Kayla had devoted her life to music. Jackie would not even exist had it not been for her obsession with music. There was so much Kayla still wanted to say and do with music, even if she could no longer perform. And yet Helen couldn't see any of this?

"Doesn't everyone? I mean, everyone musical?"

"Want to compose? I couldn't say that everyone musical wants to do any one thing."

"Let me restate that. Doesn't everyone want to create? In one way or another. Create and leave something behind, after they're gone, something which says they were once here? Something which attests to the power of their imagination and soul? A legacy?"

"And you have already done that with your compositions, haven't you? Your music is beautiful and will certainly live after you. You've already accomplished so much. Why press yourself for more? With the royalties you already get for your CDs and what you've composed, you don't need to create right now to make a living. You need to give yourself a break when it's not coming easily. You need to relax."

"Sure, Helen. Forgive me for pointing out that your advice is easy to say but hard to follow. I feel certain there's more inside of me, more that would be good, the equal of what I've composed before, if I could only get it out. Haven't you wanted to create? Some kind of art? Didn't you once sign up for a painting class?"

"And I was terrible at it and gave it up soon as a misguided effort."

"Well, you wanted to have kids too. You made a family. You have wonderful grandchildren. That's creation. That's our human instinct. That's your legacy. Could you have suppressed such a desire?"

Helen picked up a stone from beside the bench and tossed it haphazardly toward the nearest tree. It landed without a sound. "I'm not sure it's the same thing. But, honestly, no, I couldn't have suppressed my desire. Having a family was very important to me, and *Hashem* has blessed that effort. And – how shall I say this? When I was having troubles with David, and I'd met your father, he'd just arrived in the country, terribly cute, you know, learning English, and your father helped us with our problems, helped David and me – talk to each other better, maybe? – and it wasn't long after when I got pregnant for the first time. So I guess your father helping us was part of *Hashem*'s plan."

"Kids are the best legacy, aren't they?"

"You have your legacy in Jackie."

"He will probably be my only child."

"And some day, I predict, you will be a grandmother too. Jackie will want to have his own children."

"Maybe. Will I live that long?"

Helen let Kayla's question hang. No one could give an honest answer to such a question. *Hashem* did not disclose His plans for any human being. As they sat quietly, Helen's thoughts inevitably turned to Sarah, whom *Hashem* had decreed would not live the full measure of a life. Sarah had been part of the legacy Helen had hoped to leave, and now it was certain Helen would outlive her daughter.

For Kayla, the conversation about Jackie made her think of the other children she might have in the future, if only she found the right man to marry. These thoughts then made her reflect again on what had gone terribly wrong in her relationship with Aharon. The wind picked up suddenly, as did Kayla's unease. And she felt the temperature drop by a couple of degrees.

"We'd better go in. I'm getting way too cold."

El Melech Ne'eman

There was still an hour left before they would have to get up for breakfast, and Helen had wanted to sleep a bit more, but couldn't. Kayla herself had fallen asleep again and was snoring lightly, but it wasn't Kayla's snoring keeping Helen awake. Kayla's noise was like the shushing of distant waves breaking on a shore. What kept Helen awake, what she could not stop mulling over, was the dream she had just had.

She had dreamt that Sarah had come into the cell while Helen lay half-awake on her cot. This Sarah was dressed in white burial shrouds. She stood next to where Helen lay, looking down at Helen with hatred. Helen screamed and tried to reach out to defend herself from what she assumed would be a physical attack, but her arms were immobile. Then, as suddenly as she had come, Sarah disappeared. Helen became fully awake, breathing hard, feeling the rush of adrenalin. She lay still for minutes, trying to slow her breathing and allow the fear to drain from her body. Replacing the fear were her feelings of immense guilt for having abandoned Sarah.

Had she ever been so selfish when her children's welfare was at stake? Helen remembered the night when Sarah, then age ten, had been hospitalized after a bad fall and a concussion. She had spent more than a dozen hours virtually glued to the chair in her hospital room, watching her sleep, praying she would not die. Helen had insisted that

David return home, that she would be okay on her own. He had reluctantly complied. *Hashem* had been good to them. Sarah was fine when she awoke, and the doctor, after another examination, allowed Sarah to be released (under strict observation for twenty-four hours). Helen had felt a glow of unmentionable pride in her own stamina and determination.

And it had always been the same when her kids needed her. How many countless days did she take off from work to attend a teacher-conference or cancel a client so she could haul one of the kids to a swim meet or soccer match? She thought of herself as a devoted, self-sacrificing mother; it was a role more important than any other in her life. Helen could not get comfortable as she wondered whether her late-in-life marriage to Nicky had nudged her away from the role she thought she'd perfected.

Just as she was about to drift off, Helen remembered again how Sarah had asked her to pray for a miracle. She had been remiss in her prayer. Now, she thought of getting everyone together to pray for Sarah. And when Helen opened her eyes again – she had slept for only fifteen minutes – she woke Kayla to mention the idea.

"I'll do anything you want, Helen," Kayla said as she sat up on her cot and yawned. "You know that. But you don't need a group of four people, counting Dad – who doesn't believe in *Hashem* – to pray. You can freely pray by yourself for Sarah's health, and I imagine you have been. As I have, too. Ugh, what time is it?"

"Still early. Sorry to have disturbed you, but this idea is important to me."

"You can recite the prayers as well as I can. *Y'hi ratzon milfanecha …*"

"You're absolutely right, I have been saying them myself. But something is missing."

"*Hashem* hears our prayers, Helen. You know that, too. *Sh'mea tifilah.*"

"Yes, but …"

"Is that what you want, just to have Dad pray for Sarah, so he feels how difficult this trip is for you? I mean, do you see him praying? And would his prayers mean anything, anyway? He doesn't believe."

"No, maybe not. But maybe yes. Both his praying and its effect. Who knows what he believes anymore? Let's ask him on the way into breakfast. It can't hurt. If he says no, maybe Jackie will still come with the two of us. There's a nice copse of trees on the other side of the winery, which I discovered yesterday when I was walking by myself. It would be a pleasant spot, probably catch a breeze too."

"Fine."

With Kayla next to her as a reluctant co-conspirator, Helen mentioned her idea to Nicky outside the dining room later that morning. "And we can add prayers for things you want, too. The end of the lawsuit, for example. It doesn't have to be all about Sarah."

He thought for a long minute before responding. Helen and Kayla had not asked for a major favor. Even after Nicky had stopped believing in a Supreme Being, he had from time to time studied Talmud and recited prayers of thankfulness after a meal. He had even married Helen under a *Chupah* with a rabbi presiding. None of these occasions had been particularly uncomfortable for him, notwithstanding his lack of faith. The hardest thing he'd had to do was attest under oath, at Abbess Fevronia's insistence, how his life had been saved by the Theotokos, but he'd done that as well.

What caused a wave of nausea was Nicky's recognition that Helen's desire for their family to pray as a group was the tip of an iceberg he had ignored. Helen had been hiding her angst at having left Sarah; the trip to the monastery, which at one point had seemed such a reasonable thing for the family to do, now seemed like one of his worst mistakes. And, as had often happened previously, it was a mistake he'd made because he found it virtually impossible to say no to Kayla. It was Kayla who had pressed him to make this trip, and he had agreed and dragged Helen along. And now there was Kayla, holding Helen's arm, looking at him and, with Helen, waiting for his response.

"All right. We can do this after breakfast. You two lead the way, and Jackie and I will go with you."

"Where are we going, Grandpa?"

"Right now, young man, we're going to our table. And don't forget the rules: listen to the singing, but no talking. And just put on your plate what you know you will eat. I think I'll eat only an orange."

Breakfast concluded, Helen led the three others up the steep path to the winery. Before they were halfway there, Jackie complained about how tired his legs were and demanded that Nicky carry him. Nicky allowed Jackie to jump onto his back, but, after a few difficult steps, gently put him down again.

"You'll have to walk on your own the rest of the way. We're practically there, and you're too big and I'm too old. And, my dear grandson, you were strangling me. Next time we do that, if there is a next time, don't put your arms around my neck." But Jackie knew Grandpa was not angry with him. He could not remember when Grandpa had ever been angry with him, despite all the times Jackie had done something he wasn't supposed to.

Behind the winery, they found the group of trees that Helen had mentioned. It was indeed pleasant, and a steady, stiff breeze had sprung up. "Do we just sit on the ground facing each other, or what?" asked Nicky.

"Let's face east," replied Helen, arranging Kayla and Jackie next to her as she lowered herself to the pine needles still damp from the previous evening's mist.

Nicky, still on his feet, looked down at his daughter. "Do you want to lead?" offered.

"But Grandpa … Shouldn't that be you?" Jackie put his hand protectively on Kayla's arm. "*Ima* is a woman and women don't lead our prayers."

Kayla leaned over and kissed the top of Jackie's head. "Quite so. This little fellow will be the Rebbe someday. Will you do the honors,

Dad? Start with something we all know? And then we can pray for healing?"

Nicky sighed. In for a dime, in for a dollar, he thought. Best to get it over with. "Well, fine, let's all say *Sh'ma*. There's no *minyan*, so we start …"

"*El melech ne'eman*," contributed Jackie. "Rabbi Beck taught us."

"He has taught you correctly, so …"

"But Grandpa, you don't have a *kippah*. How can you pray? Rabbi Beck says we must cover our heads when we pray, even if we don't at other times."

"Hmm. I don't have a hat. I hadn't thought of bringing one with me to breakfast. So, I'll just imagine I have a hat and then …"

"Wait, Nicky. Here's a kerchief," said Helen, as she pulled a dark pink, purple. and blue silk square from her bag. "You can tie it. Or, wait, let me tie it for you."

This was the last thing Nicky wanted to wear, but he mentally gritted his teeth and resolved to do it for Helen. And he would do it for Jackie, who would have been offended had he tried to pray without showing the requisite respect for God. Nicky was now glad that their being on the other side of the winery meant there was no one else who would see his indignity, no one else who could see his wife wrapping the woman's scarf around his head. He sighed. What husbands must sometimes do for their wives. And he recalled how he'd had to put up with Adel's craziness for over two decades. It was how the world worked, apparently.

"All right," he said, knowing he looked utterly ridiculous as he could see the pink edge of the kerchief just above his right eye. "Let's get this going. The sooner we start, the sooner we finish."

"Nicky …" protested Helen, her voice telling him that prayer shouldn't be rushed.

"*El Melech Ne'eman, Sh'ma Yisroel …*"

As if guided by the same invisible puppet string, all four covered their eyes with their right hands in the recitation of Judaism's central prayer. Nicky recited out loud in a firm and steady voice; the women were reciting silently, while Jackie whispered.

At the conclusion of *Sh'ma*, as Nicky pronounced "*Adonoi elohechem emet*" ("The Lord is your God, in truth"), he heard a distant clap of thunder. Rain might not be a bad thing if it ended their prayer service, but it was not yet raining.

"And now, let's everyone pray silently for …"

"Dad, do the *Amidah*," urged Kayla. "We have to do that." She stood, extending a hand to help Helen rise as well. "Silently, of course. And we can add our prayers for healing Sarah – and anyone else – as usual with *R'faenu*."

But Kayla's proposal created a problem for her son. "I don't know the *Amidah* by heart, *Ima*. We've gotten only through *Atah Gibor*."

"That's okay, Jackie." Kayla thought for a second, then pointed. "Let's you and I move over near that tree, so everything after *Atah Gibor* I can say softly and you can listen. That way, we won't bother Grandpa and Helen."

"It's not a bother if you stay with us," offered Helen, her comment punctuated by a slightly louder clap of thunder. The wind, as if in response, notched up significantly. "We'd better hurry, though, or I think we'll get soaked."

Lightning

The weather looked threatening as Theodora walked purposefully into the vineyards. She was quite sure no one saw her do so, which was how she wanted it. She didn't want to be stopped or questioned or interrupted in her resolve. The prayers she needed to offer had to be sent up to Christ the Lord, but not from her cell. She had tried there, and nothing came together to make her feel that her prayers for Sarah were heard. Disconcertingly – since she had so often prayed to good effect from that cell – the feeling of oneness with the Lord evaded her. She then recalled the verses from Psalm 139 she'd heard sung by a chorus of angels the prior year, before her trip to America. "Captivity by the river" always led her to the holiest place at the monastery. If her prayer was going to be heard, she had to offer it by the stream, at Fevronia's grave, over the final resting place of the martyred monks. So, if she was rained on in the process, it was an annoyance she could easily bear. She resolved herself to be impervious to the elements. The Lord Jesus Christ would protect her.

It would normally take her fifteen minutes to make her way through the vineyards at her fastest pace, but on this late morning she stumbled frequently and made slow progress. After only two minutes, she began to hear the thunder and feel the wind pick up considerably. In five more minutes, she felt the first raindrops. She thought briefly about turning back but, as the rain grew heavier, Theodora knew she'd be soaked regardless. She would proceed as planned, even as the sky turned black except for those split seconds when lightning flashed. The thought that she might be struck by lightning and killed never entered her mind. Theodora had never again known fear after the Theotokos, with Her veil, had lifted her out of the closet in which she had been left to die. When Theodora mused upon the inevitability of her own death, it was only with a keen anticipation of living for eternity at the feet of Jesus.

As she finally made her way out of the vineyard into the open area near the stream, when the grapevines no longer provided slight protection, a gust of wind nearly knocked her down. Her cassock shivered around her, and yet she felt closer to God than she had felt in a long time. It was God's rain drenching her, God's lightning showing the way through the vineyard. So it had to have been right for her to come to this sacred place. At Fevronia's grave, Theodora lay prostrate, stretched out with her hands over her head, her face in a muddy spot, bare of grass. She could smell, not only the mud, but the holy blood soaking through this small portion of land for nearly fifty years. It was blood that could summon miracles. She could even smell the hatred and the fear flowing through the veins of the German execution squad, particularly the smell of the devil's agent among them. She knew the goddess's name: Phrike, Goddess of Horror. How she wished the Theotokos had been there to save the monks, but that was not part of God's plan.

"Κύριε Ιησού Χριστέ, συγχώρεσέ με, έναν αμαρτωλό." [*Kyr-u insse Christe, syncorese me, enan amartoyo.*] ["Oh Lord Jesus Christ, please forgive me, a sinner."]

She had to start all prayers with the Jesus prayer. You could not approach God without first acknowledging that you had sinned, had missed the mark, had not opened up enough of yourself to God's presence. Only in such a state of humility could one then ask God to hear a prayer for a specific person or outcome. She had been taught so by the first priest she'd ever known, her first teacher in Christ, the one who'd locked her into the closet to protect her and had then sacrificed his own life to save her.

As she prayed for Sarah, rainwater trilled against Theodora's face and into her nostrils. She lay as still as possible, waiting for a message to confirm her prayer had been heard. She might have been lying for mere seconds or for hours, she did not know how long, but finally she could hear Silenos calling out to her one word of encouragement from the murk below.

"*Nai!*"

That simple syllable of affirmation in the voice she had never heard before, but which could only have been that of Fevronia's brother, was what Theodora needed most. She was on the right track. It had been right to come through the storm. She continued to pray. She willed herself to see the stricken Sarah in her mind's eye. Then, as clear as if standing before her in the brilliant sunshine, the young woman emerged from a shadow. Theodora reached out toward Helen's daughter to learn what she could from the feel of her body. Was it too late for the Lord Jesus Christ to give her a renewed life? Or at least to take away her suffering? Would Christ even want to do so, given Sarah was Jewish?

Sarah *was* there, facing Theodora in a sunny field, on a beautiful day, the gently flowing Microdermis nearby. Theodora reached to take the young woman into her arms, and Sarah – resisting her initial urge to jump back – allowed herself to be held. Sarah must have known who Theodora was as soon as she felt Theodora's warmth flooding into her. Theodora had hugged her the previous fall, at Helen and Nicky's wedding. But now Theodora's embrace was much stronger; Sarah could not have pushed herself away if she had wanted to.

"You are so ill, aren't you, my sweet one?"

"You see through me and all which lies in me, Theodora. I don't have much time left on this earth."

"Is your heart open to God? Do you wish to be healed?"

Sarah thought for a few seconds before replying, as the sound of thunder crashed about her even though the sky was a brilliant blue.

"The idea of leaving my children gives me great pain, as does the thought that my mother should have to bury me, her child. And the knowledge my mother may not be here when I die troubles me as well. But if this is *Hashem*'s will, then it must be so."

The sky darkened. Theodora could feel Sarah's tears against her cheek and smell her fear. She kissed Sarah lightly on the side of her head, then stepped back, releasing her. She'd never tried to heal anyone before. Those were the kinds of miracles only saints could perform, and she knew she was a sinner, not a saint. But, if she could open up to God just the tiniest bit more, God could be the healer. Her Lord Jesus Christ would heal Sarah, even if Sarah did not acknowledge Him, if Theodora could serve even for an instant as a conduit between the two.

Then lightning struck them both.

A Reaffirmation

The storm assaulted them much more quickly than they had anticipated. One moment it was simply the wind picking up and dark clouds swelling above them. The next moment, the sky turned even blacker, and they were drenched in a relentless downpour. The wind, instantly ferocious and terrifying, tore branches off trees, whipping them through the air like arrows shot by a marauding army. What had momentarily been the exhilaration of being caught in the rain transformed into the urgency of life and death.

Lightning struck the top of the winery and a simultaneous blast of thunder deafened Helen for seconds. Her eyes spasmed shut as if the lightning ran through her body. When she opened her eyes, she was confused. Where was everyone? She had a dim sense that Kayla had grabbed Jackie and run off, but in which direction? Only Nicky was close, his arm around her, pushing her toward the winery. She tried to explain that the winery was unsafe, that one of *Hashem*'s bolts had already struck it and certainly would do so again in the next seconds, but torrents of rain and the howling wind hid her words. He had not heard her. Or, worse, he had chosen to ignore her. He still pushed her where she didn't want to go. He had always pushed her; he made it impossible to resist. She no longer had a will of her own.

And then, although the roar of the wind and the repeated claps of thunder persisted, they escaped. Nicky shoved Helen into a shed on the side of the winery as she struggled to catch her breath. How far had he made her run? Certainly farther than a seventy-year-old woman should run. But had Nicky also forced himself beyond his capacity? In the dim light of the shed, his appearance horrified her. His dripping wet face looked deathly pale. He gasped for breath, even after Helen had brought her own breathing under control. She thought incongruously of what the proverbial cat had dragged in, wondering which of them was the cat and which the dead mouse. Suddenly, she began to laugh.

"What?" Nicky managed to ask, as he wiped his face with the sodden pink and purple kerchief he had pulled from his head.

"Just ..." She pitched again into a fit of laughter, falling to her knees.

"What's so damn funny?"

"Don't say 'damn.' I don't think I've ever been so wet in my life." Looking up at her husband, Helen shivered uncontrollably.

"You're freezing."

"N...n..."

"Gotta get you out of those wet clothes. Me too." She was too tired to protest, but looking around the shed, she saw nothing that would substitute for her clothes, not even a stray towel. At best, there were tarps the workmen had used to cover equipment. She and Nicky would need to wait out the still-raging storm and then most likely put on their soaked clothes again for the rush back to the church. But that would be later. Now, she was ready to warm herself in the only way she could.

Helen reached up for Nicky as he knelt down next to her and folded her naked body in his. He was cold, too, and clammy. His touch, the feel of his chest against her breasts, did not bring Helen immediate relief from the cold, but in a minute their combined body heat took the edge off her chill, and with every passing minute she felt better.

Then the storm – the prodigious rain still pounding on the roof of the shed – stopped warning them of death and became a reaffirmation of life. She felt his hands cup her breasts and knew that Nicky too had sensed the change. She reached for him, aware he was already excited, as excited as she'd become in seconds. Could they? In a damp, dirty shed? Even as the question formed itself in her head, her body answered in the affirmative.

It didn't matter where they were or that the tarps on which they lay were grimy or that they couldn't lock the door or that Kayla and Jackie were still out in the storm.

A Heavy Branch

Sarah had vanished. Theodora, slowly regaining consciousness, became painfully aware that she lay in the middle of a deluge. The Microdermis had overflowed its banks. Rushing water rose toward Theodora, and she tried to pull herself up into a kneeling position, but her body was frozen in place. The weight of the water sopping through her clothes held her down. Still, Theodora felt a pleasant tingle course through her, a sensation she knew had to do with the lightning bolt that had hit nearby.

Sarah had returned to America after having met Theodora, face-to-face, over Fevronia's grave. What was it Sarah had said? She would accept *Hashem*'s will. *Hashem*. Theodora had been taught by Helen that it meant The Name. Why did Jews refuse to name God? Theodora knew God's name, and it was Jesus Christ, but the Jews did not. *Hashem* was the closest they could come. It would have to do.

It was at the instant she felt struck by lightning, when they'd both been struck, that Theodora had fully opened her heart, and Sarah's as well, to Christ; it was in exactly that moment that Christ's love and forgiveness flooded into both of them. Theodora could see Helen's daughter being granted another two years of life, her cancer going into remission. She could see Helen having time to come to terms with the loss of her daughter. And, with these perceptions, Theodora felt the strength to pull herself into a kneeling position and then to stand, if somewhat uncertainly. She looked down to see the impression left by her body on the wet grass and mud.

"Please tell me, oh my beloved Mother in Christ, whether I have done wrong. Should a sinner such as I am not have prayed for God's intervention in Sarah's illness?"

There was no response from the ground. Fevronia would not answer. The question Theodora posed was one she would have to answer for herself.

Neither the rain nor the wind had abated. A heavy branch carried by the fierce wind clipped Theodora on the head just before she could make it to the relative safety of the vines. Immediately knocked unconscious, Theodora again lay prone in the wetness before she could understand what had happened.

Respect for Privacy

The rain had slowed but was still pattering on the rooftop of the shed. Had she fallen asleep momentarily in the amazing afterglow of sexual satisfaction? Nicky was stirring. Helen was about to whisper how much she loved him when she heard the door of the shed creaking open. The light from the open door illuminated their naked bodies. There stood Kayla, and, for the instant before Kayla slammed the door closed again, Helen registered the shock and dismay on Kayla's face.

"Jesus! What are you doing here? Shit! Where's Jackie? I can't find Jackie!"

"*Gamóto!*" swore Nicky as he began pulling on his clothes and helping Helen with hers. "Kayla? Don't you have any respect for privacy?"

"How the … How would I know you were boffing each other here, in the middle of the storm? Please! I need your help."

"*Skatá!*" Nicky emptied the water that had pooled in his shoes and pulled them over his feet without bothering about the soaked socks.

It took a half minute for Nicky and Helen to make themselves as presentable as possible. Helen, who felt her blushing would never abate, pushed Nicky out of the shed first, then followed, standing next to him but trying to hide her face by leaning it into his shoulder.

"Jackie's gone!"

"What do you mean?" asked Nicky, who had never seen his daughter so distraught, even when she had suffered the worst symptoms of schizophrenia. He grabbed her by the shoulders in an attempt to calm her. She pushed him away, wanting not to be calmed or consoled. "Come on, Kayla, take a deep breath and tell me what happened."

"I was trying to lead him to the winery, but then lost my grip when I fell in the mud. He took off. It was only a second I didn't have him in my sight, but when I looked up again I couldn't see him. I've been searching all over – for an hour? – and thought he might have hidden in …" Kayla glanced at the shed but was unable to finish her sentence. "You two. I can't f-ing believe …"

"I'm sorry you had to walk in us like that," said Nicky, "but let's get back to the church and see if anyone there has seen him."

Nicky led the charge down the hill, the three of them slipping and sliding on the wet grass and stones as if they were running on ice. At the church, they discovered that the main power was out – there had to be downed lines somewhere – but no one had seen the boy. They tried to phone Andros from Abbess Zoe's office to see if Jackie had made his way back there, but the phone lines were down, too. Zoe, Helen, and Kayla then went into the dormitory to check if Jackie was in Theodora's cell, but it was empty.

"Theodora should have been here," observed an obviously perturbed Zoe. "I knew this would come to no good."

"What would come to no good?"

Zoe looked at Kayla, shaking her head, a grim look on her face.

"I should have never allowed this …"

"Look, this isn't the time to worry about what shouldn't have been done," Kayla remonstrated, markedly raising her voice. "He's my son, missing, in a storm, and we need to find him. We need to call the police, now."

"The phone lines are down, Miss Covo, as we just found out. Please, both of you, come with me back to my office. Settle down. I'll ask Dr. Covo to run to … the house of Andros. Maybe his phone is working, and perhaps Dr. Covo will find Jackie on the road to Andros's house."

At her office, Zoe instructed Nicky what needed to be done, that Andros's house was the logical next place to look. "I'm on my way," said Nicky as he darted out the door. Kayla followed him out of the building. She yelled for Jackie as she began her way around the church.

Still in the office, Helen said, "Abbess Zoe, I need to change into dry clothes. I'll meet you here again as soon as I can." She had something entirely different in her mind, however. It didn't seem likely to her that Jackie would be found at Andros's house, as the route would have taken him directly past the church, and someone would probably have seen him. Yet, someone still needed to go to Andros's house to check, and it had made sense for Nicky to be the one. Helen was glad he was heading there now.

More likely, Helen thought, was that Theodora and Jackie were together and headed in the same direction for the same purpose. If Jackie had wanted to be with anyone more than his mother, wouldn't he have wanted to be with Theodora? Helen knew, with a slight twang of jealousy, that Jackie and Theodora had bonded closely during Theodora's visit to America. Helen intuited that Jackie could confide in Theodora in a way he'd not been able to confide in her. Perhaps he'd been so frightened by the lightning and thunder, so shocked by the chaos coming from the sky, that he needed the comfort of his loving great-aunt more than that of his *Ima*. But, if Jackie and Theodora were together, where could they have gone?

Deep in thought, Helen returned to the cell she shared with Kayla, stripped off her wet clothes again, and donned her terrycloth robe. At midday, it was not a surprise that the common bathroom was unoccupied; a long shower under hot water – but not too long – was needed to stop her shivering. As she began to warm up, Helen realized the one place at the monastery where she was most likely to find Theodora, who with barely concealed pride had led her to Fevronia's grave near the Microdermis only the previous morning. Helen had not paid much attention to the exact path they'd taken. Now, as heavy, black clouds blocked the sun, could she find her way through the vineyard on her own?

And had the stream become a raging flood? Enough water had fallen from the sky to float Noah's ark ten times over.

With the image of raging waters in her mind and the grinding fear it elicited, Helen turned off the shower, wrapped her robe around her again, and ran back to her cell to dress, leaving a trail of wet footprints.

A Tiny Tornado

They shouldn't have treated him as if he was a baby. *Ima* shouldn't have been pulling him so hard to get out of the rain. If water was so bad for him, why was he always forced to bathe? It wasn't that he hated baths. Once he was in the water, with his toys, it was fun. He was old enough to take his own bath now, and, if he was in a rush, he could shower himself without the toys. Bath or shower, he knew how to make the water the right temperature, and he could wash his hair without getting shampoo in his eyes.

It was just that, whenever *Ima* or Uncle Max told him it was time for a bath or shower, he was always in the middle of something else. They didn't understand it was hard for him to step away from the clarinet, because he would have just begun practicing when they wanted him to get clean. Yes, he must practice. He loved to practice. *Ima* constantly told him how important it was to practice. They wanted him to practice and become even better than Jimmy Hamilton. But then why stop his practice? Or maybe he wasn't practicing but had just started to make up a story with his Hot Wheels. The dirt on him would last until he finished with his Hot Wheels, and the bath would be just as good later than earlier. Better, in fact.

The grownups acted as if they were scared by the storm, particularly *Ima*, but he was not. Just as lightning had struck in the nearby field, he'd looked up and caught a glimpse of the beautiful woman he'd seen at the stream, the woman whose face sparkled at him as if the sun shone from within, the woman who was not *Ima* but whose face had been painted on icons he'd seen throughout the church. It was odd that he could see her face in sunlight, even though a great rainstorm with dark clouds had come upon them. He would have gone willingly with *Ima* as she joined the rest in fleeing from under the trees, but the beautiful woman had called to him – he had certainly heard her call "Jackie" – and ordered him to follow her. She was far away, as far away as second base from home plate, but he definitely felt her tug on his body, and, as he let himself be tugged, he freed himself from *Ima* and she slipped but he didn't care and he ran and in an instant he was next to the beautiful woman – now she had a full body, glowing with the power of seven suns – and in a second she had whisked him into the vineyard. He didn't know how she'd managed it, because he had no sensation of flying or even swimming through the rain, and yet he was being guided along through the vines by the beautiful woman at his side.

He was awash in the storm's water, but felt strangely warm, almost as if he *was* in a bath. He'd been in a summer rainstorm before and remembered that the water was not awfully cold, not like the rain in winter, but still cold enough. This was a different rain. *Ima* had thought the water would hurt him, but he knew he was safe. The woman – what was her Greek name again? – oh, the Theotokos, yes, he'd heard it many times by now from the mouths of both Abbess Fevronia and Sister Theodora – the Theotokos was taking him somewhere and would make sure he got there safely. And then before him, as if thinking about her had caused her body to form, he saw Sister Theodora. She lay face down, just at the edge of the vineyard. The black veil usually covering her head, as part of her black nun's uniform, was missing.

And the little stream had become a big river and was overflowing its banks. There couldn't possibly be so much water where before there had been an empty field, but he had to believe his eyes.

Theodora wasn't moving. Was she dead?

He shuddered, remembering sadly the vision he'd had of a dead Abbess Fevronia and it was only within a day or two – or less? – that she did die, although they'd tried to hide her death from him. And then Sister Theodora had brought the dead Abbess Fevronia back to Greece, in a box.

He stood over Theodora for a second, then knelt and tried to push her over, so she'd be lying face up. It had to be easier to breathe that way. He used every bit of strength he had, but all Jackie managed was to push her sideways. The beautiful woman who had summoned him away from *Ima* and led him to Theodora was gone.

"Sister Theodora. It's Jackie. Are you okay?"

There was no response.

Then he saw she was bleeding from the side of her head, from just above an ear. He remembered a jingle from *Sesame Street* about how B was for bandage. "It can happen to you and can happen to me." That was the part standing out in his memory. But he didn't have bandages. What did he have? Just his green polo shirt, *Ima* called it, and a T-shirt underneath. He took off his polo shirt, thought for a second about wiping Theodora's blood away with it, then bunched it up and used it instead to prop her head only about an inch higher than it had been, but his effort got her nose and mouth farther away from the rapidly growing puddle. Then he took off his T-shirt and gently wiped away the blood. He saw there was a big gash over Theodora's ear, but the blood had slowed down. He shivered again from the chill.

"Sister Theodora. Hi. It's Jackie. Can you hear me?"

Still no response.

He leaned down farther to kiss her ear near the gash. Her flesh did not give off its usual heat. Was she breathing? Is this what a dead person feels like? He had seen on television once when *Ima* had allowed him to watch *Gunsmoke* that you could tell if a person was dead by listening to them breathe or not breathe. You put your ear right by the person's mouth. He tried to do this with Theodora. Kneeling even farther, he got his ear next to her mouth, which was half open.

He couldn't be sure if he heard any breath coming from Theodora. All he heard was the wind. There was wind all around him, as if he'd been caught inside a tiny tornado. And it finally occurred to him to wonder, if the beautiful lady was not with him, then where she was. He felt for a second that she was in the wind, that she *was* the wind. Had she ever really been with him?

Theodora opened her eyes and saw Jackie over her.

"Κύριε Ιησού Χριστέ, συγχώρεσέ με, έναν αμαρτωλό." [*Kyr-u insse Christe, syncorese me, enan amartoyo.*] ["Oh Lord Jesus Christ, please forgive me, a sinner."]

Brilliantly Orange

Theodora seemed in multiple places at the same time. There was the present, where she was conscious of being guided through the monastery's vineyard by Jackie. He was shorter than she, much lighter, yet had enough strength, with his right arm around her back, to keep her from falling where she wanted to fall. He kept urging her. Believe in *Hashem*, Theodora. You will be fine, Theodora. *Hashem* will protect you. Trust *Hashem*. His persistent urging was as responsible for her ability to struggle along as was his arm. But it wasn't Jackie, she knew.

It was Papa. He was leading her to his study, where a volume of the Talmud lay open on his desk, and he wanted to teach her some new words. Why had Papa picked on her? Why couldn't it have been Ada this afternoon whom he needed with him? Why did he want any of his children with him when he studied? But she would never resist Papa. He loved her, he protected her, and it was her solemn duty to obey him. She had never been one of those disagreeable, obstinate children, like her friend Lara Yahon, who lived across the street. Lara would have run and hid, laughing, if her father had urged her to study Talmud with him. Kal could not do that to Papa. She would comply with his wishes.

How had Jackie become Papa? How did Papa find himself at the monastery? Papa's soul ... did it even still exist? Papa would never accept Christ, so his soul could not have become immortal. Papa had been murdered at Auschwitz.

And then Theodora found herself at the death camp, but not as a prisoner. She watched the pathetic scene unfold from above. What struck her first were the awful sounds of children crying, children screaming for their parents, parents screaming for their children, and the Nazi guards barking orders. But Theodora saw as well as heard. There was the boxcar from which Papa and Ada emerged. Where was Mama? Theodora remembered then that she had once killed Mama, pushing her down as they fought when Mama sent her away with Alex. But no. Mama hadn't died then.

Theodora forced herself to jump back twenty hours and was now in the rattling boxcar packed with the dead, the dying, and the frightened, watching in anguish, unable to help anyone. She saw Mama die there, Papa holding her, Mama easily letting her soul fly away as she slumped against Papa, Ada crying at her side, so many people crying and praying out loud and the echoes of *Sh'ma* echoing through the boxcar as its dazed occupants felt how close they were to their end. Papa wouldn't let them pile Mama in the corner with the other three who had died, an old couple – how good neither would live to suffer without the other – and a baby. Theodora saw that Papa would hold Mama until he was compelled to let go.

And then back at the camp, Theodora saw the bodies, Mama's too, dumped out like so much offal. And there was Ada, sent off to die immediately, and Papa, who might have lived because of his skill as a physician, choosing instead to go with Ada, to comfort her. And then Theodora saw Ada pulled out of the line by a Nazi guard and thrown onto the hard ground, where she hid her face and tried to make herself invisible. And, Theodora saw, Papa continuing with those doomed to immediate death, not caring anymore whether he lived, preferring to die, having lost Mama, and having sent Nicky and Kal to disappear into the unknown, and knowing Ada too was on her way to death or worse, whimpering, screaming for him – "Papa, don't leave me" – and understanding with horror that it was all useless, and having the strength only to keep walking toward his end. The Supreme Being had decided, and he, Mordechai Covo, would not fight God's will.

The stench of death was awful. It made Theodora gag. It corroded her lungs. Why had Theodora never smelled it before? Or had she? She now recalled the priest and his acolyte, who had saved her and perished for their efforts, when the smell of decay first reached her nostrils, as she was locked in a closet for days near their decaying bodies. But the odor assaulting her at the camp was much stronger.

And, at the same time, Theodora found herself with Sarah. So young. So tragic to leave such a beautiful family. They were around her bed and knew the end was near and had tried to call Helen back but had learned the telephone lines were down somewhere. Sarah would have to face death without her mother. Why should she die anyway? This was not the right time. Theodora had been sure her prayer would be answered, that Sarah would have more years to live, and now it looked like Theodora had been sadly mistaken. Again. Mistaken about the Second Coming. Mistaken that her prayers had been answered in the affirmative. God, the Lord Jesus Christ, had heard her prayer but decided not to grant it. She had not prayed with enough sincerity. She, a sinner, had presumed to ask for something she was not entitled to. Instead of praying for forgiveness, as she had been taught was the only true prayer, she had tried to influence the Lord's justice.

She wanted to reach out to Jonah, Sarah's husband, who sat on the edge of Sarah's bed, holding her cold hand, feeling for her pulse. She wanted to scream out her sorrow that her prayer had not been granted, but there was no way to form the words. The Lord had condemned Theodora only to watch in great sorrow as Sarah died.

And then Theodora was back in the vineyard, struggling along with Jackie, her body telling her it was impossible to take one more step. The pain in her head, where she had been struck by something as hard as a brick, was intense. Yet, as much as she tried to lie down, ready to die, just as Papa had been ready to die, just as Sarah had been ready to die, she could not fall. She turned to her right, knowing there was another force – a force she had to see – helping Jackie bring her back out of danger. She was not surprised to encounter the glowing, hot, brilliantly orange aura of the Theotokos.

The Theotokos and Helen were one of a kind, devout Jewish women who had brought life into the world only to see their children unjustly taken away.

Leaning

She pulled on the light green New Jersey Devils sweatshirt with the garish red logo, thinking now she'd probably should have put it on earlier in the day. Maybe she should have known she'd be caught in a deluge. But, even if she'd known, she felt the logo – indeed, the whole idea of devils – was inappropriate for a monastery. She kicked herself mentally, angry that propriety hadn't been a concern when she was packing. Now, with a fine drizzle still falling, she cared little about what others might think. She would not get chilled again if she could help it. Wearing the pullover probably wouldn't have mattered earlier, she mused, as nothing could have protected her from the massive amount of rain. Against the drizzle, the pullover was at least marginally useful, and maybe the wrench-like red "J" on her chest – with its tail pointing to her midsection – would make her more visible in the gloom.

Had she seen one of the nuns on her way to the vineyard, Helen might have asked for company on her search for Theodora and Jackie. But she saw no one, and no one saw her.

She made her way into the vines, guessing as best she could the correct row. The thick mud threatened to suck off her tennis shoes. Helen grabbed one of the vines for support, then crouched to untie her shoes, pull out her feet, and roll off her socks. She crammed the socks into her sodden shoes and, with difficulty, yanked the shoes out of the mire. She then wedged them together in the crotch of the nearest vine. All right, she thought. Barefoot it will be. Get the shoes and socks later.

Helen prayed she was on the right track to "the graves," the term Theodora had used because that's where the murdered monks were supposedly interred. That's where Abbess Fevronia's body had been placed for its eternal rest. But to Helen a cemetery, Christian or Jewish, was a place hallowed out for that particular purpose before burial of the first body. It was typically a place with boundaries, a section of earth that might be fenced to protect against accidental entrance. It could not be a place where murderers hid their victims, a place where the victims were forced at gunpoint to dig their own graves. Babi Yar was not a cemetery. So even though Sister Theodora had seemed to take great pride in her choosing to bury Abbess Fevronia there, the small field bordering the Microdermis was still not a cemetery.

In the distance, Helen heard what she thought might be the brook, but it did not sound like the tame brook she and Nicky had recently seen. It sounded more like the rapids she and David had once attempted on a raft while vacationing in the Poconos, bouncing and swirling whitewater that had terrified her and induced her to swear she'd never go rafting again. But now – with Jackie missing – there was no choice but to come as close as she could. Please, *Hashem*, she prayed, don't let the waters pull Jackie away and drown him. She feared the unspeakable had already happened and that her prayer was in vain even as she uttered it.

The voices of the rushing waters rose ever higher – she had to be going in the right direction – and yet Helen was not close enough to see the Microdermis. She felt she'd fought through the mud more than far enough to have reached it, and yet it was still too far away. Each step was an agony of effort. She held onto the nearest vines for support, and clumps of grapes fell where her hand had banged against them, as if the wind had weakened the thin branches connecting them to the heavy vines. Her breathing was labored. This was not what a seventy-year-old woman should be doing, and what if she, too, were swept downstream by the powerful forces *Hashem*'s storm had unleashed? After that horrible episode in the Poconos, she feared death by drowning more than any other kind. David's face flashed through her mind. Why should she see it now? Was this her life passing before her eyes? And then it was Sarah whom Helen saw, not the healthy Sarah, energetic mother of Helen's grandchildren, marathoner, gardener, no, not her, but the dying Sarah, lying pale and weak on her bed, Jonah and the rest of her family around her, even David, all except for Helen herself. And she saw with blazing clarity that it had to be a choice between the life of Sarah and the life of Jackie. *Hashem* might spare one of them, but could not spare both, and yet she could not bear to lose either.

She saw them struggling toward her. There were unmistakably three people on the path between the vines, fighting their way through the mud. There were two nuns and Jackie. One nun had to be Sister Theodora, and the other, wearing not the traditional black habit, but some kind of maroon veil. Or maybe the veil was dark crimson, but in the poor light it was difficult to make out colors. Theodora was in between Jackie and …

It must have been an illusion, a trick of the shadows, a hallucination brought about by extreme stress. That was the only way to explain it. There were not three, but two, just Jackie and Theodora. It looked as if Theodora was leaning on Jackie, who was having trouble keeping himself from being pushed down by her weight. They made agonizingly slow progress.

Helen called out, but she could not be sure they had heard her over the roar of the wind. She waved frantically, but could not be sure they saw her. They seemed in a separate world.

Helen offered a silent prayer to *Hashem* in thankfulness for the sparing of Jackie's life, and she knew then that Sarah had died.

A Sucker Punch

Somehow, Helen managed to pick up speed, if only slightly, as the mud fought hard to suck her down. She screamed again at Theodora and Jackie, continuing to wave her arms. Yes, now it looked like they had spotted her, and they seemed to move more quickly in response. Or maybe not. Maybe Helen just wanted to believe that. In her mind, it took forever for them to close the gap. In reality, it was about twenty seconds.

Helen gasped for breath, her heart a snare drum on steroids. "*Baruch Hashem*! You're alive! I was afraid you'd been washed away …" Then Helen saw the ugly gash on the side of Theodora's head, the blood on her face and cassock, which ran in rivulets with the falling rain, and Theodora looked deathly pale. "What … We have to get you back the church. Jackie, are you all right? Your *Ima* is worried to death …"

"There was a lady helping us!" Jackie panted. "Did you see her?" He still had his arm around Theodora, who leaned on him as a crutch.

There *had* been three, at least for a couple of seconds, but Helen didn't want to admit what she'd seen; there was no rational way to explain the woman's disappearance. Yet her instincts as a mother and as a social worker told her she could not call Jackie a liar or otherwise contradict him and make him distrust his own senses.

"A lady? My goodness. It must have been another nun. But quick! Let me get on the other side of Sister Theodora. Put an arm around me, Theodora. Put most of your weight on me. It looks like the storm is picking up again." Indeed, the rain, which had at one point slackened, now again fell with renewed anger, its enemies not yet vanquished. "Jackie ... we've got to get her back to the church fast as we can. She needs a doctor. And you need dry clothes, and ..."

"You're wet too, Helen. You look funny in the Devils shirt."

She looked ghastly. That much she knew.

"Sister Theodora, let's ..."

Helen never finished the sentence. Theodora had passed out, her limp body too heavy for Helen to hold up, even with Jackie's help. Theodora slipped through Helen's grasp, collapsed as if knocked flat by a sucker punch. Lightning tore through the sky, and the simultaneous crash of thunder reverberated through her body, her nerves pulverized by the storm's insane energy.

There was no air to breathe, and Helen knew she would die. With Sarah already dead, it was just as well.

——

Only a minute later – but it seemed much longer to Helen – Nicky, Kayla, and Zoe arrived, agitated and worried, but relieved they had found everyone they'd been looking for. Theodora was already coming to. After carefully questioning her about pain and palpating for broken bones, Nicky slowly got Theodora to her feet. With Zoe helping, he was able to get Theodora back to the church in ten minutes. Kayla was too relieved that Jackie was apparently fine to say anything. She just held his hand tightly on the way back, and Helen held Jackie's other hand. The three of them stopped momentarily to allow Helen to retrieve her hopelessly drenched socks and shoes.

Once the group arrived back at the church, Zoe directed one of her employees to drive Theodora and Nicky to the Serres General Hospital in the monastery's pickup truck. There, two emergency room doctors patched up Theodora. Luckily, she had needed only four stitches and otherwise checked out well. The doctors told her to take it easy for a few days. They remarked on how fortunate Theodora was not to have been hurt more severely in the storm. The storm had been ferocious in Serres, too, the doctors told them. The hospital was running on its emergency generators.

The Only Conceivable Result

Things couldn't be grimmer, thought Max, as the plaintiff wrapped up her case. Two experts had been allowed to offer highly flawed opinions on medical causation. Their rationale for blaming Maripulol as the cause of death was the proximity of its ingestion and Mr. Lodge's seizure. No real science connected the drug to seizures: no epidemiology, no toxicology, not even a mechanistic theory. And, after Judge Metcalf had overruled Phil's objections, Max had stayed up all night drafting a motion demanding the judge reverse herself and exclude the testimony. When Phil tried to file the motion in open court, the judge angrily threatened him with contempt and instructed her clerk not to accept the papers. It was clear to Max that Judge Metcalf couldn't be bothered with trying to learn the science, with Rule 702, or with any semblance of legal analysis. It was likewise obvious she thought she could prevent a successful appeal if she interfered with the defendant's ability to make a record.

Turning away from the courtroom clerk, with the court's papers still in his hand, Phil tried to hand a copy to Bradworth, plaintiff's counsel, who ignored him. Phil gently placed the plaintiff's copy on the corner of her counsel's table and turned back to his seat at the defense table. Throughout all this, Phil smiled, acting as if things were proceeding exactly as he had planned. Max could tell the smile was achieved only with great effort. Max knew that, inside, Phil was boiling mad, as he had a right to be.

At the next break, Max suggested to Phil that they file the defendant's motion, not in open court, but directly in the Clerk of Court's office down the hallway, get a time-stamped copy of their filing, and then be ready to attach that to the appellate brief they would have to file if the jury found for the plaintiff. Phil complimented Max on his creative solution to the problem of making a record and did as Max suggested. Still, both knew that losing at trial would be its own major disaster with the client, who could always take its business elsewhere; scores of competent defense-oriented law firms would be happy to take over the case and the client's other business. But Phil and Max had done their job; they had laid the groundwork for an appeal.

The sole good development was the shrinkage of the original eight-person jury. One juror just failed to show up for duty on the fifth day of trial and could not be reached by phone; his employer advised the upset Judge Metcalf on the telephone that the juror hadn't returned to work, either. After a two-hour delay, the judge resumed the trial with just seven jurors. But later, at lunch, another juror became violently ill, with a stomach bug or food poisoning. She'd been rushed to the hospital, and the judge had no choice but to continue the trial with only six jurors. Now, the plaintiff and judge, who was clearly on her side, were in trouble. A federal court jury could not return a verdict with fewer than six jurors, unless the parties stipulated to a lower number, and there was no way Phil and Max would allow their client to stipulate.

The second week saw Phil putting on the defense experts. He was constantly being called to the bench for conferences as Bradworth objected. Often, Judge Metcalf sustained the objections, forcing Phil to struggle to get his witnesses' opinions before the jury. During one of those conferences, Max had an idea. The jurors were bored, unable to hear what was going on at the bench, disgusted with the repeated interruptions of their entertainment. Max noticed Juror Number Five, an unemployed man of twenty-two who lacked a high school degree, begin to doze. Phil apparently hadn't noticed, even as he returned to the podium from yet another bench conference and continued questioning the expert then on the stand. Max carefully kept an eye on Number Five. Within a minute, there could be no mistake; the juror was asleep. Now, the question for Max was how to let Phil know, what Phil might do about it, and what, if anything, the judge might do.

The first part was easy. Max wrote a note, casually walked up to the podium, and slipped it to Phil as if the slip of paper held another question to be asked. Phil glanced at him angrily, but then read the note, and his demeanor regained its nonchalance. Okay, step one accomplished. Phil had been advised. Step two was up to Phil. He asked another question, looked at Number Five now and held his gaze there long enough for the judge to follow it. At first, Max feared the judge wouldn't care, but after another ten seconds – during which the juror snored loudly – she interrupted the testimony and ordered the witness to step down from the stand and leave the courtroom. Max saw that the five awake jurors, confused, watched as the witness left. They were wondering yet again, Max surmised, what kind of crazy courtroom they had had the misfortune to wander into. They were wondering what sin the witness had committed, to be so abruptly banned from their presence. After the swinging doors to the hallway closed behind the witness, the judge directed her next order to the U.S. Marshal.

"Take the jury to the jury room. All but Number Five."

Number Six nudged Number Five in the ribs, and the young man woke with a start. As he saw his fellow jurors rise to leave, he rose as well.

"Number Five, you will remain in the courtroom for now."

"But, Judge, I need to use the bathroom."

"You will remain here until I tell you to leave. You may sit."

Number Five resumed his chair, perplexed.

The judge waited until the other jurors were gone, then continued, "Madame Clerk, administer the oath for a witness." Max held his breath as the clerk required Juror Number Five to swear he'd tell the truth, so help him God. Max hoped beyond hope that somehow the judge would have no choice but to excuse the juror and declare a mistrial. Not a full defense victory – the case could always be retried – but damn close. "Juror Number Five, I noticed you sleeping. Would you agree that's what you were doing?"

"No, Judge, I …"

"That's quite enough. You don't need to add lies to the disregard of your sworn duty to listen carefully to all the evidence."

"I *was* listening."

"You were snoring. Loudly. Who was the last witness? And, don't forget, you're under oath."

Juror Number Five looked at the empty witness box, then scanned the gallery section of the courtroom, investigations not seeming to aid his memory. He furrowed his eyebrows, as if thinking hard. Then he shrugged.

"Uh …"

"What explains your failure to know who was on the stand?"

"Well, I'm taking epilepsy medication, Judge. It does make me sleepy."

"I see, and …"

"And this morning, because I was nervous, I took extra pills." With that, the juror rested back his head and amazingly closed his eyes again.

"Sir …? Juror Number Five? Wake up." But Number Five did not hear. Metcalf banged her gavel, loudly, to no avail. Indeed, Juror Number Five was out cold, snoring again.

Phil rose and asked for a mistrial, noting that Juror Number Five was still asleep, had overmedicated by his own admission, had not heard all the testimony, and was useless as a juror. Bradworth was too stunned to say anything, but sat quietly, seeming to massage his scalp through his hair, as if he were trying to stimulate his brain. The judge, obviously disgusted at the likely loss of more than a week of her valuable time, barked out, "I will have your written motion by 2:30 pm and the plaintiff's response by 4:00 pm. Court adjourned for today. Mr. Marshal, take Juror Number Five into custody."

Max was greatly amused, watching the marshal wake up Juror Number Five, handcuff him while the juror protested loudly, and march him out of the courtroom.

The paperwork was a formality. Max knew a mistrial was the only conceivable result. As they left the courtroom, he felt Phil's hand on the shoulder and heard him say something about "work." It was either to compliment him or to tell him to immediately write the motion asked for by the judge. Max thought it had to be the latter. But it was not a problem. Max had already written most of the motion in his mind.

The Wrong Woman

They knew they had won. Max easily drafted the motion as soon as he and Phil had gotten back to the Sonesta Downtown Chicago, where they shared the news with the three associates and three paralegals in the war room. They would be packing up soon, re-boxing the documents and word-processors and computers, and what seemed like miles of interlinking cable, but all that could wait until the next morning. Yes, Phil and Max made clear, in a few months, when the judge again had time on her calendar, they would reverse the process and set up again for the new trial – unless the case settled cheaply in the meantime – but this was an evening for celebration. The clients – in-house attorneys for the drug manufacturer – were delighted with the day's results, and Phil and Max were directed to take everyone out for a great dinner.

Phil knew Chicago well, as he'd tried a case there earlier in his career, and chose Catch 35. It was the best seafood restaurant, he confidently announced. There normally would have been a problem getting a table for ten people – the clients had to be included naturally – but the promise of an extra hundred-dollar tip to the host magically greased the wheel.

Max was in a giddy mood, helped along by his second Beefeater martini. Sitting immediately to his right was one of the paralegals, a young woman who'd recently graduated from Manhattan College with a degree in English and who'd pledged to work at their firm for two years before deciding whether to attend law school. Her name was Ann. Not Annie. Max knew at least that much about her.

Without realizing how it happened, Max saw Ann would laugh no matter what stupid thing he said to her. He was trying to be funny, and it was working, because she too was letting the alcohol get to her. He had gotten amazing guffaws for his attempts to imitate the voice and demeanor of the clueless Judge Metcalf. She loved the story about how Metcalf at one point had dropped a pen or something else and then got off her chair to search the floor, disappearing from view for a minute while everyone else in the courtroom waited. She loved the story about how Metcalf was entirely ignorant about the hearsay rule.

Ann was the only one with whom Max could have realistically had any conversation, because to his left was Bill, a senior associate who seemed morose. A sober Max would've anxiously tried to engage Bill in conversation and find out why he was so grumpy. It was so much more rewarding, however, to keep young Ann in a laughing mood. Now he realized she was beautiful as well as young. Was she flirting with him? Was he flirting with her? As he drained the martini – the appetizers were being cleared by the attentive waiters – he realized it didn't matter who was flirting with whom. He leaned closer to Ann to say something only she would hear and was caught in pleasant surprise by the aura of her flowery perfume, so much so that he forgot what he had wanted to say.

"Do you …?" he asked, letting the question drift into nothingness.

She giggled and asked, "Do I what?"

He thought he had wanted to make a plan with her, to get together back at the hotel after dinner. But before he could formulate the right words, Phil would have to stand just then and make a speech. Max was annoyed. It was long past time for toasts. But he could see that Phil wanted to further ingratiate himself with the clients, sitting on either side of him, opposite to where Max sat around the large circular table. The interruption would have to be endured. Would there even have been anything to celebrate this evening had Max not been particularly alert in the courtroom?

"I just want to say … well, thanks to all of you here, but particularly thanks to Don and Amanda, the two best clients any law firm ever had. Let's drink to that. To our clients!"

His martini glass empty, Max raised his water glass instead. This was all a show for the clients. They controlled the purse strings. Scores of firms ached for their business. If you sucked up to them – and you had to do a slam bang job and win all your cases – they would keep the business flowing your way. Business. There had been a time when Max, first becoming interested in the legal profession, thought that it was all about doing good for the downtrodden. Like his sister. Well, maybe Kayla wasn't downtrodden at the time, but she had been a victim. It had taken Max's good common sense to see what was happening, he'd been able to rectify the bad situation before the end of Kayla's career, with the help of real lawyers – he had only been in college – and he'd somehow convinced himself that a legal career would be much more of the same. But then you get stuck. Not that he had a mountain of school debt; he had none, due to his father's substantial income as a psychiatrist. It was the damned alimony and child support he'd been paying for years. It made a necessity of continuing to run on the law firm treadmill.

By the time Phil sat, as the main courses were served, Max had lost interest in continuing the game with Ann. Women, well, at least one woman in particular, had been his downfall. Fooling around with a subordinate in the firm, beautiful though she was, as interested in him as she was, would be much worse than just marrying the wrong person at the wrong time. Any complaint against him for sexual harassment and he'd be thrown out of the firm on his ass; his legal career would be in shambles.

And there was Kayla to consider.

No Possible Way

Still buzzed by the alcohol, Max found it impossible to sleep. He was simultaneously replaying what he now considered his great success at the trial, Phil's warm acknowledgements, and his flirting with Ann. He regretted not having followed up with her. Her invitation to do so had been so obvious. He felt once again as he had in high school, inept with the opposite sex. He was both on top of the world, or at least getting near the top, professionally; he was at the bottom of the world socially, without even the vague possibility of a girlfriend, burdened by an ex-wife who had stolen Joseph and Rosina from under his nose.

Did he even know who he was supposed to be? His father was his main role model, sensible, devoted to his clients … no, to his patients, but it was the same thing. And how rotten that his father should be afflicted with this ridiculous lawsuit so late in his career. Maybe, though, there was something Max could do about it. He was a lawyer. He was creative. He was diligent. What are defense lawyers supposed to do but fight frivolous lawsuits? He had new confidence in his sense for what was practical in a given situation.

Max got out of bed and found the small pad of hotel notepaper on the desk. He reached into his briefcase for a ballpoint pen. It was the same pen with which he'd written the key message to Phil earlier in the day. No. Past midnight, it was technically the day before. Whatever, it seemed like years ago now. He drank a full glass of water to help clear his head. And he started his thinking by drawing small pictures – stick figures – on the paper in front of him. Two of the figures, standing close together, he labeled "Y." One, standing apart, he labeled "C." Gradually, through the early morning hours, the diagram grew more complicated and spread over three pages. At about five o'clock, though, he crumpled them all into the wastebasket, lay down again, and promptly fell asleep.

——

Directed to take off from work for a while, as a reward for a job well done, Max spent the morning of his first day back home doing an extra thorough cleaning and organizing of the house. Kayla would be pleased when she returned. It looked as if Jackie's artwork and toys had wandered into every conceivable corner. There were even tiny Legos under Kayla's piano. These he collected and returned to their box, which he found under Jackie's bed. When he thought he had done a reasonably good job, he stopped to make himself a cheese sandwich. The Muenster cheese was moldy, but he cut off the bad parts, hunted down the small jar of mustard in the back of the refrigerator, found the last slices of desiccated rye bread, and slapped everything together. He opened the June 19 newspaper to the sports section as he ate, to read with dismay that the former San Francisco Giants pitcher, Dave Dravecky, had just had his cancerous arm amputated. The story reminded him of Sarah's battle with cancer. He found her phone number in the small phonebook Kayla and he kept in the kitchen odds-and-ends drawer and called but got only a busy signal.

He wondered whether he should try to reach his father in Greece, both to give him the good news of the trial's outcome and to inquire about Sarah, but then decided against it. It would be nine in the evening in Greece, his father would likely have been ready to go to sleep, and in any event Max had only the monastery's number. But as his thoughts turned to his father, ideas arose once more about how Max could now do something important.

Exactly how was the question. He picked up the copy of the malpractice complaint he'd left on his desk and read through it again. He concluded it was imperative he set up a face-to-face meeting with the plaintiffs, the parents of the deceased, at a time and place where they might be amenable to hearing him out. That would be hard, as he knew nothing about them other than what he could glean from the complaint. Certainly, they wouldn't have filed anything had it not been for their lawyers, who must have convinced them they could get rich and, at the same time, honor the memory of their lost son. A suicide. Max could not fathom why any normal parents would want to prolong the grief process and display publicly at a trial the troubled nature of their offspring. Obviously, the Yahons had been severely depressed, not in their right minds, and suggestible. Max felt he could talk to the Yahons about these things in a caring, understanding way. Not as a lawyer – that would have been unethical – but as the son of the man they were persecuting.

The name Yahon might have been common in Salonika – according to his father – but it was hardly common in Brooklyn. A few telephone calls were all it took to locate the parents of the deceased. When he reached them, it was the father who answered. Max stated clearly his relationship to Nicky and made his pitch for a meeting. Any public place in which they felt comfortable. He had information for them. Yes, it was about the lawsuit, but he wouldn't say more until they were face-to-face. No, he wouldn't meet them at their lawyer's office, but, after their meeting, if they wanted to bring their lawyer into the picture he had no objection. The father was dubious, but when the mother came onto the phone and Max went through his spiel again, he detected a note of interest, almost a note of hopefulness. The Yahons conferred with each other for two minutes, during which Max could hear only the mumbling of their voices. He was encouraged they hadn't hung up immediately. Then, the father came back on the phone and agreed. They could meet him at the Information Desk of the Williamsburgh branch of the Brooklyn Public Library at six that evening. He would have five minutes to say everything he had to say.

Max checked his watch, quickly calculated how long it would take for the trains to get him into the city and to Brooklyn and to the library. He thought he could make it by six, but just barely. By car, it would be just as slow. He was on his way.

——

They had selected Williamsburgh branch library because it was just a few blocks from the Yahon's home and one block from the subway. As it was Tuesday, the library would be open until eight, more than enough time for their short discussion. He would make his pitch, the Yahons would respond, and then they would part ways, most likely never to see each other again.

Max passed a basketball court, still bathed in sunlight, and stopped for a second to watch six kids playing a cut-throat game. A boy wearing red basketball shorts and a white tee-shirt had gone in for what should have been an easy lay-up but was viciously fouled with an elbow to the head. He fell flat, dazed, but his comrades laughed, helped him up, and continued their game. Max sighed and kept walking; in less than a minute he had climbed the library's concrete steps and entered the red brick building through the arched doorway. Inside, across from the circulation desk, stood a woman who appeared to be in her early sixties, her hair hidden under a black scarf. She wore a long gray dress that couldn't have been comfortable in the heat. Her face was deeply lined and without makeup. She looked at him as if she knew him immediately, as if her eyes had been following him since he'd left his house in New Jersey.

"Mrs. Yahon?"

"Yes; you are Max."

He nodded. "Your husband?"

"Decided not to come. So say what you want to say."

He indicated that they should sit at the closest table, conveniently vacant. Even as he sat, though, he felt the first pangs of hunger. He would have to find something quick to eat in the neighborhood before getting on the subway again. It was a huge effort, Max now realized, to try to help his father, and it would probably be for naught.

"Mrs. Yahon. I want to say first how sorry I am about Shimon."

She looked at him with immensely sad eyes, but said nothing.

"My father, Dr. Covo, is terribly sad as well. As always, when someone has died."

"Who are you again? You said this had to do with our lawsuit." There was a look of confusion on her face.

"I thought I explained on the phone. Um … my father is one of the doctors you and your husband sued, because of Shimon's death."

She shrugged and waved a hand briefly, as if to suggest that she had more important things to consider.

"Mrs. Yahon, I am begging you and your husband to drop this action."

"You're his lawyer?"

"No. I am a lawyer, but not here as his lawyer. I'm here only as his son."

"Then why don't we hear from his real lawyer? Why don't we hear about how much money the insurance companies will pay us? Our son is gone."

"Yes, and that's a tragedy, but my question to you and your husband is whether you want to compound the tragedy of Shimon's death. Because …"

"Nothing matters to us anymore. Your father has no idea what it's like to lose a son. Let him suffer too."

Max paused for a few seconds, allowing her words to linger in the air. Perhaps Mrs. Yahon would hear them as well and be shocked at the depth of her desire for revenge. Finally, Max continued, softly and conspiratorially. "My father lost virtually all his family in the *Shoah*. He knows pain." He paused to think for another second, to watch her. He thought he saw a slight sign of uncertainty. She was waiting for him to go on. "He went back after the war to his house in Salonika to find that it was occupied by strangers, Bulgarians, people who had helped the Nazis, people who had never received good legal ..."

"Salonika? My family was from Salonika too. I was born there. And Yosef, too. We were lucky our parents left in the thirties, but I don't see ..."

"Mrs. Yahon ..."

"Please call me Nehama."

"Nehama, fine. Please call me Max. All I want you to know is something your lawyers probably haven't told you. If they have, and you've already accepted it, then I will leave and our business is done. But you should know that a trial ..."

"Trial?"

"Going to court. Asserting negligence in front of a judge and jury. That's what you have to do if you want to win a lot of money. In the legal profession, we often say 'rolling the dice' because the outcome is often not what we expect. In a trial, Shimon's memory, his legacy, will be ... how do I put this? ... will be harmed. Sullied. Dirtied is the way some people might put it."

"The doctor, his psychiatrist, was an animal."

"Dr. Waller. So your complaint alleges. And I have no basis to dispute that, nor do I want to. But my father was not an animal and tried his best to help your son. He just took one overnight shift at the hospital. He couldn't have known at the time what Dr. Waller was doing with your ..."

"Doing to. Doing *to* Shimon."

"Doing *to* Shimon. Exactly, Nehama. Exactly. My father couldn't have known about Shimon having been abused. But, at trial, Shimon's diary, with all the details, comes into evidence. The jury hears it, reads it, holds it. The press hears it read out loud in court, and they can write about it."

"Our lawyers say they will keep it out."

"Sure." Max shook his head gently, as if sad to hear her response. He sighed, visibly burdened by what he had to say next. "They will tell that to you, when they have no possible way of really knowing whether the judge will agree with them. Judges are … unpredictable, at best. Sometimes they're mean in ways you can't predict. Often, they don't even understand the rules of evidence. They take it out on the parties if they feel a case should have settled. You don't want Shimon's diary out in the public, do you?"

Mrs. Yahon rose suddenly from her chair, and for a second Max was sure she was going to strike him. But she sat again, as quickly as she'd risen. Max took a deep breath to calm himself; he was determined to act as if nothing had happened.

"Nehama … please. You don't have to continue the suit against Dr. Covo," he continued. "You have every right to tell your lawyer to dismiss him or to dismiss the entire suit, even against Dr. Waller's estate, to protect Shimon's privacy. Or you and your husband can agree, I guess, to a small settlement. The insurance companies would most likely be happy to get rid of the case cheaply. It's only the greed of your lawyers preventing that, but you, as the clients, have control."

"We signed papers with our lawyers. And our lawyers don't seem greedy at all, but …" There was more than a hint of question in her voice. It seemed to Max that Mrs. Yahon was begging for legal advice.

"Nehama … I am deeply sorry for your loss, and I'm sorry as well I haven't been able to say the same thing directly to Mr. Yahon. May Shimon's memory be for a blessing. I have two children, twins, young. Yet, I can't imagine the grief you are suffering. But if the worst thing happened with them – as with Shimon – I wouldn't want to prolong my agony by a big fight in court … and I wouldn't want their good names tarnished. And, honestly, I wouldn't trust my own lawyers, because they're in it only for the money they can make. They will say they care about you and your husband, but it's an act. The lawyers who represent you are good actors. That's how they make their money. They don't care the least about you or your husband or your son."

She looked down at the table. He waited a full minute, but she was immobile, a stone. As far as he could see, she wasn't crying. She was in fact hardly breathing. He couldn't tell whether she was suppressing her anger or her grief or her confusion at their meeting.

Max waited, hungry, sorry he was there, suddenly regretting he'd chosen to interfere, yet glad at the same time. He was at least trying to do something helpful for his father.

Too Wired

Nicky didn't hear the telephone ring in Andros's house. It was just after midnight, and he'd been asleep, dreaming of Adel. In the dream, he was still a young doctor, she was still his patient, and they sat together in a place vaguely resembling Nicky's office, listening to music coming from a vinyl record spinning on a turntable, Kayla performing a Chopin mazurka, slow and painfully sad. And then her music was joined by a big bass drum, banging out an erratic rhythm. Not what Chopin intended at all, Nicky thought in his dream, until he awoke to realize that Andros was rapping on the bedroom door and calling him. Nicky glanced over to see Jackie still fast asleep, his thumb in his mouth.

In Greek, Nicky spoke to Andros, who was opening the door. "What is it?"

"It's the telephone, Dr. Covo, from America, and I wish kindly you would explain to them the time difference."

"Quite sorry." He got out of bed, wearing only boxer shorts and a tee-shirt; he didn't bother to look for his robe, but strode out of the bedroom and picked up Andros's telephone.

"Yes?" he asked with more than a touch of irritability.

"Nicky. Martin Edelmann here. Sorry to bother you, but …"

"It's past midnight here. What couldn't wait until morning our time or next afternoon?"

"Damn, Nicky. You gave me this number to call if anything happened. So, I have good news, if you care to hear it."

"Okay. Shoot."

"The plaintiffs caved. They wanted to drop the case for peanuts. Five thousand from Waller's carrier and nothing from ours. It's amazing. I had to let you know as soon as possible, because I knew you were worried."

"Holy shit. I mean ... that's fantastic, but how the hell did this happen?"

"That's what I wanted to ask you. When Mark told me, he was, well, totally pissed. Something happened with his clients, he said. Here's where it gets fuzzy. They told him they had talked to another lawyer, some lawyer who convinced them to give up the lawsuit. Mark demanded to know what I'd done, whether another lawyer from my firm had approached his clients, because someone certainly has. Of course, I told him no one from my firm would ever do such a thing."

"It's not kosher?"

"Not the least bit kosher. So, anyway, Mark grumbled he was thinking seriously of starting a Bar investigation and wanted to know what I knew and, like, I don't know anything. He sputtered on about misconduct and such and finally said he hoped he would annihilate me in court if we ever had a case together again, he hoped I would be fucking disbarred, as he put it, and hung up. Weird."

"Well, yes weird. But are you sure this is final?"

"His motion to dismiss the case with prejudice was filed yesterday, and the judge signed off on it today. I wanted to wait to make sure before I called you."

"As Adel used to say, fuck a duck. Thanks for the call, and I guess I don't have to warn you not to call here again at this hour. But I appreciate the news."

"You could sound happier about it. Goodbye."

Nicky hung up and had to explain to Andros what had happened, as best he knew. All Andros could say in response was that he was going back to bed and would Dr. Covo and Jackie please try to be quiet in the morning if they got up before he did. Then Nicky had to explain it all, in simpler terms, to Jackie, who had by then gotten out of bed to see where Grandpa had gone.

With both of them back in their beds a few minutes later, Nicky realized he was too wired to sleep. Some other lawyer had gotten involved in his case? It had to have been Max, yet Nicky couldn't believe his son had jeopardized his entire legal career by involving himself in a case that wasn't his. Bar investigation? Nicky wasn't sure what might come of it, but it would likely not be good for Max. Part of him was greatly annoyed that his son had felt it necessary to intervene. It was just like Max, thinking once more that he knew better than his father about everything. It forcefully reminded him of how Max had involved himself in Kayla's contract woes, long before he'd even gone to law school. And, yes, he remembered as well how Max had been right about Kayla being cheated and that he, Nicky, had been, if not wrong, then at least negligent. Still, he was the father, Max the son, and the son should have stayed out of his father's business.

Despite his growing anger, Nicky couldn't help but feel greatly relieved the lawsuit was over. He'd not expected to escape harm so easily. At best, he thought there would have to be a trial. Now, he could give up his worries of being asked to lie, in order to save the remnant of his career. It was Max whose reputation and career were possibly on the line, not Nicky's. And what would Nicky say to Max when they were together again, in just a few days? Chastise him? Accuse him? Feign ignorance of his involvement? Let the matter never be discussed again? And what should Nicky tell Helen of all this?

It was more than an hour before he fell back to sleep. When he awoke, just before dawn, he looked over to see Jackie sleeping peacefully, apparently without a worry in the world.

Lightness

It was the last morning of their visit. Shortly before nine, a telegram had been delivered to Helen, advising that her daughter had died the day before. Jonah had offered, with their rabbi's permission, to put off the funeral until Helen got back, but Helen objected vehemently. She was a traditionalist about Jewish practice. There had been a long, emotional telephone conversation, and ultimately Jonah had given in. Helen would visit the cemetery when she returned and put a stone on Sarah's grave. She would be there – *Hashem* willing – eleven months later for the unveiling. Sarah, of blessed memory, would not be denied her burial at the proper time.

Nicky had feared that Helen might collapse at the horrible news, but Helen seemed to have expected it and maintained a stoic, if subdued, demeanor. It was barely all she could do to respond to the people who offered her condolences and hugs. In private, with Nicky, she allowed herself to cry. But it was time to pull herself together, she knew.

Andros agreed to keep Jackie occupied at his house for a while with a game of rummy, as Nicky, Helen, and Kayla, sitting on the bench in Andros's small garden, discussed their departure plans. They each had things they wanted to say privately to Theodora. They agreed that, in the early afternoon, they would say their goodbyes in some fashion. There wouldn't be time for long conversations, as they needed to get back to the airport in Thessaloniki and catch their flight.

Kayla decided that she and Jackie would say their farewells to Theodora together. She worried about what Jackie – if unsupervised – might say to Theodora about another nun who had helped Jackie and Helen fight their way through the mud of the vineyard as they carried Theodora back to the church. She worried Theodora – if unsupervised – might try to extract a promise from Jackie to someday turn to Jesus Christ and that her impressionable and loving son might so promise. Jackie accepted Kayla's dictate without complaint, but reminded Kayla that he wanted to give Theodora something to remember him by, because, as he said, he wouldn't ever see her again. Kayla had assured him that one could never know what the future might bring; the best gift he could offer Theodora, the gift she would appreciate more than anything else, was a strong hug.

Helen would make her farewell first, with Kayla and Jackie nearby, but not too obviously waiting. Nicky would be the last. He would try – against the monastery's rules – to meet Theodora briefly in her cell before his departure.

Nicky had already said goodbye to Abbess Zoe, thanking her for her counsel and making an overly generous donation to the monastery, more than twice what he'd paid to secure the women's room. In return, Zoe had thanked Nicky profusely "in the name of Our Lord Jesus Christ," and Nicky had merely smiled, recognizing it would have been rude to argue about who was whose lord.

With the plan set, it was time for the Divine Liturgy, the last service the visitors would attend. Kayla stood at the rear end of the church and listened to the nuns' chanting. She had with her a pad and pen, as Theodora had invited her to do, and waited for inspiration, but she heard nothing even remotely inspirational. Frustrated, she put her writing implements into her purse and closed her eyes, the better to listen. Maybe she could just enjoy the music for what it was, for its spirit, instead of worrying about her own lack of creativity. She would let herself feel the music rather than analyze it.

Her focus on the nuns' chanting led Kayla to think about Theodora's solemn advice of two days before. Kayla remembered verbatim. "God is everywhere. God's spirit is to everyone if they reach out. God the Creator brings His creation of music to the world through you." Well, perhaps such had been true for Kayla once, and it had stopped being true, but maybe it might be true again. So where was *Hashem* in the nuns' music? That was the place to start. Their voices were strong and certain. But wasn't it mere ornamentation, a pretty way of saying what they needed to say? *Hashem* wasn't in the music at all, because *Hashem* could not be *in* anything, although the music was in *Hashem*. Could the church itself, could the monastery, could all of Greece be in *Hashem*? Could she feel *Hashem* in this church? Theodora had told her to feel *Hashem*'s spirit, to let it in.

Kayla opened her eyes, startled to see that the inside of the church looked different, lighter than just moments before, and the lightness couldn't have been just a trick of the sun's angle. It had been bright sunlight already when she'd entered. The sunlight couldn't have grown any brighter. Kayla blinked a few times, trying to make sure nothing had gone wrong with her eyes, but the sensation that the church had grown lighter remained. Indeed, the lightness grew, not only to be perceived by her eyes, but a lightness to be felt, a lightness of spirit. And Kayla realized what had changed wasn't lightness inside the church as much as a lightness inside herself.

Kayla's gaze traveled slowly up the center aisle toward the nave. At the front, Theodora knelt before an icon of the Mother of God and her Child. Theodora crossed herself and kissed the icon. Theodora was part of the music, even though she wasn't singing. Theodora was part of the light. For a second, Kayla thought Theodora was light itself, a light spreading into Kayla when she least expected it. Kayla knew then that Theodora was the holiest of all the people she'd ever known, the closest to *Hashem*. The power of Kayla's realization knocked her back a step, and she had to sit on the edge of the window sill behind her. Hadn't Theodora told her to let the music seep into her, to feel its power?

Then the nuns began repeating a fifteen-step melodic sequence. It was in B-Minor, of all possible keys. Kayla saw the notes on the page even as she heard them, and the page of music implanted itself in her memory. No need for pad and pen. The harmonies, which bathed the melodies in light, spoke of *Hashem* and were part of the music *Hashem* had brought to the world at the time of Creation, when the world had been formed from chaos by *Hashem*'s word.

The music that Kayla would write from these beginnings – it would have to be a sonata for clarinet and piano – took shape and grew beautiful in her mind, with no effort. She listened carefully, with every fiber of her soul, and now she knew it wasn't the nuns' singing she heard but the singing and stillness of her own heart.

Nothing More to Say

Sister Theodora suggested that the best place for her to say farewells to her family was in the monastery's small library, a room little bigger than two cells conjoined. She had pushed a small folding chair into the room, its back to one of the three bookcases. There, she sat and waited for Kayla and Jackie; she prayed silently, with her eyes closed, until they entered.

"If this is a good time, Sister Theodora ..." began Kayla, but her aunt interrupted her.

"This is fine. Please to sit." Jackie made himself comfortable in the large upholstered chair across from Theodora, while Kayla took the smaller wooden rocking chair at Jackie's side.

The three looked at each other expectantly for a few seconds. Kayla wondered who would start and was not surprised when Jackie was the first to speak.

"Sister Theodora ... we're supposed to say goodbye, but I don't want to. I want to stay here, with you." He looked sheepishly at Kayla, who smiled, recognizing she could not directly contradict her son's emotional expression. He would have to be allowed to say goodbye in the way he wanted to.

"So sweet of you, Jackie. And I feel ..." Theodora stopped, trying to figure out how to best express in English what she would have found difficult even in Greek. "I will miss you very much. Even before we met, I knew you were special. I know this still to be true. But your place is with your *Ima*. The monastery, here, is my place. It's special for those who believe in Jesus Christ the Lord and you wouldn't be happy here if you stayed for a long time."

"But ... I know ... but the beautiful lady, the one who helped us in the storm. She's here."

Theodora rose from her chair and reached out toward Jackie. As if pulled by a magnet, he rose too, accepting her embrace. Theodora could feel his small body trembling. She could sense he was trying not to cry, but without success. It would be good to let him cry it out, whatever troubled his soul, she thought. After a minute, when she felt he could control his tears, she lovingly led him to sit again.

"The lady," Theodora continued, "is the Blessed Mother of God, the Theotokos, who in your language is called the Virgin Mary. And, yes, she does visit St. Vlassios, not often. The monastery -- my home – is holy to her, and I pray every day for the strength to see her. And to see my Lord Jesus Christ."

"He was the man in the picture *Ima* took away from me, the one you gave me."

"Yes, your *Ima* told me she had taken it from you. And ..." Theodora stopped and glanced at Kayla, who nodded slightly. "And I now see I was wrong to give you that gift. I wanted to return a gift to you because of the model piano you gave to me, which I still have in my cell. But I gave you the wrong thing." She sighed, still struggling for words. "You are Jewish. You have your own faith, your own tradition."

"Yes."

"Your tradition is much older than mine, but I believe in a newer and different faith. I believe in the Lord Jesus Christ."

"Jesus was a Jew."

"Yes, he was. Your rabbi has taught you well."

Theodora could see Jackie was on the verge of tears again. "But I can't have that picture of Jesus, even though he was a Jew and his mother was a Jew. She was the lady I saw in the sunlight. The lady who helped me carry you." The statement sounded like a plea and a question rolled together.

"You're much better off with pictures of your *Ima* and Grandpa and Helen, all who love you and are trying to teach you well. You are much better off to have people teach you ideas meant for the special Jewish boy you are."

"But ..."

"Jackie, if there's anything I know right now, because of spending this time with you, because you helped to save me, it's that your *Ima* and Grandpa and Helen – and your Uncle Max too – are everything you need. This picture, the icon, which is so important to me, wasn't the right thing for you, not the right gift, and I'm glad your *Ima* found it and returned it to me. And that means I will find you another present, one that is more ... one that is better for the wonderful person you are."

"What kind of present?" he asked eagerly.

"I don't know. I haven't decided yet, but when I decide, I will mail it to you in America."

"Will I ever see you again, Sister Theodora?"

"If that is God's will, then yes."

"And ... what if God says no?"

"Then we will accept – you and I – what God wants us to accept. In that, we have no choice."

"God is *Hashem*, you know."

She nodded and smiled. There was nothing more to say. But yet, as the seconds passed in silence, a new question arose in Theodora, a question she would never have thought of asking even a minute earlier. Yet, it had to be asked now, urgently.

"Jackie, will you please to forgive me, for what I did, for giving you something that wasn't meant for you?"

He smiled. "Sure. I forgive you. But now can I have one more hug?"

La ketubah de la ley

When Helen arrived at the library to say goodbye to Theodora, she was surprised that Theodora met her at the door and told Helen to follow her. Theodora placed her hand gently on Helen's arm as they walked. "It is better if we talk in my cell. No one else can listen."

"But listen to what? Why your cell?"

Theodora smiled. "You will see."

When they reached the cell, Theodora crossed herself, lit her lampada, and knelt to pray. Helen sat on Theodora's cot, wondering if Theodora was expecting her to pray too, wondering how long Theodora thought it appropriate to make Helen sit silently, waiting. She didn't have long to wait, though. After only a minute, Theodora rose, retrieved her well-worn copy of the Bible from a drawer in her night table, and sat next to Helen.

"You know the Book of Rout, *nai*?" asked Theodora, as she found the pages.

"Of course. We pronounce it 'Ruth.'"

"Ruth. Very well. I have been reading it – this is in Greek – during your visit here. It is a beautiful story, *nai*?"

"Well, I agree. But couldn't we have talked about this in the library?"

Theodora chuckled. "Yes, but I wanted to find my own copy of the Bible and ..." The sentence drifted off as, it seemed to Helen, Theodora's thought became distracted.

"And?"

"I love this passage: '*Laos sou, laos mou, kai tou theos sou, theos mou.* Your people shall be my people and your God my God.' This Moabite woman was a convert to the Jewish faith?"

"That's the only logical interpretation."

"She did not know Christ."

"No."

Theodora repeated the passage from her Bible. "*Laos sou, laos mou, kai tou theos sou, theos mou.* It's so pretty in Greek, isn't it?"

"Yes."

"It rhymes so nicely. Does it rhyme also in Hebrew?"

It was a passage Helen knew well, one she had studied with other women in Congregation Aish Ahaim. "No, not quite the same way. Let's see ... it goes '*amech ami, v'elohaich elohai.*' But still most poetic."

Theodora smiled and nodded. Then she sang the verse in Greek, softly, with a chanting melody Helen recognized from the church service, a monotone except for the last "*theos,*" which elevated a step before declining on the last "*mou.*" Theodora put down her Bible and continued, "I am too a convert. And I wonder about Ruth, whether in some way she missed the faith she grew up with."

"Nothing in the story suggests she did."

"Don't you find that hard to believe?"

"Honestly, Theodora, I never thought about it. But, as I think about it now, I would say no. I think the point of the story is to establish the devotion of the convert to the worship of *Hashem,* a devotion leading to the existence of King David."

"Yes. And through David to the Theotokos, the Holy Mother of God, and thus to Jesus, Our Savior."

"That is what Christians believe?"

"It is the truth. For me. It's what I chose to believe because I wanted to live. Because I didn't want to die locked in a closet. But, Helen, something had to be lost too. Do you see? Ruth had to give up her belief in other gods, in Chemosh, I think was the name of one."

"You feel that, despite your strong Christian faith, you have lost something?"

A puff of wind seemed to come from nowhere. The lampada sputtered a second, then went out. Theodora crossed herself, relit the lampada, and prayed for another minute before returning to the cot.

"No. I think Ruth lost something, even if the book doesn't say so, but, inside of me, there's a … how should I say? … there is still my Jewish family. I have not lost them. They brought me into this world. Ever since you and Nicky came last year, I have been thinking about my family, about Papa and Mama, and about Ada. I have watched their horrible deaths. I took myself to the railroad car and to the death camp, to watch them die. I have been praying since to Christ Our Lord for the salvation of their souls. For the peace of their immortal souls. I feel Christ has answered my prayer, that they are saved."

Helen pondered this for a long time, as Theodora looked at her, apparently expecting a response. Then Helen thought of at least one thing she could reasonably say. "It's so good of you to pray for them."

Theodora nodded ever so slightly. "So, I wonder if you know this song. I wanted to sing it for you. I remember it, somehow, from Shavuot. Maybe the last song Papa tried to teach me." In her sweet voice, Theodora began. "*La ketubah de la ley* …" [The writing of law …]

Helen knew the song well, as it had been her family's favorite when they celebrated the festival commemorating *Hashem*'s gift of the Torah to *B'Nai Yisroel*, the children of Israel. She joined in with Theodora, their two voices much stronger than one voice alone. When she could, Helen tried to harmonize. It sounded amazing to her ears. Now she understood why Theodora had wanted to meet in her cell and not the library.

"*Por muestra relasion con el Dio, toda esta en la Tora.*" [Our relationship to God is all set forth in the Torah.]

As she sang, Helen focused her sight on the flame in the lampada, entranced by its uncanny flickering. When the women finished singing, Helen looked back at Theodora to see tears streaming down her face.

One More Time

Nicky was not waiting outside her cell door as she thought he might be. After saying goodbye once more to Helen, Theodora returned to the library; there, she saw her brother waiting. Without saying anything, he engulfed her in a long hug, much longer than propriety allowed. She hugged him back, weakly at first, then with greater strength. When he finally stepped away from her, he kept hold of her hands. He was surprised to see that his sister had been crying.

"Why the tears, Kal?"

She shook her head slightly. "Your wife made me cry, singing with me, in my cell."

"Helen?"

"She has a lovely voice. We sang '*La ketubah de la ley*' together."

"I remember it well. I used to sing it to you."

"You did?"

"It helped put you to sleep."

Kal nodded. "I believe you, but I don't remember."

"Of course not. You were tiny."

They say facing each other, Theodora in the rocking chair and Nicky in the upholstered chair.

"You were going to come to my cell."

"I know. I chickened out. Against the rules. But this library is fine. So, now I guess it's ..."

"Goodbyes are hard for me, Nicky. This will be the hardest. Last year, for some reason, when you and Helen left the monastery, it was easier. Maybe, even then, I knew I would visit you soon. I could feel God telling me I would see you again."

"Is God saying something different now?"

She drew in a deep breath. It was a full minute before Theodora was able to respond.

"I don't know. I don't feel the same confidence I felt before. Even when we said goodbye in America, when I was coming back with …"

"You don't have …"

"With Abbess Fevronia, I thought we would see each other again. I had the sense there were things we still had to say. I thought maybe it would be years, but that there would come a time. And the time came, didn't it? Much sooner than I imagined. You brought your family. You brought Jackie. And that has made me happy beyond words, to be with all of you. To see him again. Now, though, saying goodbye … something has changed. I don't know what."

"Nothing can change that I love you, my sister, and always will. Nothing can change the miracle of finding you again here – when I was certain that you had died long before. It has been the main blessing of my life. And confessing to you helped me so much in dealing with guilt, about the lives I took and the lives I couldn't save." His smile broadened. "And a part of me still wishes – although it can't be – that you come to live with me in New York."

"You're right. It can't be."

"I accept that, yes. But you could visit us again, maybe in another year. Maybe two. Maybe five. We will write to each other."

"As you have learned, my dear brother, I am not much of a writer."

"Well, you have a point. Still, I can write to you. And, as for your not writing back, I understand, and I forgive you, which is why I think more likely we'll stay in touch – as closely as possible – by telephone. Are you crying again? This is the first time I've seen you cry, since you were … six."

Theodora forced herself to smile, as she wiped tears away with a tissue. "How could we not cry? Helen's daughter has died. I have sinned in wanting Jackie to be someone other than who he wants to be. And I will miss you very much."

"Will you visit us again?"

Theodora looked down, not being able to bear Nicky's hopeful face. "I don't think so, as much as you would want me to. Not unless I am commanded to do so by the Lord Jesus Christ. My Lord wants me to stay here at the monastery, where I am needed, and where I feel I am home, truly at home. And on my last trip, there was such bad luck … death."

"But also good. Please don't forget that."

"Nicky … this is where my heart sings, where I can hear the music of Heaven."

He nodded, resigned. "I understand, Kal. You are in the place that God wants you to be. I accept that. You made the right choice, and we are all blessed by your being here and being who you are. I will miss you terribly, too, Kal. And someday I will be back, I promise, if Abbess Zoe gives her blessing for such a visit. So, Kal … hug me one more time please before I leave."

The Half-Melody

Grandpa would drive down soon, and Jackie had been told to pack his suitcase, carefully put his clarinet away in its case, and wait with Andros. Then Grandpa, *Ima*, and Helen would pick him up, and the four of them would go back to the airport. In a little less than a day, he would be home again. In less than a week, he was sure to see Rabbi Beck at the *Chabad*, who would ask about his trip to the monastery, and he would see *HaMoreh* Aharon as well.

He felt sad their visit was ending, although Theodora's promise of a new, better gift lightened his spirits a bit. The grownups all seemed sad, too, but for another reason. Helen's daughter, Sarah, had died, he knew, and Helen was crying a lot, although she tried to hide it. And *Ima* and Grandpa were sad because Helen was sad. They had tried to explain to him about cancer, but it was hard for him to picture. He had always been taught that growing was good. He was supposed to grow up. *Ima* always complimented him on how well he was growing. So when he learned about cancer, that something growing in your body can make you terribly sick and cause you to die, it made little sense. Yet, it had happened. Ezra's *Ima* was not alive anymore. Ezra would be very sad, too. When Jackie got back home, he would have to say something to Ezra and worried what he could say.

First Abbess Fevronia, now Sarah, and he wondered whether he himself had done something to make them die. Was it because he had not been strong enough in obeying *Hashem*'s laws? Sister Theodora was involved in all of this. Because of the things she had done – encouraging him to pray with her, giving him the icon, taking him to visit Fevronia's grave – *Hashem* might be punishing him and his family, and now Helen and his good friend Ezra had suffered as well.

Filled with nervous energy, Jackie opened the clarinet case and looked over at Andros, who had been reading the newspaper. "May I play again? Until they come?"

Andros smiled, putting down the sports section of the *Kathimerini* and reaching instead for his pipe. "*Nai. Ecso apo,*" was Andros's response as he pointed toward the door.

So Jackie moistened the reed as he walked outside and wondered what he might play. Then he thought he remembered the half-melody of the nuns' chanting. He would try that. It was music that sounded like how he felt. Sad. Seeking. Pleading. Needing to know. A prayer perhaps.

Jackie could not be sure *Hashem* would listen or, if He did, whether He would care.

Salachti

Shiva

It wasn't technically a *shiva* service, because seven days had passed after Sarah's burial. Delays had interfered with the return of Helen and the others from Greece. The fierce storms had both messed up the airlines' schedules and damaged the main runway at Thessaloniki's airport. And, after they had gotten home, Helen had wanted a few days of relative isolation. Finally, when Helen felt sufficiently able, Jonah scheduled another *minyan* at his house, and he knew many fellow members of Congregation Aish Ahaim would attend. It would give Helen – who had spent a very quiet week with them, mostly sleeping in their guest room as far as Jonah could tell – a chance to receive the condolences of her friends. When Kayla told Jackie that Grandpa was picking her up to go to Sarah and Jonah's house for the *minyan*, he insisted on coming along, and Max said he would go as well.

The *minyan* would combine *mincha* and *ma'ariv* – afternoon and evening prayers – and begin at eight. When Nicky and the others arrived ten minutes before the appointed hour, they encountered a house that was already jam-packed, everyone forced to squeeze past one another if they needed to move. Nicky wondered how he would find Helen in the mess of visitors and family when, happily for him, she reached a hand past a large man wearing a blue sweater and grabbed his arm.

"Helen. Glad you found me. So many people."

"There's a lot," she agreed. "Some I worked with twenty years ago … wow, there's Bill Newman. Haven't seen him in ages. It's comforting they're here."

"Can I do anything for you?"

She tried to smile, but the smile faded quickly to the somber expression Helen had worn since receiving the news of Sarah's death. "Just be here with me."

Despite her grief, Helen looked okay to Nicky. Yes, although sadness enveloped her, her hair had been washed and combed, and her dark gray dress was attractive, flattering Helen's slim figure. Nicky marveled at Helen's extraordinary strength. By the time she'd gotten home from Greece, she seemed to be keeping it together. They'd talked quite a bit about Sarah on the flight, and Nicky had tried to convince Helen – who was miserable with self-doubt – that she'd done the right thing by insisting on no delay of the funeral.

Jonah himself led the *minyan*. Prayer books for a house of mourning had been passed around, but there were twice as many people as books, so some visitors shared the books, and the more knowledgeable attendees – Nicky included – recited the prayers by heart. During the first mourner's *kaddish*, as Nicky watched her closely, Helen looked a bit shaky on her feet. But it was when Jonah asked Helen if she wanted to say a few words about Sarah before *ma'ariv* – it was not yet dark enough for the evening prayer – that Helen broke down. Her heartrending sobs caught everyone by surprise; Nicky had his arm around her in an instant and stopped her from collapsing. She pressed her head into his chest as he led her upstairs through the throng of visitors. Kayla followed, but Jonah stayed among his guests because he had to lead the service. It was now just dark enough to begin.

Helen had been doing so well, everyone said.

———

After the service, the crowd did quick work on the bagels, lox, and cream cheese that Jonah and the older kids had set out; holding paper plates and plastic cups of Dr. Brown's cream soda, they chatted about nothing in particular. It would be rude to rush away. Their presence there was necessary to bolster the spirits of the bereaved. Nonetheless, within twenty minutes after the service, the last visitors made their sorrowful goodbyes to Jonah and the kids.

Little Ezra offered his hand to whoever reached for it and allowed himself to be hugged by visitors willing to bend to his level. He wore the black wool cap that Jackie had given him upon returning from Greece. It was too large and fell to the top of Ezra's eyes. Still, he wore it with pride, a treasured gift from his step-cousin, just like the black wool cap Jackie himself was now wearing. Both had been acquired at a shop in the Thessaloniki airport.

When it was quiet, Helen returned downstairs. Jonah came into the living room from the kitchen, glanced at Helen, and, convinced she was not going to collapse again, moved to clean up the plates and cups left on the coffee table.

But Nicky intervened. "Sit down, Jonah, just a minute." Jonah pulled the bench away from the upright piano gracing one side of the room. As he sat, Jonah thought it had been years since anyone had played the piano. He'd wanted to sell it, but Sarah had refused, thinking that she might start piano lessons again if she had the time. And now, Jonah worried, how could they ever sell it? It was as if it had become a part of Sarah that could never be allowed to leave the house.

Jonah turned to face Helen, who sat next to Nicky on the sofa, and took a deep breath. "Today, all the friends here, has been hard on you. Perhaps we shouldn't have planned this last *minyan*."

Helen took her son-in-law's hand. "No, Jonah. Our friends wanted to come back again. They needed to come back when I was here. I'm glad we did this and ..." Helen stopped to wipe tears from her eyes with tissues clutched in her right hand. Everyone waited, recognizing she needed time to say whatever it was she wanted to say. There was a minute of silence, broken only by Jonah's oldest child Rivka, a college senior, coming in to clear away the trash. Rivka, too, had red eyes. When she saw Helen crying and everyone watching Helen, she too sat and waited.

Finally, Helen spoke. "Jonah, I am so sorry I was not here when I needed to be. Such a terrible, terrible mistake for me ...."

"Helen, please stop. You've told me many times how sorry you are, but, as I've said, no one could know that Sarah would go ... so quickly ..."

"Can you ..."

"And I do forgive you. I do forgive you. The whole family forgives you. And there's nothing to forgive. What's done is done. We just want you to get through this as well as ... as much ..."

Jonah left the piano bench and moved to the sofa; Nicky got out of the way. There, Jonah and Helen hugged. Nicky could not bear to watch Helen cry so freely, so he turned to Kayla, but she was also crying. He reached out and took Kayla's hand, then noticed Max and Jackie staring at the scene from the doorway. Max had a comforting adult hand on Jackie's shoulder. Catching Max's eyes, Nicky gestured toward Kayla, and Max gently pushed the boy toward his mother.

"I wish Sister Theodora was with us now, too," Jackie said. "And her friend too, the orange lady, the one I saw in the sunlight, the nice lady I wasn't supposed to see." His comments had them all smiling for a second.

Kayla hugged her son, kissing him on the top of his head. They would be a family and help Helen get through this, she thought.

Coffin

Jackie and Ezra had made their way to the large basement playroom of Ezra's house as soon as the *minyan* started. Other than his wearing the too-large black cap Jackie had given him, Ezra seemed normal. Jackie wasn't sure what he'd expected. *Ima* had told him that Ezra would be sad and depressed. She'd had to explain to Jackie what she meant by "depressed." But Ezra didn't seem like a person who had no energy, who might not even want to get out of bed in the morning. It must be, Jackie concluded, that Ezra was sad inside. There were times Jackie was sad inside, too.

Jackie was sad when *Ima* had told him that Aliyah should stay with Ezra a couple of extra weeks, that Ezra needed her. He'd protested mildly, he needed Aliyah to sleep with, as always, but *Ima* was firm on the subject. Two more weeks, she said, and they were almost over. He'd soon have her back. Jackie looked over to see Aliyah curled up inside a tipped-over carboard box pushed up against the basement wall. The cat seemed to be ignoring both of them.

"Do you want to play lightning tag?" asked Ezra, as he kicked a blue plastic ball – the size of a soccer ball – toward Jackie.

"Sure."

"I'm it first. You run, but only when I count from three." Ezra picked up the ball, held it over his head, and began counting. "Three, two, one, the game starts now!"

With that, Jackie ran to the other end of the room, Ezra chased him, threw the ball at him but missed, and for a few seconds Jackie had forgotten he was supposed to say something to Ezra. *Ima* had tried to coach him. Then he remembered what was happening upstairs, why Helen had been crying so much, why others were crying. Jackie stopped trying to escape Ezra as he worried about what he was supposed to say, and Ezra took the opportunity to throw the ball with surprising strength at Jackie's midsection from three feet. The ball bounced hard off the boy.

"Oh! You got me!"

"Now you're it."

"Okay, but wait. I have to say something."

"No, let's play."

"I will, but I'm supposed to say I am very sorry … for your loss. Let's sit on the floor and shoot the ball."

"Okay, but I go first."

They sat on the tattered green rug that occupied a corner of the room, eight or nine feet from each other, and started their game, rolling the blue ball at each other as hard as they could. Ezra was as playful as ever, and Jackie felt that he might not have heard the first time.

"Ezra, I am very sorry for your loss, about your *Ima*, you know."

Ezra picked up the ball rather than shooting it back toward Jackie. "Why?"

Ezra was going to make this difficult, but Jackie had promised *Ima* he would say to Ezra what she'd instructed him to say. "Because she's … You know. Because she died."

"Oh, I know." He rolled the ball back to Jackie with a little less force. "That means she's just on a long trip."

Did Ezra not understand death? Did he not go to his *Ima*'s funeral and see the coffin, the word Jackie had learned the previous year, when Abbess Fevronia had died, the box they used to bury dead people? That would explain it. Maybe Ezra wasn't sad because he was too young to see the truth of what had happened. But Jackie couldn't just leave it at that. He was much older. He had to share what he knew of the world. Ezra looked up to him. He couldn't lie to Ezra, even if everyone else had.

"Your *Ima* was sick, right?"

"She threw up a lot. But she's better now. *Abba* told me that she doesn't hurt any more. That's why she went on this long trip, to keep feeling better. Let's run around, I'm tired of sitting here. I'm it. You run to the other end while I count."

Standing, Ezra again held the ball over his head.

"Come on! Get up and run away from me!"

Jackie did as Ezra ordered. *Ima* would ask him later if he'd told Ezra how sorry he was, and he would need to explain that Ezra didn't understand, that he had tried to help Ezra see the truth, but Ezra wasn't ready yet. Ezra might be depressed inside, but his outside wasn't aware of it.

"I said run away! You have to play by my rules!"

Ezra could be bossy. Aliyah chose that moment to run out of her cardboard box and up the stairs to the main floor of the house.

"Three, two, one, the game starts now!"

Ten Minutes

Kayla told Rabbi Beck of her decision and that she still needed one more well-supervised meeting with Aharon, and he'd agreed again to let them use their porch. Then she'd called Aharon, asked him without more comment if he could join her there, and it was arranged.

As the hour approached, Kayla felt her nerves were electric wires that had crossed and were sparking madly before shorting out. She was angry at herself for feeling so out of joint. She knew what she had to do. She knew she had to be strong, but felt she could also be kind. The meeting would be short, for there was nothing Aharon might say to dissuade her. Although cutting herself off from what had promised to be a meaningful relationship made her sad, although she feared never having another opportunity, she knew Aharon was not the right man for her. There was too much about him she could not trust. She told herself it had nothing to do with his sexual problems. She sensed deeper problems that he had not come close to revealing. She sensed issues that would always underlie their relationship and that she would be powerless to overcome. If she were to live with him, share his bed, maybe even bear his children, she would still always be distant from Aharon's inner core, and she didn't want to live the rest of her life fearing what might lie there.

Could she come to love him, if they were married and lived together for years? She laughed to herself, thinking of the song from

Fiddler on the Roof where Tevye wants to know if Golda loves him. It was true that love might come after living with a spouse as opposed to before. But was the possibility of such love enough to keep a relationship together if, at the bottom, there was no trust? If, at the bottom, there was just fear? Kayla doubted it. The fear of the unknown, the fear of coming to harm at the hands of another, was never far from her consciousness. She knew that fear was also a symptom of her illness, but sometimes, she thought with dismay, a person can be both paranoid and in real danger.

The meeting went off as well as Kayla could have imagined. She stated simply that she did not feel a long-term relationship would work. She didn't try to explain why. She didn't try to blame herself, nor did she try to blame Aharon. They both began their meetings in good faith, they both had treated each other fairly, and they both would now be better off opening themselves to other relationships. She didn't even try to pretend that they could continue as friends. Yes, Aharon might end up being Jackie's teacher at *Chabad* for a year or two, and she would treat him with the respect and attention any teacher deserved. That would be it.

For his part, Aharon acted honorably. He was visibly hurt, he asked a few questions testing the firmness of Kayla's rejection, but he seemed relieved at the end.

In ten minutes, it was over.

In Search of a Pulse

Sarah had refused all painkillers, wanting to be fully aware of what was going on. It felt as if every one of her organs had turned against her. She imagined at times that a swarm of invisible ants had invaded her, climbing through her mouth, nose, ears, and vagina and, once gaining entrance, releasing poison into every cell of her body. There were moments when the pain mounted from a dull ache to utter agony, and she came close a few times to begging for relief, but always gritted her teeth and waited until the severe pain passed. She had endured the greater pain of giving birth to three children. She would stay awake and cognizant as long as she could, relishing every second *Hashem* granted her to remain alive.

So she knew that the rest of her family had gathered around her, taking turns sitting next to her bed and holding her hand. Everyone was there but her mother, whom Sarah had urged not to come home. Sarah well knew she was lying when she told her mother she was doing well. Her time left alive was very short, and Sarah reasoned it would do no good for her mother to start for home, only to find on arrival that she had been too late. And if her mother could make it to her bedside before the light left Sarah's eyes forever, what then? Sarah knew her mother well, knew she would suffer the most by watching for the end. As her father lay dying, Sarah had seen the anguish her mother suffered; she wanted to spare her that kind of torture.

Despite having foresworn the offered narcotics, Sarah drifted in and out of awareness. When she could focus briefly on the faces of those around her, she could easily see their fear. Danny seemed to turn away whenever Sarah looked at him. Only Ezra seemed his normal self, repeatedly begging Sarah to get out of bed and play with him.

She tried to talk to Jonah. There was so much she wanted to say. But the power to speak had left her. She could muster only one weak word – "home" – and was not even sure herself what she meant by that. She was home, with the family around her.

During the months since her diagnosis, she had tried many times to tell him how lucky she'd been to meet him and to have created with him their family, but the right words would never come to mind. There had been times when they had calm and deliberate conversations about what was to come, but always with the express hope if not expectation she would be the miracle, the one in five to beat the odds. Yes, the children's futures were relatively secure; they'd had the foresight a decade earlier to insure Sarah's life for five hundred thousand dollars, what seemed then to be ridiculously excessive. Now, every penny would be needed. Yes, down the road, if Jonah was really lonely, then of course he should feel free to involve himself in new relationships; Sarah would not begrudge him that from the grave.

As death lurked nearby, only minutes away, Sarah knew she had waited too long to say to Jonah the things she should have said. That Sarah would not have had any meaning in her life had she and Jonah not found each other. That their kids were gifts from God, amazing human beings with the potential to change the world for the better. That Jonah should make sure their kids had the best possible education and a solid home to return to whenever they needed it. That they should remember always how much she loved them and enjoy the fullest possible lives without her.

How long had her eyes been closed? It seemed like ages since she had last forced them open to see who was still in the room. She thought everyone had been there – everyone but her mother – but that had been so long ago. But where was her mother? Why hadn't she come? Couldn't she understand how badly Sarah needed her?

She knew her breathing had stopped minutes earlier. That was one less thing to struggle with. Then, Sarah listened inside herself to the weakening beat of her heart, listened carefully until she realized her heart had stopped beating. If she'd had the strength to speak, she would have announced to all around her that she'd reached this major lifetime milestone, her heart's cessation. And she badly wanted to tell them about the strange flash of warm orange light around her.

She felt someone take hold of her left wrist. It must have been Jonah. He pressed two fingers tightly into her flesh, in search of a pulse. "She's gone," she heard him say. She wanted to argue with him. She couldn't be gone yet, if she had felt him, if she had heard him. And yet she knew he had spoken the truth.

No Easy Answers

Sitting at her piano, Kayla carefully reviewed her notes from Greece, now and then playing a short segment of the possible melodies for the first themes of her sonata-form movement. To write for the clarinet – an instrument she knew only because Jackie was addicted to it – was a challenge. It struck her at times as an absurdity. The clarinet part would end up sounding not as a clarinet part should at all; no one would want to perform it, even if Kayla herself accompanied. But these realizations did not dissuade her from making the effort. For the first time in months, she felt she had musical ideas worthy of being developed. She could feel the blockage crumble, as a dam springs one leak, then another, before caving in entirely and allowing a cascade of water. Water was exactly the right metaphor, she thought as she immersed herself in the task of composing.

Kayla was unaware of the passage of time, the light dwindling from mid-afternoon brightness to dusk. She looked again at the staff paper on which she had been composing for hours. How was it possible? The first movement of a sonata had been roughed out. There were smudges across the pages where she had erased many notes, but what lay before her was legible. She played again the piano part, ignoring the clarinet lines, to hear whether it was worthy in its own right, and smiled as she did so, sensing she'd made good progress. The music sounded like her, what she believed music should be, what the piano could express in its complexity, emotions of longing, frustration, and ultimate resolution.

Then she played again more slowly, as she sang the clarinet part. Her voice was weak at first, reflecting her fear of expressing the full power of the music. But then she let her voice get stronger. The clarinet would indeed be like a song telling of the mystery of *Hashem*. It was exactly what Kayla had hoped she could create.

There was enigma in the union of the two instruments. It was not an entirely happy relationship. The clarinet wanted to dominate and struggled always to gain an upper hand, and so Kayla had to force her voice louder over many measures. And there were the discordances. Kayla's music would not always go where one might have expected it to go. Her music was neither tonal nor atonal. She thought of it, in places, as a race, the instruments complementing each other, yet bouncing off each other, as they fought for the lead. She thought of it, in places, as lovers trying to mate. She had imbued it with a romantic yearning for union. And then the movement ended abruptly, on the pleading note of a question, just when a listener might have hoped for a more definitive answer.

Kayla finally became conscious of noises coming from her kitchen, of Max fixing dinner for Jackie. How had it gotten late so quickly? She should have prepared the meal. She was chagrined, yet thankful the two men in her life had left her alone, recognizing she was absorbed in her composing. They had made a large space in which she could work, and she'd taken advantage of it. What she'd written, albeit rough, was something she could refine over the next days and weeks, and a second and third movement would follow quickly. She no longer doubted that she'd be able to continue. Whatever had blocked her had moved out of the way. Or been pushed.

She read through the first movement again and could hear it clearly; the two instruments played together in the room with her. As she listened, her thoughts drifted to Aharon. Yes, there were turns in the music that undoubtedly sprang from the turns of their relationship. She realized she'd been conscious of Aharon throughout her composing. It was certainly why she'd let the first movement end as suddenly as she had, uncertain, with the emptiness of longing.

There could be no easy answers. No direction, either to or away from Aharon, was possible. But there were two more movements of her sonata to craft. The notes she'd saved from hearing *malachim* in her dream, which she thought might be good for a second movement, were sufficient to start with, but would the second movement be a song of love never consummated or would the two instruments find their answers in each other? And would the third movement be a tumultuous explosion, an exposition of anger, neglect, and sorrow, or would it be a riotous dance of hope? She knew she could go either way. Both would work.

The Smartass Lawyer

Nicky and Helen had casually discussed the matter a few times, but Nicky felt he now had to make a firm decision. After *shloshim* – after Helen's thirty days of saying *kaddish* were over – he told Helen they were going out for dinner and chose what he knew would be a quiet restaurant, where they could talk without being distracted. They had been to Miriam once before, and it would be quiet enough.

They made small talk and ordered. Helen nursed her glass of sparkling water, eyeing Nicky as he sipped his bourbon. Then they fell unusually quiet, both waiting for each other to speak. Finally, Helen broke the silence. "So, you wanted to talk again? Seriously, you said. Here we are."

Before he could respond, the waiter brought their meals, grilled Halloumi cheese and artichoke heart salad for Helen and latkes with extra sour cream for Nicky. Their conversation again subsided as they tasted their food, smiled, and agreed that everything was amazing; Miriam had again done an outstanding job. But soon, Helen put down her fork deliberately. "Please, Nicky. Get started with whatever you want to say. Let's get it out in the open."

"All right. I think I'm done … No … I am done with psychiatry. What I want to do is give notice to all my patients tomorrow, maybe see a few over the next week, and then put my office up for sublet. Or try to sell the practice."

Helen nodded. "I thought that's what this talk was about, and I won't tell you not to, if you're committed, but I expected you'd try to just slow down and phase out over a longer period."

"Yes. Well, it's what I expected too, for a while."

"The Yahon thing got to you badly, didn't it?"

"You know it did. But it wasn't only this fucking lawsuit. It's what I almost did to get out of it and, then, it's how it *did* go away; I didn't like any of it."

"You're losing me."

"I should have told you this much earlier, but I didn't understand what was going on. I wasn't sure."

"But now you're sure? About what?"

"Edelmann wanted me to lie in an affidavit, or that's how I saw it. I seriously considered doing that, anything to avoid the burden of having to go to trial."

"But you didn't, obviously. They dropped the lawsuit without you having to lie." There was definitely a touch of a question in Helen's response.

"I wanted to," Nicky sighed.

"Nicky, if you wanted to, you would have done so immediately. The only thing holding you back was your conscience. But, go on, about ... how did it go away?"

"When the case settled, Edelmann told me that the plaintiffs' attorney was royally pissed, because some lawyer – some unidentified lawyer – had improperly contacted his clients and convinced them to drop the case. The plaintiffs' lawyer begged his clients, the parents, to say more specifically what had happened, who had approached them, but they clammed up. They won't cooperate with their own lawyer."

"And ..."

"It was Max."

"How do you know?" Helen was certain Nicky had to be right, but she needed to hear the whole story.

"I confronted him two days ago, when you were visiting Jonah and the family, and I begged off with a headache."

"I remember doubting you even then, but I didn't feel like arguing."

"By the time I got to their house, Kayla was putting Jackie to bed, and I just sat Max down in the living room and asked him directly. Or accused him, I should say. I could tell from the look on his face he'd done what I suspected, and he admitted it. I don't think I've ever been so angry at him, but … I didn't lash out. I kept my cool and just asked him why. I asked him why he'd put his entire legal career in jeopardy. I told him what Edelmann had said, that there could be a Bar investigation. I told him – although he knew this already, I'm sure – that he could be disbarred." Nicky drained the last bit of bourbon from his glass.

Helen shook her head, dismayed by her recognition of the threat to Max's career. "What did he say?"

"Something to the effect that he knew I wouldn't help myself. He knew, unless he took action – those were his exact words – 'took action' – that I would let this lawsuit crush me."

"And did he say anything else?"

"He scoffed at the idea there'd be an investigation and, he said, if there was, he would beat it. He sounded like the smartass lawyer he always wanted to be. I can't say I have a lot of love for the legal profession. And I'm so disappointed in him. He's proud of what he did and doesn't see it as dishonorable."

"He loves you, Nicky. He admires you so much, and, well, what he did was wrong, from one point of view, but right when you consider it was a son doing what he could for his father."

"I know he loves me, but … I can't imagine why. I feel like I'm always coming up short in his estimation."

"Nonsense. You're not coming up short. He's very proud of what you've done, what you've accomplished in life, how you've helped so many." Helen tried to make her voice soothing and encouraging, but thought while she did so that Max did often see himself as superior in many ways to his father. "So, how did this sit-down with Max end?"

Nicky shrugged. "I thanked him, even though – as I made clear – he'd done something stupid. I forgave him, although I'm not sure if I was the one who needed to forgive. The Yahons are more likely the ones who need to forgive him. This might not be over for them – if they are called to testify at a Bar hearing – even though, thanks to my son, they obviously want this whole thing to end."

"You forgave Max. That's the important thing."

They finished their main courses in silence, and by the time it came to order dessert, their moods had lightened. Nicky ordered a second bourbon, and Helen asked for another glass of wine. They shared a Greek lemon-olive oil cake.

NJ Devils

It was already past midnight, and Max was unable to sleep. Too many things were on his mind. As soon as he stopped thinking of one thing, he began thinking of another.

Foremost was his concern he'd placed his career in jeopardy. Of course, he knew it was unethical for him to act as he had. He was not a friend of the Yahons. He was not even an acquaintance when he pushed them to drop the case against his father. He had in fact told them he was a lawyer, claiming for himself a professional expertise and undercutting the relationship between the Yahons and their own lawyers. And then he'd relied upon his expertise in the advice that he'd given. Did he deserve to be disbarred? He wasn't sure, but, if there was an investigation, he imagined he would be disciplined in some way, even though he'd professed a lack of concern to his father. He knew that, even if the Bar decided merely to slap him on the wrist, his firm would fire him in a heartbeat. Maybe they'd fire him even before the Bar took action, just on the basis of the investigation. It didn't matter if he had helped Phil dodge the bullet in a big case. It didn't matter that his efforts at trial had helped the firm keep one of its most important clients. Nothing mattered other than the firm having to keep its nose clean and disentangle itself from a lawyer under suspicion for having acted unethically.

And when these ruminations subsided, they were replaced by concerns about Kayla's life. He knew she'd broken off with Aharon; she'd admitted as much. But why she had done so was another matter. She refused to say, seemingly embarrassed by the question, and Max did not pursue the issue. So, without having a reason, Max felt guilty himself, fearing he must have encouraged Kayla to reject a perfectly reasonable suitor. He tried to replay in his mind their conversation at dinner they had shared with him. Had he manifested antagonism toward Aharon? Had he at some other time conveyed the idea that Kayla's departure from his house, taking Jackie with her, would be a major, irredeemable loss to him? Then it came to him with a shock. He had specifically warned Kayla against Aharon. He had said … what was it? Something bad. He'd said Aharon was weird in some way. Off. Yes, that's what he'd told Kayla. He'd planted a seed that had taken root and in its full flowering had broken them apart. Just because of … what? His jealousy? His fear of inconvenience?

And when neither his situations in the law firm or with Kayla were uppermost in his mind, he thought about the twins, missing them terribly, still wanting to understand, after so many years, how they had been stolen from him by their mother. It was a permanent stain on his life that he could not see them grow up on a day-to-day basis, that he was left with inadequate phone calls and annual, frustrating, and too-short visits.

As he finally got drowsy, he heard a noise in the hallway. It sounded like Kayla's footsteps. Was she just on her way to the bathroom? Then he heard her make her way downstairs, presumably to get something warm to drink. She would do that occasionally. He got up, put on his bathrobe and slippers, and followed her.

"You can't sleep either?" she asked as he walked into the kitchen. She was pouring milk into a Brooklyn Dodgers coffee mug. She, too, was dressed in a bathrobe, light blue. He could see she wore dark purple pajamas beneath her bathrobe.

"Not my best night." He reached into the open cupboard to take out his favorite NJ Devils mug, poured milk himself, and they heated their mugs together in the microwave.

"What's on your mind?" she asked a minute later, sipping carefully.

He shrugged. "Not important, I guess."

"If you don't want to talk, fine."

"Except …"

"Except what?"

"A lot of what was keeping me up was about you."

"Oh," she said, looking away suddenly toward the window, where nothing could be seen in the night's darkness, not even lights from the street or from the house next door.

"I wonder if it was something I did, something I said … you know … why you and Aharon have stopped meeting. I feel so sick, now as I think about it, that I suggested Aharon was peculiar in some way. I'd feel terrible if my comments were why you've stopped seeing him."

"That's silly, Max. That's not the reason at all. I thought I'd assured you weeks ago. Honestly, you were right about Aharon. But I had to discover his problems for myself. It took me too long to understand."

"Look, you don't owe me any explanation."

They fell silent as they drank their milk. Kayla was mulling over how she might give Max a more complete explanation, so he wouldn't have to imagine her breakup with Aharon was his fault. It was just like him, she thought, to feel the world revolved around him, that nothing could happen near him unless he himself was responsible. And, damn, Max *had* been right.

"Max … Aharon was … no, let me say this correctly … you sensed it somehow. Aharon is a troubled man."

"What do you mean?"

"I mean … he's solid in some ways. I think he's probably a good teacher. He must be talented, although I've never heard him play. He's outwardly observant."

"Outwardly?"

"If I said he has inner demons, would that make sense?"

"It might."

"I shouldn't be saying this, not to you, probably not to anyone but a therapist, but … he wanted to use me. Physically. I don't think he cared about me as a person, nor would he ever have cared."

"Kayla, please, you've said …"

"No, Max. I'm going to finish. I've got to say this, particularly to you, because you tried in your best way to warn me, and now you're the one losing sleep." She waited a second or two. When he no longer objected, she continued. "I wanted him, too. I was willing to, you know … let him. We were in a hotel room, when I told you I was going to *Chabad*. It was because of his urging me, but I was a willing participant, may *Hashem* forgive me. And then it turned out … he couldn't do what he wanted to do. And I knew it was a sign from *Hashem*, who was trying to keep me from sinning further."

"That's … I don't know what to say. But this isn't the kind of conversation a brother and sister should be having."

"Well, we're not just any brother and sister. And who else I should talk to instead … to Dad? Who else but you *could* I talk to?"

"Helen?"

"You talk to Helen it's like talking to Dad. Do you know I walked in on them, *in flagrante*, at the monastery? Not even in a bed, but on the floor of a shed!"

"Holy shit."

"You're worried about the two of us having a conversation about sex, and yet you're looking at a grown woman who basically saw her elderly father doing it with his wife. *That* is something that should never happen. I mean, my seeing it. It wouldn't have happened had it not been for the monster storm."

"Still …"

"And I wasn't *looking* for them. I was looking for Jackie."

"That's horrible. That you had to see them."

"Well, I mean, it's not the worst thing in the world. It was kind of funny, to be honest, to see Dad so embarrassed." As she thought back to those few moments, she blushed deeply. "Jesus ...."

"But, about Aharon … you said something about demons?"

Kayla gently bit her lip, wondering if she could explain better than she already had. "At his core, or so I sensed, he doesn't believe. He's lost, if you will. Sexual problems are only a small manifestation of something troubling him. At least, those were the vibes I finally got. Well, there it is. Do you think you can sleep now? I've been honest and said things maybe I should've kept private, but I've told you. I owe you at least that much, I hope you believe me, and I hope you'll be able to sleep."

"It's not because you're afraid of marriage and what that would mean for our relationship? I mean, the relationship here, in this house, of you and Jackie living with me?"

She didn't answer. Instead, she moved from her chair to where Max sat, leaned over, kissed him on the top of his head, and hugged him. She could sense a tenseness on his part, but he seemed quickly to bring that under control and relax. Then he stood, and when he tried to hug her, she allowed it for a half second, but stepped back abruptly, making sure the belt of her robe was tightly knotted.

"Maybe. Maybe I'm a little afraid after all. I need you, Max. I love you. The life we live here."

"Because … you know. I would manage."

"You would, you've always been able to find a way to manage, no matter what trouble found its way to you, but I'm not sure about me."

Another Unwanted Change

I've debated whether to add a short note here. This story, all about family, has left me little more than an afterthought. Fine, but there are things I need to get out of my fur.

A story about family? I don't remember my mother or brothers or sisters. My earliest memory is of living in a shelter and then one day being picked up by Kayla. She was going to adopt me, for which I was very glad, but the thing is, as I soon discovered, she didn't want me for herself. She wanted me for her father and gave me to him as a surprise. He was surprised, all right, but not in a good way. Look. His apartment was fine, oceans of milk better than the shelter. And it's not that I was ungrateful for having been rescued. Indeed, I had plenty of room to run around in and hide. But the thing is that her father didn't want me. He ignored me as best he could. You could tell that it was a big chore for him to put down my food and clean out my litter box. Oh well, I thought. I knew things could be a lot worse. But I was a kitten (still am, as a matter of fact), and I would have liked a bit of play.

Then, to my surprise, Kayla's father gave me back to Kayla – or to her son, Jackie, to be exact.

Jackie is a bit more playful, he tosses me his used reeds, and he lets me sleep with him, which I will do every once in a while. Honestly, his bed is too soft for my liking, so I prefer to sleep on the floor underneath. At times, though, he's so needy. He will beg me to get under the covers with him, and I know it will be easier for me to get to sleep if I just give in. I say to myself: "Aliyah, this is a good life. Be happy about it."

Then, just weeks ago, another unwanted change of ownership. It was like being sent down the river. Jackie brought me over to Ezra. Now, that was weird. No one there was in a playful mood, least of all Ezra. In fact, I was downright afraid of him. Little kids can decide to be mean to cats, especially to kittens, if they are angry at the world, if they want to lash out. I don't know how I knew that, but I did. As if all that wasn't bad enough, his mother decided that it was time for her to die. Everyone knew it but Ezra. If I could have talked, I would have sat down with him and had a heart-to-heart. I would have told him to get over it. I would have pointed out that I never even knew my mother, who hadn't wanted me in the first place. But I'm a cat. I can't talk. So, I tried to stay out of his way. It was his older sister who fed me and cleaned out my litter box.

I'm happy to say that I'm back with Jackie now. I've forgiven him for dumping me with Ezra's family. The short absence – it started when he was on vacation in Greece, I think – has even improved our relationship. When he gets out that big black tube he blows into – the one that screeches and squeaks, the one that makes him sound as if someone has caught his ear in a vice – I'm more tolerant. I know that life can change in an instant. I stick my head under his pillow, which helps to dampen the sound.

A Journey

Helen broached a topic she'd been wondering about for weeks. "Why did you want to read that book, Nicky?" she asked, as she brought into the living room of their apartment their copy of *The White Hotel* and put it on the end table next to the sofa. They sat there in silence for a few seconds, while Nicky contemplated an answer.

"Honestly? So I could read the end again. So I could imagine what Thomas had in mind when he wrote 'The Camp.' So maybe I could feel some joy in his vision of an afterlife, where the tragedy of the Holocaust led only to reunions and new promise."

She shook her head. "I thought that chapter was silly at best, even though I do believe in *ha'olam haba*, a world beyond this one, but silly can't be the right word, either. The part about Babi Yar is blood-curdling. I read it for the second time last night in bed, when you were snoring. I had to get out of bed to cry. I didn't want to wake you."

"The chapter about Babi Yar is more than terrible, but, when I reread it at the monastery, I didn't want to cry. I wanted to … I wanted to kill a Nazi again, or a Ukrainian collaborator. It put me in the mindset of killing the Greeks who worked with the Nazis. If I cried at all for my family, it was in 1944, and not since. I cried it out a long time ago. But it still affects me; I can imagine my parents and Ada, being thrown into that pit in Kiev, even though they met their ends elsewhere, and I just … what's the expression? … I just see red."

"So why did you need to take *The White Hotel* with you to the monastery? Why on this trip?"

"Because of 'The Camp.' I wanted to see if the monastery was ... was the camp? A form of the camp? Because ... you see the connection, don't you?"

"No. I'm not following at all, sorry to say."

"It's a place ... they are both places of reunion. Places where something magical happens, and you find what you thought you'd lost forever but hasn't been lost at all ... you find what has just been misplaced, to be found again. Places where you can hug someone you thought you'd lost for all time. Where you can literally suck life's milk from your mother, at least in the case of *The White Hotel*."

"Utterly weird."

"The book is a fantasy."

"And the monastery is a real place."

"Still ..."

"But there's a connection, Nicky, I grant you. You found Kal alive there when you thought she'd been murdered, the way Lisa is murdered in the novel and returns to life again in the last chapter."

"Yes. I think you're right. That's what I've been trying to say."

They fell silent. Nicky deliberated how he might even explain more to Helen. Because there was more, yet Nicky wasn't sure he knew how to say what he had to say, what he'd been thinking about and feeling for weeks since their return from Greece. But there was no way around it. He would try.

"Helen ... this is going to sound strange."

"A lot of what you say is strange. But what are you talking about?"

"Something happened at the monastery. It crept up on me. I didn't know it was coming ..."

"What on earth are you talking about?"

"It was happening, and yet I didn't know it."

"What was? You're worrying me, Nicky."

"When we gathered to pray for Sarah, and the rain, the lightning ... you remember?"

"How could I not remember?"

"And then ... you and I ..." Here, to Helen's great surprise, Nicky blushed.

Helen laughed. "I know what we did, Nicky. We made love and were caught. By your daughter." It was Helen's turn to turn red. She looked away, trying unsuccessfully to hide what was obvious.

"And that instant, when I was inside you, all the clatter of rain and wind and thunder, all of that, I started to believe again."

She thought she hadn't heard him correctly. The Nicky she knew, the confirmed lifelong atheist, would never have admitted to belief in *Hashem*. At least, she didn't think so. "Excuse me?"

"I knew you would think I was joking."

"I don't think you're joking ... but ..."

"I started to believe again. It was like I was thirteen. Just like that. Boom. I knew there was ... *Hashem*. And how this happened, I don't know ... but it's there. It's now the truth of my life."

She took him into her suddenly strong arms, her warm body conveying the unequivocal message she was beyond happy to receive his confession of faith. All she could say was "Oh, Nicky." He returned the hug as fiercely as she gave it. They kissed each other deeply.

After a minute, he pulled back. "Why, Helen? Why after all this time? Why there at the monastery? Why in the middle of the worst storm I can ever remember being in?"

"You just decided it was time."

"Just like that? I decided?"

"That's what belief is. That's what belief has always been. Your choice. Your decision."

"And how do I ask *Hashem* to forgive me for all the years I was away?"

"You were simply on a journey. *Hashem* knew all along where you'd end up."

Acknowledgements

I am so blessed to have a supportive family: my wife, Laurie; my children Marty and Jean; my grandchildren Cole and Neely, and my dear and beloved children-in-law, Drea and Eyal. Without their love and unconditional acceptance of my desire to write, I would have given up this pursuit (some would say obsession) long ago.

There are many other people to thank. I would like to extend my deepest appreciation to those who read an earlier draft of this novel and gave me their honest criticisms: Steven Berger, my dear cousin and the source of my best information about Orthodox Christianity; Pierre Dugan, who as a faithful friend has read everything I've been working on and always been generous with his time and guidance; Nancy Rankin, a friend for more than half a century, the first editor of a literary magazine to whom I submitted my work and a perceptive critic; Elliot Rosen, yet another close friend, who has supported my creative efforts from the beginning; my fellow author Bonnie Suchman for her close read of the manuscript, and Rabbi Ethan Seidel, not only a spiritual guide and friend, but someone keenly receptive to the many religious themes in this novel. He's probably the only rabbi in the world who would have invited me, a congregant, to read a story about the Theotokos during a Shabbat service. To these readers and supporters, I owe an enormous amount. And, to Jean, many thanks for encouraging me on the short chapter written by Aliyah.

Let me not forget the amazing mentors I had as a student in the M.F.A. program in Creative Writing at American University: Kyle Dargan, Stephanie Grant, David Keplinger, Patty Park, Dolen Perkins-Valdez, Rachel Snyder, and Roberta Rubenstein. Without their guidance and support, I would not have been able to write these novels. And I must also mention with gratitude Carolivia Herron, the novelist, scholar, and friend who long ago encouraged me in my writing and who has invited me so many times to be a guest on her radio show.

Many thanks also go to Black Rose Writing, the publisher I have been so lucky to find, the place where all my novels have had a happy home. And thanks also Mary Ellen Bramwell of Black Rose Writing, for her edits and suggestions.

Finally, I would like to thank the thousands of readers who have enjoyed *The Flight of the Veil*, *The Music Stalker*, and *To See God*. With the publication of *Forgiven: A Novel*, I feel the saga of the Covo family may well have come to its logical conclusion (or maybe not, because I have sprinkled throughout this novel many seeds that may yet germinate). To you readers who have accompanied me on the journey thus far, and might do so in the future, my utmost gratitude.

About the Author

Bruce J. Berger, author of three previous award-winning novels about the Covo family, received his MFA in Creative Writing from American University and has taught college writing and creative writing there since 2017. In his previous career, after graduating from the University of Connecticut and Harvard Law School, Berger practiced law for forty years. For fun, he plays baseball in a senior league, something he's done for about thirty years. Berger lives in Silver Spring, Maryland, with his wife, Laurie, and their dogs, Whiskey and Savvy. He loves to spend time with his two grandchildren, Cole and Neely, who live just down the street.

Other Titles by Bruce J. Berger

The Covo Family Saga

Note from Bruce J. Berger

Word-of-mouth is crucial for any author to succeed. If you enjoyed *Forgiven: A Novel,* please leave a review online — anywhere you are able. Even if it's just a sentence or two. It would make all the difference and would be very much appreciated.

Thanks!
Bruce J. Berger

We hope you enjoyed reading this title from:

BLACK ROSE writing™

www.blackrosewriting.com

Subscribe to our mailing list – *The Rosevine* – and receive **FREE** books, daily deals, and stay current with news about
upcoming releases and our hottest authors.
Scan the QR code below to sign up.

Already a subscriber? Please accept a sincere thank you for being a fan of Black Rose Writing authors.

View other Black Rose Writing titles at
www.blackrosewriting.com/books and use promo code
PRINT to receive a **20% discount** when purchasing.